A Cast of Spaniards

A CAST OF SPANIARDS

stories by
Mark Jacobs

Talisman House, Publishers
Hoboken, New Jersey

Published in the United States of America by

Talisman House, Publishers
P.O. Box 1117
Hoboken, NJ 07030

Several of these stories were first published in magazines and journals: "Eusebio's Spaniard" in *Buffalo Spree Magazine*, "Stone Cowboy on the High Plains" in *The Atlantic Monthly*, "The Necessary Plane" in *The Sun*, "Sixto in Harvest" in *Farmer's Market*, "Lover's Leap" in *North Dakota Quarterly*, "The Murder of German Morales" in *The Nebraska Review*.

Library of Congress Cataloging-in-Publication Data

Jacobs, Mark, 1951-
A cast of Spaniards : stories / by Mark Jacobs
p. cm.
ISBN 1-883689-19-8 (cloth) : $33.95. — ISBN 1-883689-18-X (paper) : $12.95
1. Central America—Social life and customs—Fiction. 2. South America—Social life and customs—Fiction. I. Title.
PS3560.A2549C37 1994
813'.54—dc20
94-37430
CIP

For Jacqueline and Anne Jacobs

Remembering my father, Thomas Jacobs

Contents

Eusebio's Spaniard

There arrived a morning in early winter when Andrea woke from an eyeless sleep knowing the names of all the steps on the dark staircase she had been going down for so long. First came the loss not of faith but of God Himself; in her fifth year in Peru He had simply gone away. After that went the old, hard habits of faith; of those, hardest to lose was prayer, because it was like forgetting how to talk, how to say important things. Later, she experienced what she called willful indifference. What good was a God who only let you know He wasn't there? She continued down, until she reached a place in which all she did was wait. Work and wait. The absence in which she worked was absolute, and it was enormous. If God were ever to show Himself again, she thought, it must be in such a place. In this Peru. She knew she would never leave.

After the luxury of warm covers, she felt winter sting through the tile floor as she dressed. From her window in the clinic she looked out at the inhospitable mountains, the high expanse of canted plain lathered with a dry sweat of brown dust. It was just the sort of place, really, one would expect to find an apocalypse. In such thin soil guerrillas who loved to kill might well flourish, and their military counterparts.

Little Maria Elena brought her a cup of *mate de coca*. Andrea wrapped her hands around the mug of steaming tea. She felt momentarily weak. Her body, she had learned, was composed of three unstable elements: fire and ice and a volatile blue gas. She was not old, but her body had lived long enough to imagine with some precision how old age was going to feel.

"Cold this morning," the girl said. "You did not sleep well, Sister."

She had given up asking the Peruvian staff at the clinic not to call her Sister. She had defrocked herself years earlier when the Shining Path terror had driven her order from the Altiplano. But perhaps Maria Elena knew better than she; maybe the transplanted North American woman who ran the clinic was still inescapably a nun.

"I slept perfectly," she told the girl patiently. "What about Eusebio? Is he here?"

The girl shrugged her hump-bladed shoulders and looked at the floor. That meant the handyman was there and wanted trouble. Which Andrea would be happy to provide, thank you.

A sleepy peace still dulled the ward when Andrea began her morning rounds. She consulted in a professional whisper with the night nurse, then sent her to bed. No one's condition had worsened in the night, and the late-rising sun allowed some of the children to sleep a little later. The trick, in such a life, such a place, was to find satisfaction in the smallest victories. It was an art in which Andrea was skilled. By the time she worked her way through the clinic the sun was up.

In the kitchen the wood stove was drawing poorly. Chewing a heel of hard bread at the table, Eusebio told her with unconvincing indifference, "The pipe must be clogged with soot again." His dark eyes stared at her, challenging. His skin was at once ruddy and dark, as though someone had pounded red and brown into a paste that lost nothing of either color. He had the power, in his hostility, to make her foreignness feel like guilt.

Eusebio called himself a pagan. Less a pagan than a skeptic, in Andrea's view, he drew pleasure from scoffing at the Christian God, to Whose defense he assumed she must always spring. He drank sporadically. During a binge he would disappear into the mountains for a week or two. When he reappeared at the clinic he was calmer, still more aloof, but less inclined to bait her. When he was gone she missed him, missed the hard edge of his hostility. She told him she would help him clean the pipe.

Bundled against the weather, she followed Eusebio outside to the back wall of the kitchen where the stove pipe issued from a square hole. A wind full of needles pricked the town raising a thin cloud of brown dust. In the glazing light of early morning she took in the mountain overshadowing the clinic, the wide stony plains that lay like slag, the brown-dirt town that seemed to have been pushed up from the earth in a long, painful labor. The town meant a few dozen mud-brown shacks with thatch or tile roofs, distended along narrow streets that splayed out from an oversized church at an arbitrary center. A black and white spotted llama grazed on the stones in the plaza of the church. Notwithstanding its barren aspect, the place radiated its own peculiar, stark beauty.

"Cold this morning, Sister Andrea," Eusebio grunted as he scraped at the soot where it lay clogging the pipe.

"It is. This pipe is filthy. We mustn't allow the dirt to build up so much."

"It will draw fine in a few minutes. Why do you suppose your God makes His world so cold, do you imagine? If I were a believer the cold would make me doubt His goodness."

"Here, draw the soot into this sack."

"I understand; some questions have no answers. Did you hear? The Shining Path attacked the town of Quilaquepa yesterday."

"Did they kill anyone?"

"They lined up the mayor against the church and sprayed him with bullets from machine guns. And his family, children too. Of course to them all killing is political. They are political surgeons removing cancers."

She flinched, wished she had not, or that he had not seen.

"Let's grant your God the cold; perhaps He had His reasons. But how is it He would permit such terror to consume a country like ours? The existence of such a God inspires repulsion in me, I confess to you."

The needle wind gusted at them, blowing the soot that the handyman scraped from the pipe. "Hurry, please," she told him. "It's too cold to be outside doing this now. You should have looked after it months ago."

"You are not the only foreigner to suffer winter in the Andes," he advised her.

"I don't suffer it."

"My grandfather once guided a foreigner, a Spaniard, through these same mountains looking for gold."

"How long ago, Eusebio?" She assumed she was being set up. This was why she enjoyed him, put up with his hostility, which was real enough to touch, to be touched by.

"Not so very long ago. It happened in my own lifetime. This Spaniard was apparently the third son of a duke. His eldest brother inherited the family fortune, and the middle son joined the army. This third child was to join the church but he rebelled. Perhaps he was plagued by the question of cold, or the question of terror. At any rate he came to Peru to seek the fortune he did not inherit. At that time also there was war in Spain, I believe. In Lima he met a couple of Chilean adventurers who had been exiled from their country for certain crimes."

"What crimes?"

"That we never knew. But they convinced the Spaniard there was gold to be had in the mountains hereabouts. He put up the cash for the expedition."

"They found no gold," Andrea anticipated him.

"But they did. A fair quantity. They followed the course of a creek in which they found a few nuggets, and they dug into the mountainside at the place where the creek began. They filled two sacks, though to be honest I cannot tell you the size of the sacks. Finally, the night before they were to come down from the mountains, the Spaniard set the two Chileans to arguing. He had been hinting to each one separately that the other had plans to steal away with the gold."

"The Spaniard hoped to get the gold for himself, then."

"What would one expect, Sister? Inevitably, a fight with knives broke out. My grandfather said it was the ugliest spectacle he witnessed in his life. The two thugs cut each other to pieces until both went weak from loss of blood. When they were completely exhausted, the Spaniard pushed them both over a cliff."

"What a horrible story."

"The Spaniard threatened to shoot my grandfather if he said a word. Not that my grandfather would have mixed in what was no concern of his. Anyway, the Spaniard fell asleep with the bags of gold under his head. In the morning, however, things had changed. My grandfather woke to the sound of the Spaniard crying. He was sitting huddled by a fire hugging his gold. It appears that the man underwent a trial during the night. Maybe your God visited him and promised him hell; who can say?"

"Well, when the sun came up the Spaniard walked over to the cliff in a trance. My grandfather thought he must be going to jump over. Instead, he began to throw the nuggets over the cliff, one by one, until the sacks were empty. Then he threw the sacks. When my grandfather moved to stop him he shot at him with his pistol. The bullet hit a stone by his foot, and a chip from the stone hit his ankle and made a deep cut."

The pipe was clean. Smoke blew freely overhead, and Eusebio tied shut the sack of soot. He seemed at the same time to cut off his story, as though she had contracted him to talk by the hour and his time was up.

"What happened then, Eusebio?" She was sure there was more.

"Ah, well. In time the foot healed."

Before he walked away to dump the soot, he hesitated a moment before asking his question. "Do you know how far Quilaquepa is from here, Sister Andrea?"

She nodded.

"Seventy kilometers," he told her anyway. "So close. The terror is maybe seventy kilometers away from us. You should go home. What is happening in Peru is not for foreigners anymore. It never was. Go home to a warm safe house in the United States of North America."

"This is my home, Eusebio. Seventeen years. Isn't that enough time to claim this place?"

"You're a fool," he told her harshly, his anger pushing him past the limits of irony and civil enmity with which he usually treated her. She let him go.

Though winter-short Andrea's day was tediously long. She put Eusebio's odd story out of her mind, but the impression of being insecurely rooted in the stony soil of the Peruvian high plains remained. A dozen times she went to the window to stare at the wind-riddled town: children playing in a puddle with an emaciated spotted dog; free-ranging alpacas and llamas and black pigs; women in bowler hats and dark dresses enlivened by colored slings in which they lugged their infants. This was Peru, this was slow apocalypse. It was the place in which the world's most sustained and fanatic terror carried out its patient program of logical ideological destruction. It was home.

In the afternoon a jeep brought mail, including a letter from Alva. Her friend seemed to have been listening long distance. Years ago, before the terror closed their mission, Alva had left the order and gone home to the tumult of North America, taking with her a friendship and a power of understanding that were not to be replaced. Sometimes Andrea thought the years of separation would end up estranging them from each other. And the language of Alva's letters was increasingly foreign to Andrea. Though she could follow the track of this new language intellectually, she felt distant from a life whose experience was described as a process of taking risks, of becoming vulnerable, of learning to assert oneself positively. This time, though, Alva was talking about Job, and Andrea read hard.

They're wrong, she read, when they tell us that Job is about patience. Or if he is then patience is secondary. What's primary, what really matters in Job, is the quality and the depth and the nature of his suffering. Job is a diver. With his eyes open he keeps diving down and down and farther down into a place where he can know nothing at all except his own emptiness. He dives down into the place where God isn't. And it seems to me, Andrea, that if he hadn't, then God Himself would not, could not, have known how deep was the sea He created. Is that heresy? Let the cardinals debate in comfort. In a world in which *Sendero Luminoso* kills *campesinos* in the name of *campesino* liberation we are permitted heresies. If they help. I'm worried again for you; can't help it. Surely you must see that no one, nothing, will keep *Sendero* and the military together from destroying Peru ...

Surely she must. In response, she absorbed herself in the work at hand that had to be done. Marshaling her crew, she wound bandages, had the wardroom floor scrubbed, then cut vegetables for the cook, who was making a chicken stew. She was relieved when darkness came and she could no longer see out the window.

In the evening, the fire in the cook stove dwindled to embers, she drank a cup of *mate de coca,* sitting in a chair before the open door of the stove. The heat made her doze. When the kitchen door was thrown open with a bang she jumped startled from her chair. Eusebio, of course, standing in her doorway wrapped in a dark wool poncho and wearing a pair of castoff army boots. He was smoking a cigar, which meant he had also been drinking.

"Good evening, Eusebio. Do you want tea?"

He shook his head but moved into the room a little farther.

"What do you want then?"

"You did not hear the end of the story I told you this morning," he told her, recrimination coloring his alcohol-blurred voice as if the fault were hers alone.

"Then tell it to me."

"In fifteen minutes Manuel will be here with his Landcruiser. He'll take you away."

"Don't be ridiculous. I'm not going anywhere, Eusebio."

"You'll go, Sister," he told her in a voice whose cold, flat certainty irritated her mightily. Why did he continue to hate her? The injustice of it galled her. She watched him pace the kitchen energetically until a wing of his poncho caught a cup from a shelf and sent it crashing to the floor. Then he stood over it, kicked the chips, ground them with his boot heel. "No one heard a word of him for a long time," he was saying. "Then, in the spring, he showed up at one of the villages with a newborn alpaca in his arms. He paraded through the streets of the village with the little beast. When he met someone in the street he would lift the alpaca before him and proclaim, 'This is the Lamb of God, Who takes away the sins of the world.'"

She threw a handful of sticks on the embers. No story he could remember or invent, she told herself, would convince her to leave when there was nowhere else to go.

"The Spaniard was shoeless, and his European clothes were worn to rags. After he had travelled for some time like that through the villages with his alpaca people began to accept him as one more crazy foreigner. The animal grew, but the Spaniard continued to carry it. Of course exposure and bad food and hard weather wore him down and he got sick. People pitied him. They gave him food and let him sleep near their fire, but all he did was get worse. And the alpaca, which slept with him, grew bigger and heavier."

When Eusebio paused they both heard the wind brush the kitchen walls. The broken cup was ground to powder.

"By winter the Spaniard was close to death. He trembled when he walked, and he scarcely had the strength to lift his alpaca. But he carried on. He had become a missionary. He had joined your church after all."

"That's not the end of your story, though."

The wind brushed. Eusebio studied his boots. "He came here," he said, "looking for my grandfather. He had trained the animal to walk behind him like a dog. My grandfather gave him some shoes and let him stay in our house. He was more dead than alive, at first. He lay by the fire and prayed. I didn't understand what that was about, it was Latin. But as the winter passed the Spaniard grew a little stronger. He moved from a pallet to a chair by the fire, and he drank soup all day long. Soup and prayers, soup and prayers. He drove us crazy.'

"I remember one night waking from the cold. I saw the Spaniard awake, kneeling with his head next to the coals trying to read his Bible by the glow. His body rocked, his head nodded, and saliva dripped from his mouth. I was afraid, but I was also disgusted.'

"Then in spring the alpaca died. It had been sick along with the Spaniard but never recovered. That night I stayed awake to watch him but he didn't pray. He sat by the fire with his head cocked to one side, like an animal's head when it listens. Once he saw me watching and made the sign of the cross at me. In the morning he found me in the street and told me to go along with him."

"And you went? Just like that?"

"Who can explain why? I was a boy, and maybe I was curious. But I went. Yes. Moreover, there was something commanding about him, like a soldier. So in his rags and bad shoes he led me through the streets out of town, out onto the plain. Do you know the place out there people call El Nido del Loco?"

"That enormous flat rock to the east?"

"That's it. That's where we went. By then I was suspicious enough to be afraid. But I had lost my will, I couldn't cut and run. So I followed him. There was snow on the plain, just enough to make it look like dust. The sun flashed on it and blinded me. The sun was white, too, the color of a white stone in a stream bed. There was nothing else around. No animals, nothing.'

"At the rock he held me by the neck and tied my hands and feet. Then he shoved me flat onto the rock, on my back. The sun burned into my eyes, and the Spaniard pulled out his Bible."

"Eusebio," she interrupted, but he waved away her small sound.

"'Little one,' he said to me, 'do you believe it was an angel who held back Abraham's hand?' What could I say? He told me it was no angel, it was old Abraham himself wanting to believe that God is not terrible, but Abraham was wrong. He babbled on like that and without my noticing where it came from there was a long knife in his hand. Half a meter long, I believe now, with a black handle and a thin straight blade that looked like white fire with the sun on it. He told me to pray, but I heard other sounds then. Behind us, fanning out on the plain, I saw my father, my grandfather, my uncles, and some of the other men from our village. They had rocks in their hands. The Spaniard watched them come as if he couldn't get it into his head that they had something to do with him. When the men got into good throwing distance they stopped.'

"My grandfather called out for him to untie me. His voice carried a long way out there but it sounded thin, like water. Sweet but thin. My head turned, I could see a line of men with rocks in their hands. I don't remember what the Spaniard said, must have been more Latin. But he seemed not to remember I was there. With his left hand he placed his Bible next to me on the rock. The long knife was in his right hand. When he raised his right arm over me a rock hit him hard in the shoulder. He dropped the knife, and more rocks hit him. As the men came closer their aim got better. The Spaniard bled like any stuck animal bleeds. By the time they reached us he was on the ground and mostly dead, but my father ran the long knife through him anyway. Then he untied me and shook me hard. He told me it was my fault."

"I'm sorry," Andrea told him quietly.

He looked at her as though that were a stranger response than he had expected from her. "You have to go," he said.

"I won't. This is my home, if I have one."

"The Shining Path is coming this way. Now. Tomorrow, maybe tomorrow they will be here."

"You're lying. You're lying to force me out, Eusebio."

But he wasn't, and she knew he wasn't. Nevertheless she tried to talk him out of what he knew. "Does *Sendero* always warn people before they attack a place?"

He shrugged. "This is Peru," he told her, as though that explained it. "People here are not like you."

"Are you saying you have contact with them, Eusebio?"

"I'm only saying I know that they are coming here."

"I believe you. But I'll stay. I'll take my chances."

"Then you're willing to sacrifice the children? All these children … "

"What do you mean?"

"Sister Andrea, they are contaminated now. You have contaminated them. The *Sendero* know that, and they will kill them to prevent the disease from spreading."

"What disease, Eusebio?" She was aware that she was hissing, that the red anger rising in her was squeezing off her vision, her voice, pressing her flat against the back wall of herself, but she could not shut up. "Tell me the name of the sickness, will you please, that I have communicated to these children. Tell me now." She slapped the table with the heel of her hand, but the sound it made was also flat. It went nowhere.

"You are a foreigner," he said, and she assumed she would never forgive him.

They gave her time to pack a bag, but there was nothing she wanted to take because there was nowhere to go. Outdoors in the wind, in a deep puddle of darkness next to Manuel's Landcruiser while no one was there Eusebio kissed her hand, and the shock of that weakened her. She sagged against the jeep and wept. "Your going," he told her in a masked voice, "impoverishes my life." He walked away.

Manuel didn't talk, which was good. He owned a store, gave credit, had, she supposed, a stake in the postponement of the apocalypse. If he had said a word she could not have responded. For several hours they jolted along across the high plains, the wind constant, evocative, terrifying in its breathy emptiness. The sky was clear and cloudless. It was like driving across the bottom floor of heaven. The stars pulsed white, leaving a little ring of blue around them when the light contracted. If she opened the window of the jeep she could reach up and pluck one, they were that close. But then what would she do with it when she had it in her hand? It did not occur to her to ask Manuel where they were going.

In the middle of the night, the deadest hour, the road passed through a town sealed against the weather. No lights, no life, no nothing. In such a place, she told herself, unable to complete the thought.

"I want to stop here," she told him.

"We can't stop, Sister Andrea. We have to keep going."

"Stop now. I insist. I am going to be sick. Find me a place to be sick, please."

He stopped, parked, knocked on a door, terrified someone then spent ten minutes cajoling in Quechua to have them open up and let the sick foreigner inside for a moment. Perhaps the people inside knew his name, or owed him money, or thought he would shoot them if they didn't open up. Andrea heard the bar sliding, wood on wood, as they unbolted the door, and she rushed inside drawn by the smoky orange light of the kerosene lamp they had lit to receive her. A miniature woman in a black shawl gave her a squat, dripping candle on a saucer, pointed to a room in the back of the house, and Andrea went in and closed the door after herself just as if she had known what she was doing, what she wanted.

She was not sick. What she needed was to stop moving, get out from under the vast hostile sky with its billion pluckable bright stars. The empty vastness had made her dizzy, was all. She needed to think. Of course she would not sacrifice the children. But losing them so suddenly, losing her place, created a grief like that of bereavement. She had no urge to cry, but it would have been wonderful to be able to think, to construct a sentence in her mind that told her, began to tell her, what was happening. No such luck. Her going, Eusebio had said, impoverished his life.

"Sister Andrea?" Manuel, decent but worried, was on the other side of the door.

The worst part of this apocalypse, after all, was that it went so slowly, so slowly. Surely but so slowly. Its work of destruction seemed to take so much time. But she knew what she wanted. She wanted, somewhere inside the terrible emptiness of that slow-moving apocalypse, to find the God Who had abandoned her, abandoned Peru, abandoned the children in the clinic to be cured by the Shining Path terror of the disease she had inflicted on them.

"Sister Andrea? We have to get going. We have to keep moving."

"I'm coming," she told Manuel, and she was. Not that there was anywhere to go. For a moment she was aware of a tremulous quiet outside. Then the wind returned with a separate voice for every gust. She was coming, but before she turned the handle on the door she heard a serene voice intone persuasively in her ear: This is the alpaca of God, Who takes away the sins of the world. It was the kind of voice, she figured, she must accustom herself to hearing.

She turned the handle, opened the door, sensed more than saw the sleepy suspicious people in blankets in the shadows watching her wanting her to go away. "I'm ready," she told Manuel. "Let's go."

Stone Cowboy on the High Plains

Two days before he was released forever from El Panóptico Prison, in La Paz, Bolivia, Roger the Stone Cowboy became aware that he had been talking to God. A Swedish mercy nurse who spoke terrible Spanish was binding up his forearm where one of the troll crazies had sliced him, in an argument in which Roger himself had played no part. As the earnest, homely blonde woman worked, he could feel his pulse thunder the length of the hurt arm. They were in a room the trolls called the infirmary, which meant it had a bed nobody slept in. (All Bolivians were trolls, Roger had decided a long time ago. They were short and dark and strange, not like people, really, but human like to a certain extent.) Light the color of clear, thin honey came through the single window high in the prison wall and dripped down on them. Roger felt sticky.

The honey light dripped, his pulse thundered, the mercy nurse babbled bad Spanish. An odd lull had occurred in the afternoon bitch and hum in El Panóptico. Before the woman released his arm, Roger became aware that he was saying something into that lull: Give me back my heart. It was not really what he would have thought of as a prayer. Definitely it was no prayer. He didn't care what it was. More interesting was where he was sending it. In a slow roll, like revelation, he realized that he had indeed been mumbling to God. No answer came back, of course. That would have been too much to expect. He returned to his pallet in a kind of daze.

He was giving up dope. All kinds, not just the coke cigarettes the trolls smoked, called *pitillos*. All shit, shit in all its manifestations. That was a lot for a Stone Cowboy who had made himself high, by his own best estimate, in twenty three countries and twenty five American states over a period of more than ten years. So he was giving up a lot, and that was hard. He had some insurance, but he wasn't touching it. He wished he had remembered to keep track of how many days he had stayed down now, but he hadn't. His mind had become his body, and it was acting funny. Then that mumbling.

"When they let you out, in two days, what are you going to do?" the Swedish woman asked him.

He shook his head, not because he didn't want to be sociable but because he was preoccupied. His mind had become his body.

"Did you hear me?"

"I heard you." You you you you you ... Et cetera. "Do you have any idea of where you are going to?" she persisted.

Give me back my heart is what he thought, but he said nothing to her, because he did not want her to misunderstand him.

"Will the people from your consulate help you?" No way, Josefeen. He would not go back to Gringolandia. Not until he had calmed down a little more. He knew the trolls wanted him out of Bolivia, but when the vice-consul showed up to escort him to his doom, he slipped, skipped, did not trip. It was easy.

He had only a few bucks in troll money, so he had to get a job. First to eat and sleep, then money to move on with. He had his insurance but wasn't touching any of it. So he took a yellow unpsychedelic bus with black stripes up out of the canyon of La Paz, up the highway toward the Altiplano. He wanted to get a good view of the Andes, something he had craved his whole time in jail. The Altiplano was a desert that had gotten lost, squeezed in between two ranges of the Andes at 14,000 feet. The ultimate natural high was what a French doper in El Panóptico had called it. Real people couldn't survive long at that altitude, just llamas and alpacas. And trolls. Real people needed air with something in it their lungs could chew on.

Three quarters of the way up the *autopista* the bus broke down. The engine shuddered like the French doper had done one night, and that was it. The trolls filed off the bus like religious fatalists, and Roger followed last, because he had to. Most of the trolls went up the hillside on a footpath alongside a concrete culvert down which no water coursed. A few walked the highway in hopes of a ride. The driver, who apparently had no plan, sat by the roadside and chain-smoked cigarettes. Roger watched his face for a sign of distress, but none was there. That was a troll for you. He wished the man would offer him a cigarette, but forget that. When his half pack of smokes was gone, the driver stood up and left, walking on the highway berm without looking back or hoping for a ride. No good-bye, because no hello. Give me back my heart. Roger crossed the highway and sat down cross-legged on an outcropping of shaley rock. Below him, in the brown bowl of the canyon, the lights were going on in La Paz. The skyscrapers downtown looked ridiculously little in the vastness of brown earth around them. Toothpicks of light.

On the far horizon the outlines of the mountain Illimani were filed smooth in the twilight. For all the smoothness, the mountain dominated the city. The Indians worshipped the mountains as gods, someone had told him, but that might have been pure bullshit, some tourist's stone fantasy. He sat and watched the night fill up the canyon as if he had no place else on earth to be, nothing better to do. The air had begun to get cold.

Eventually he recognized a certain pressure inside his head, as if he were not alone, or as if he had been trying to communicate something to someone without knowing it. It was not a prayer. He remembered the way his body had looked when he had seen it in a mirror by chance at the prison: dead-white skin, pudgy like pastry. A real shock. He looked like weakness in the flesh. He was thirty-seven years old, but ten years' extra wear seemed to have been compressed into every one of those years. That was the dope, no doubt. He was a veteran cowpoke, a long-time outrider of the world's high plains.

The pressure and the indefiniteness of the sensations he felt bothered him as he sat. The entrancing scene of La Paz at night, even after his long confinement, could not hold him. Though he wasn't hopeful, he went back to the highway and stuck out his thumb. Anyway, he felt better moving.

After ten minutes a pickup truck stopped, and the troll driver motioned for him to get into the back, which he did, happily. The truck engine laboring, they climbed the last quarter of the highway out of the canyon and passed through the toll booth, after which Roger expected the driver to stop and let him out. The man, a fat-bellied troll Indian with a flat hatchet nose, did not stop. Because he could think of no convincing reason to get out at any particular place along the road, Roger acquiesced.

They went slowly through the muddy urban sprawl of the city of El Alto. The pickup, whose shock absorbers had died in 1970, bounced like an amusement-park ride. Welcome to El Alto, the City of the Future, read one enthusiastic mural, which displayed troll workers in an attitude of defiance, holding their tools like weapons. If this is the future ... Roger said to himself archly, but could think of nothing compelling to complete the thought. What it was was an Altiplano mud village multiplied several hundred times: the same crumbly adobe huts and walls, the same mud streets, the same Indians in their Andean stupor going about the business of surviving. The city lacked only llamas in the streets; he saw plenty of pigs and dogs, and a few oxygen-starved chickens.

The sign said Rio Seco—Dry River—but they were all dry in this part of the country. A real river hadn't coursed through the Altiplano since the dinosaurs used to wander down to the banks and lap up the polluted water after a hard day defending their territory. With no warning the troll driver stopped at an intersection of two crater-pocked streets. Roger jumped out and down.

"*Gracias*," he said to the man, who waved an enormous hand as if irritated and drove off trying to avoid the craters, which were full of dust that rose up in clouds like smoke signals.

Although he felt weak, Roger was not hungry at all, not even thirsty. He liked walking, so he walked, keeping careful track of the things he saw. A blind man with no legs sat on a street corner, holding his upturned hat for change. He must have been a miner: dynamite victims were strewn all over La Paz, like debris from an unnatural disaster. Next to the man was a crippled yellow cat. Roger put some change into the hat, at the same time resisting a strange urge to kick the helpless, ugly cat, whose fur was stiff with dirt.

As he walked he kept up his inventory: A blonde-haired doll like Barbie, with no limbs, lying on her back in the mud like a rape victim. Three men teetering as they shared a bottle of beer, with the one glass building a communal buzz. An underemployed hustler with bad teeth and a tight skirt that could flatter no one. Boys playing soccer in the street with a scuffed ball that needed air. A woman in a heavy shawl, baggy skirts, and a black bowler hat, sitting in a huddle alone in her corner store, next to tall bottles of soda pop in rainbow colors. Alongside those bottles the woman had no face in his imagination, and probably didn't feel the lack.

Attracted either by her or by the almost cheerful yellow light inside her store, Roger went inside. He bought a small bottle of warm Coca-Cola and poured it into the greasy glass the woman handed him. She had a face after all, but it was the typical face of a troll, illegible and hostile in a disconcerting blank way, just like the Altiplano and the Andes. For a moment Roger wanted not to go, but to be, home. In prison he had learned a little Aymara, so he spoke to the shopkeeper woman politely in that language.

"Can I find a hotel nearby?"

Surprised to hear the Aymara, but unwilling to show the surprise, she shook her lowered head.

"Anyplace to rent a room?"

"What for?" she asked him in Spanish.

"To sleep, that's all," he said in Aymara. He had a good ear; he knew that his accent was pretty good, and that she must be impressed. The pressure in his head was unsettling, as though he had lost his equilibrium. He had felt like this his first few days in La Paz, before his body adjusted to the dehumanizing altitude.

"Why to sleep?" she asked him. Stupid damn question, but that was her way of holding up the conversation. She had spoken in Aymara, which minor triumph of diplomacy pleased Roger unnecessarily. "Because my body is tired." His mind was still his body, and it had been invaded.

"You're a foreigner," she said, also unnecessarily.

"Guess from where."

She shook her head. She was about forty, maybe, and she had a striking, angular, womanly face, if you could get used to the idea of the shape of her body, which was a bunch of connected lumps below all those mysterious cloaking skirts.

"I'm a Russian," he said.

"Liar."

"Then what?"

"A gringo."

Something in the way the trolls said that word was offensive, as if they were the human ones and Americans were some low breed of dog.

"Why to sleep?" she asked again, so that he knew she liked him.

"Because I'm tired."

"I have a room in back."

"I don't have a lot of money."

"All the gringos have money."

"That's a lie. I was in jail."

"In El Panóptico?"

"That's right."

"Then you're a drug addict."

"I'm not. It was a mistake, a case of mistaken identity."

"Liar."

"I'm not a liar, and I'm not a drug addict, but I am a gringo. Is that wrong in some way?"

The last he had to say in Spanish, because he was reaching the end of his dexterity in Aymara, which was a backwards, upside-down kind of language.

"All the gringos have lots of money. How did you come to Bolivia?"

"On an airplane."

"See?"

"How much for the room, for one night?"

She told him a price that was half what he had expected to hear from her, and he accepted by pulling change from his pocket and placing the coins flat on the wooden countertop.

"I'm really a Russian," he said. "I'm a Communist. We're going to invade your country. I'm the first of the first wave. Shock troops, you know? Follow that?"

His body was three hundred and seventy years old. He had his insurance but wasn't touching it, so he bought from the woman a bottle of troll wine, terrible stuff but strong enough, strong as Robitussin. Because he liked her, he wanted to tell her that he had once been raped by identical redheaded twins in a county jail in Alabama, after he had been picked up for possession of a little dope, but he could not bring himself to that confidence. The twins had had ugly freckles all over their similar fish-white bodies. Fuck that noise, he warned himself. He let himself be led through the back room of the store to a dirt patio, where a couple of detached rooms were suspiciously hidden. She showed him into the first, which had an iron-spring cot and a comfortable cotton mattress, better than anything he had slept on in EL Panóptico except for the week when some troll disease had made him sick enough to get into the infirmary, where the consul had visited him with old *Time* magazines he never read. All news was bad news.

When the woman left, he lay on the cot on his side and opened the bottle of wine, which he drank very slowly, sucking on it almost, like a nursing baby. Soon the alcohol began to reduce the obnoxious pressure inside his head. He could feel the mellow redness seep into the cracks between his nerves, where all the irritation was, like a rash. He would not go home to Gringolandia until he had sorted through some things and could think in a straight line.

He must have drifted off, even though a little wine was left in the bottle. When they shook him awake roughly, he wanted to hit.

"This is my husband," the store woman said to him in Aymara. "His name is don Eloy."

Don Eloy looked down with tremendous disdain at the Stone Cowboy on the cot. He was big for a troll, as wide as he was tall. He looked the image of a decadent Indian on a reservation in the United States, dour and sour and dreaming of eagles. His black eyes were fierce, his ruddy face fiercer.

"What are you going to do tomorrow?" he asked Roger, as though he had a right to know.

"What do you care?" After the initial urge to strike out, he felt halfway okay. Enough wine had filtered between the nerve cracks to prevent chafing. No use resenting a troll.

"You want a job?"

"Doing what?"

"At my lumberyard."

"But doing what?"

"Working."

"How much will you pay me?"

"Ten pesos a day."

"I'll try it."

"I'll pick you up in the morning. Listen, little gringo, you shouldn't get drunk. My wife tells me you're a drug addict."

"I'm not."

"When we are working, you are going to tell me about life up north."

That sounded fine. Even on ten pesos he could save money to leave Bolivia. It was a question of discipline. He didn't have it, but he would find it. Before he fell back to sleep, he imagined the way he'd feel crossing the border, knowing that he would never see an ugly troll face, never have to talk to a troll again in his life.

The work at Eloy's small-time lumberyard was not too bad. He had done the same sort of thing in dozens of places, dozens of times: lift fetch carry, drop hold hammer, bend push pull. The dust was awful and the hours longer than you would work anywhere in the States; those were the only bad parts.

"How much a day are you going to charge me for the room and my food?" he asked Eloy his first day on the job.

"Don't worry about it, *gringuito,*" the big man said, pulling on his long front teeth with one dirty hand.

Roger, formerly the Stone Cowboy, tried to pin him down but did not succeed. And he was too tired to persist. He was weak. Not for years had he worked for so long with his hands and all his body. El Panóptico and the world's garden house of dope had run down his three-hundred and-seventy-year-old body considerably. The little strength he had left over he used to defend himself from Eloy and his men—scurvy trolls, all of them, who derived a deep, stupid satisfaction from riding him. He was not just the Gringo, he was the Worthless Gringo, who could not keep up by half with the trolls when they were lifting and stacking boards, let alone do anything requiring more skill of body.

Decadence was Eloy's explanation for Roger's miserable condition. During a break he explained his theory both to Roger and to his other hired men. Roger was not sure whether he was trying to be sarcastic, but he thought not.

"Alienation," don Eloy said. "It's obvious. Capitalist society produces alienated individuals, because the workers are alienated from their work."

"Bullshit," Roger said, defensive though he did not have to be.

"Shut up," Eloy said. "Alienated people take drugs to escape their alienation. That's a false escape, of course, but they can't know that, can they?"

They were sitting in the lumberyard on wooden chairs. Don Eloy's chair had a fabric cushion. The hired men's chairs did not. Roger had no chair. He sat on the ground and tried to breathe slowly. The exertion had made him weak. It was July, what the trolls called winter: cold and windy and dry. The dust swirled in the yard, coated Roger's body, got down into his throat so that he coughed.

"Where did you pick up ideas like that?" he asked his new boss. Couldn't let them get away with more than the minimum of trash. "University of Moscow?"

Baiting him worked. The break was stretched appreciably, and Roger sensed the satisfaction of the other men when Eloy wound up and delivered. The basic idea, from what Roger could discern, was that Bolivia and the trolls were dirt poor because the imperialists up north—the Yankees—were filthy rich. It was that simple. The standard of living and conspicuous consumption that characterized the United States were the consequences of an economic arrangement that made the trolls dependent for crumbs. Nothing new there: Roger had heard the same song sung in El Panóptico when they wanted to get down on him there. Look at the tin, Eloy ranted. Bolivian miners coughing their black lungs out produced cheap tin so that the United States could win the Second World War, and here in the Andes only a few families, oligarchs in cahoots, made any money.

The break lasted for half an hour.

He wanted to get straight with Eloy about the pay arrangement, but that night he was too tired. Looking for discipline, he bought no wine. Eloy's wife's food was about the same as prison food, to which he had become accustomed, so he ate and went to sleep.

The second day and the rest of his first week were more of the same. Eloy got puffed and holy talking about the crummy way the gringos had treated the trolls. The other men laughed like first-graders about how weak the drug addict from El Panóptico was, but they didn't push as hard as they might have, because they appreciated the long breaks they got when Eloy started spouting. At night he drank at most a little wine, no more than half a bottle, and some nights he had none at all. Roger's body felt like Bolivia after it had been tromped on and raped by a hundred thousand imperialist mineral pirates. But even that exhaustion became the cause for a little self-satisfaction: he would ride it all out.

He had his insurance but wasn't touching it. Whenever the day was quiet, he felt the pressure in his head, but he had almost become used to that: the pressure was company.

After a week he asked for his pay, and got it. Six days times ten pesos should have been sixty pesos, but don Eloy gave him thirty.

"Thirty pesos for room and board?" Roger protested. "That's outrageous."

"Do you have a better offer?"

They were standing in the little store that fronted the dusty street. Roger was part, now, of the yellow light that had attracted him the first night. Little tremors of weakness ran up and down his legs. Don Eloy's wife hung her head, so Roger could not tell whether she was ashamed of the way her husband was taking advantage of him.

"This is your idea of a political lesson," Roger said to Eloy. "That's what it is, isn't it? You're trying to prove something."

"You have a better offer?"

"I have black lungs."

"From smoking drugs."

"I don't do drugs."

"Liar," piped up the wife.

"I'll get my own place to stay," he told them both, feeling almost as stubborn as he was tired.

"Go ahead."

"You'll pay me ten pesos a day without taking anything out? No more screwing me?"

"Ten pesos."

"Guaranteed?"

"Where are you going to sleep? It's cold."

"That's my problem, not yours."

The next day was Sunday, a day more or less of rest. Eloy closed his lumberyard and sat in a contraband chaise lounge in his wife's corner store, drinking beer slowly and growing predictably sullen. The problem, evidently, was the lack of an adequate object for his anger, for which frustration Roger almost pitied him. But he was glad to get away from the big man's domestic sulk. He went walking.

On earlier walks he had seen the blue tents, and that was what gave him his idea. Out-of-work miners had come to El Alto looking for relief or a job, and those who found neither would sometimes shelter their families in tents of blue opaque plastic that they set up in the empty fields that could still be found in El Alto. No rent, no room deduction, no one taking unfair advantage. They carried their water in jugs from a tap somewhere and hunkered down into a refugee's life.

The Altiplano wind was blowing hard, stirring dust devils all across the shabby brown city. The day was still young. The sun was flat in the east and the shadows were cold, making Roger think of mornings in El Panóptico, a memory like death itself. He walked with his hands in his pockets, head down, until he saw one of the blue tents, in front of which a troll picked something from his wife's long black hair. She leaned back peaceably in the man's lap as he poked, while around them a handful of midget trolls lolled like unimaginative slaves. A quality of domestic intimacy about them impressed Roger powerfully. So he asked them for help.

When they understood that he was not making fun of them and that he had no intention of taking over the land on which they had squatted, they helped him locate some plastic and build his tent, smaller than theirs but big enough for a single man to live in. At the nearby Sunday market they helped him buy two blankets, a tin pot, and a plastic jug for water, all at reasonable prices. He spent the day with them, feeling as if he had stumbled upon the family of some uncle whom he had not expected to like.

When the sun went down, early, he crawled into the new tent, almost at peace but feeling maudlin and alone. For a long time he lay on his back and listened to the wind bang through El Alto, the City of the Future. It was not much colder than the room at Eloy's, but it was damn cold. Though he was tired, he could not sleep. The desolation of this place wanted to overwhelm him.

For the first time since he could remember, he began to plan, gingerly—the way a person might exercise after a broken leg had healed. He would not walk away from don Eloy's exploitation yard, because his body, inside which his mind still stalked nervously, had begun to crave work. Just as important, next week he would have the entire sixty pesos, and he thought he could save more than he would spend. He would work a few more weeks, buy some dollars, and get out of Bolivia. In Peru he would do the same, getting stronger and more disciplined. He would go north, working his way and getting younger. The trip would take maybe three months, with luck, but once over the border into Gringolandia, he would buy a hamburger and a milkshake, and then hitchhike home to Flint, where his high school friend Danny was probably still working as a foreman in one of the car plants. Danny would wangle Roger a job, and Roger would grow up to be President of the United States of America of the North. His first official act would be to bomb Bolivia off the fucking continent, starting with El fucking Alto.

That night, when he eventually got tired, he had reached a weird equilibrium that balanced the wind outside with the windy pressure inside his head. Danny, he realized, would never believe this, nor could the story be told. The desolation wanted to get at him, get him good, but he was learning stubbornness. In a way he was glad it was too cold to get out of the tent and go find a bottle of wine somewhere. Thus one dollar saved.

Eloy and his men sucked the marrow from the big bone of pleasure when they learned that Roger was living in a blue-plastic tent in an empty field. His fortune was their revenge for all the miners who had died from black lung, for the hundreds of years of eating small potatoes, for their condition of perpetual trollhood. At the end of the second week, however, Roger felt as if he had beaten them all. Don Eloy handed over sixty Bolivian pesos--no discount, no comment. Roger sewed an extra sock to the inside of his jeans, at the waist, into which pocket he tucked the money. He was a miser, and no bottle of bad wine tempted him. He went to sleep early, stronger and younger than he had been for years.

At the end of the third week he asked for a raise. In response he received a boring, gritty lecture from his employer about economic dependence, about the inhuman face of imperialism, about the revealing analogy between workers against capitalists and poor countries against rich countries. When don Eloy offered him one peso a week extra, he accepted the offer and felt that he had won a tactical victory.

By September the weather had warmed, at least during the day, and the nights were bearable, even on the Altiplano. The change of season made Roger restless, and he decided he would work another week and then take the bus to Peru.

"I'm leaving next Sunday," he said to Eloy.

"Where to?"

"The United States."

"They'll never take you back. They were glad to see you go."

"I just thought I ought to tell you."

"You're going to start taking drugs again, I bet."

"You bet wrong."

"You're an insolent bastard."

Roger cursed him in nicely accented Aymara, and the troll lumber man bellowed with pleasure.

That night in his tent Roger thought seriously for the first time about destroying his insurance: two hits of windowpane acid that a disconsolate gringo had passed to him in El Panóptico as a way of vicariously celebrating Roger's release. Too soon. He felt more superstitious than vulnerable, but he could not yet let them go.

Thinking made him restless, almost nervous. He crawled out of his tent to take a walk, and found the city in the grip of a power failure. Rio Seco and all of El Alto were as dark and desolate as his worst mood. Overhead the southern stars were splendid, Orion lying on his side like a drunken veteran. For some reason the sight of the stars robbed Roger of his confidence. For a long minute he considered doing the acid, after which he felt unreasonably tired. Rather than walk, he crawled back inside the blue plastic cocoon and slept. The pressure and the presence in his head had diminished as he grew back into health, and that almost disappointed him. He felt more abandoned than ever, as if some important quiet self inside were sitting with his legs crossed and his hands folded, waiting for an answer, and all he got back was the silence, on the far side of which was nothing. Give me back my heart, he heard rather petulantly.

Although they were careful not to speak a word, Roger knew that Eloy's men were the ones who broke into his tent and took the money. He remembered nothing unmistakably identifiable about any of them. Not a human smell, or an individual cough. They fell on top of him and clamped a hand over his mouth, and for a moment he thought that they were going to rape him. Impatient hands tore down his jeans, but what they grabbed was the small wad of his money, which he had changed into dollars the week before. Before they left, Roger wondered how they could know so surely where to find his money. In another life he would have cried.

Instead, he went after Eloy, whom he found stumbling drunk in a broken-shouldered restaurant that smelled of garlic. A single woman from one of the Altiplano towns worked there in the evenings. For no reason that anyone who knew Eloy found convincing, she liked to flirt with the married lumber man, even though she had no expectation of any kind of gain from the transaction.

"I want my money," Roger told him, wondering whether the man could hear or understand him through the alcoholic vapor.

"Fuck you, little gringo."

"I want my money."

But Eloy was not capable of holding up even that much conversation. Maybe to impress the woman on duty, whose one gold tooth shone strangely in the lamplight, he dove at Roger and hugged him like a lover. The force of the embrace knocked Roger down, and don Eloy fell on top of him. Sitting on his chest as if sober, he began to slap Roger in the face, while cheerful Altiplano pipe music bubbled in the background. Left side, right. Left side, right. No punches, just hard slaps. Roger felt the blood begin to run somewhere. Concentrating intensely, as if doing some Oriental meditation exercise, he drew his strength to a single point in his arms and pushed the heavy troll off. Don Eloy rolled along the floor like a barrel with arms while the waitress screamed theatrically. Roger kicked him hard once then left running.

His mind had become his body again, after a long period of improvement and strength and great discipline at saving money. Walking after he became winded, Roger began to age again, and the speed at which he regressed terrified him. At the same time, the pressure came back into his head, stronger than it had been before. Why are you doing this to me? he asked, conscious of aiming the question precisely, an arrow into a void.

No answer, none expected.

The lights had come back on in the city, what few were there. The yellow domesticity seeping through cracks and over transoms both attracted and repelled him. He got lost. Better not to go back to his tent. If Eloy sobered up he might remember who had kicked him and send his hired trolls back to mess him up. Anyway his brain worked better with his legs moving. Before he found a place out of the wind to lie down in, he had his plan.

He woke at about nine o'clock, judging by the feel of the morning around him. Someone gave him water to wash his face with, stinging cold and slightly oily. Then he went directly to don Eloy's, knowing that what he needed might take several visits. But he was lucky. Eloy's wife was tending her little soda-pop-and-cracker business alone, dozing in her chair. She smiled enigmatically at him as he came in, as though she wanted to tell him a joke.

"I want to see the old man," he said abruptly.

"He's asleep out back. You treated him bad last night, Roger, and his body is hurting him."

"Go get him."

She shook her head.

"Go get him or I'll get the police."

She clucked skeptically. "Don Eloy knows all the police."

"Not the police in the American Embassy." A stupid enough bluff, but it worked. She scuttled.

In the drawer below the cash drawer below the counter he found and took a pistol. He remembered to check to see that it was loaded, although he knew it would be. Eloy would not protect his place with an empty gun. He closed the door to the street, and, more quickly than he'd expected, Eloy came, scratching his fur like a bear roused in winter and ready to curse. As he came into the room, Roger pointed.

"I want my money."

"What money?"

A rage that was deep and satisfying and happy came over Roger. He would have been delighted to shoot the bear in the chest, and don Eloy must have been able to see that.

"What money?" he asked again, but that was only a stall.

"Don't you think I'll shoot you? What do I lose? Without the money I'm as good as dead here."

"It's out back, in a box I have."

"Let's go. I may decide to take back my money and shoot you anyway, though. Just warning you. That's politics, you know. An example of your goddam imperialism at work."

Just in time he remembered not to let the woman escape. He heard moving-around noise as they walked out behind the little house to the bedrooms, and he took her in tow easily. She went with him readily, falling in step behind her husband as if she were amused.

In one of the little rooms they found a small green metal box fastened securely with an oversized padlock. Roger could feel the reluctance of his former employer to unlock the box, could feel the effort that almost but not quite balanced the odds of getting shot against the intense disagreeableness of giving up the money. The strength of that sensation in the man, whom he hated more than Bolivia, was in itself worth experiencing, worth a trip to the land of the trolls.

"One hundred and forty five dollars," Eloy said, when he had finally opened the box. He carefully handed Roger the same small wad that had been taken from him the night before.

"What else is in there?"

"The rest is mine."

"Not anymore. Yankee imperialism in action. See it? Give me the rest."

Don Eloy shook his head ponderously several times.

"I can shoot you and take the money, or I can just take the money. How come you think I wouldn't shoot you, old man? By the time anybody pays any attention, I'm gone."

He insulted the man in Aymara, but the words made no evident impression on him. The wife had shrunk into herself, her shoulders hunched, her head bent way low.

With a truly wrenching effort that might at another time have gentled any stone cowboy in the world, don Eloy passed him the money, all in dollars. No way to count then, but maybe several hundred dollars more. Roger put the money into the front pocket of his jeans and began to back away, the pistol still pointing.

"I'll mail you the gun," he said.

"Please," don Eloy pleaded.

Roger wanted badly to say something that cut hard, something his enemy would be able to chew on as he worked in his lumberyard for the next twenty years, but nothing came. "Troll," he said softly in English, and he was gone. Running. The strength in his legs and lungs made him feel clean as he went, clean and getting younger.

He had a few bad periods on the way to the Peruvian border, doubled up with worry. If don Eloy really knew the police, they might be looking for him. But like everything else in Trollandia, controls were lax, and the Altiplano bus he was riding crossed over at the Lata-Lio checkpoint into a country that was one step north toward home.

Leaving Lata, Bolivia, to enter Lio, Peru, all passengers were required to step down from the bus and file in line past uniformed customs officers, who quizzed them and looked at passports. At the end of the line Roger turned back toward the adobe shed in Lata, in front of which stood a little cluster of Bolivian soldiers in green uniforms, gray ponchos, shiny black boots. He picked up a sun-warmed, sharp-edged rock, hefted it, and felt the itch in his palm that was the urge to throw. But he had learned discipline, and he let the rock fall back onto the ground. He maintained the last place in line.

Because of the tremendous pressure inside his head, he was scarcely aware of filing back onto the bus and moving again, of being safe. He had a window seat, and he had discipline, an acquired skill. He was conscious, however, of taking the dirty square of paper to which the acid was fixed, tearing it in two, and letting the two halves flutter out the window. He felt both clean and empty. After the satisfaction of beating don Eloy, and with hard-earned money in his pocket, the demand returned: Give me back my heart. The pressure in his head, luckily, was still there. But he heard no answer. Planning a little ahead, he calculated how soon he would get to Lima, how much that would cost. Give me back, he heard repeated with some insistence, my heart. He settled back and rode.

The Necessary Plane

Cherokee had worried that Johnny's top hat might draw terrorists, but they were lucky. He rode out of Lima on a bus with money in his pockets. He even gave Cherokee a fifty to hide in her bra. By the time the red-and-blue bus had crawled out of the gray city the money had become a secret part of her skin. She decided she would lose the bill in case she needed it later, even though Johnny might interrogate her body inch by inch. Flame, she reminded herself, not Johnny. Johnny was his name before he discovered magic. But Flame was his true name, his aura name, just as hers was Cherokee. It was the name she should have been born under, he told her when he discovered her at the Stop-N-Go in Lockport, New York. Even to think of their old names meant a lack of faith, and she needed that fifty.

In the United States the old bus they were riding would have been crunched into beer cans. But it was exciting to ride this wreck as it shimmied its way up the Andes, past Lake Titikaka. The higher they went the more exotic the landscape. There was an immense amount of mud and rock, and miles of high sky. The llamas were humpless camels. The high plains Indians were mysterious; they moved their bodies as if they were hiding secrets no privileged, backpacking gringo could ever learn. They hulked when they walked, and when they sat in the dirt guarding the little pyramids of oranges and batteries and contraband soap they had for sale, their shoulders bent toward the earth.

Flame had his theory about the strangeness of the land. "You can't expect things to be logical or rational or to make sense the same way you would in Gringolandia. The Industrial Revolution killed the magic up north. But the Andes are pre-Industrial Revolution. The magic is still alive down here, Cherokee. All we've got to do is wash the shit out of our polluted eyes so we can see it."

He had been talking that way about the Andes for months. He was always reading books on magic, and she figured he got the idea to come to South America out of one of them. At first, Cherokee didn't believe he took any of it seriously. She figured it was just the private nonsense he needed to stay in character for the next show. At least once during every performance he conjured up the Andean magic men, who read coca leaves and burned ceremonial llama shit. But one night when she heard him talking about the Andes in his sleep, she realized he believed what he was saying. They were lying in a patch of grass beneath an overpass on a superhighway going west of Chicago. The grass was brittle and stiff with road dirt, the filth of the Industrial Revolution. Cherokee listened in awe to his naked, unconscious voice as he communicated with the Andean magic men. For the next week she watched him more carefully and was moved when she realized that she had in fact taken up with a zealot, a man who believed his own rap. She felt, if not honored, a little lucky to find herself inside his glow.

It was his glow that first attracted her at the Stop-N-Go. Flame believed in glows; he called them auras. He said if she was capable of sensing his aura in a convenience store, without training, she must be capable of understanding magic.

When he found her she was stacking cans of dog food on shelves. Outside the city there were ducks invading family picnics, flowers wilting in the woods, a million things she would never see, but the air conditioning in the Stop-N-Go enclosed her in a cool cocoon of unreality around her as she stocked cans. He materialized next to her and asked where the natural foods section was. Cherokee's idea of natural food was jalapeño taco sauce.

Flame was skinny. He wore a black t-shirt decorated with a silver moon and a ring of stars looping like flowers. His hair—and this gave her a little start, like waking out of a sex dream before it was finished—was exactly the same shade of yellowy blonde as hers. The long shape of his bones was like hers, too. They could have been brother and sister. He was always impressed by what he never admitted were coincidences. On the back of his left hand a small green snake was tattooed. Its tongue was a red knife. The plain silver hoop earring he wore seemed neither defiant nor effeminate, but simply a necessary decoration. It was summer, and his small feet wriggled in sandals the way a child's feet would. Later it seemed odd that she hadn't noticed the peculiar green of his eyes, clear as a cat's.

He didn't want taco sauce. He explained how the chemicals in processed food jammed up the body's pores and caused spiritual depression. He asked if she was married.

"Sort of," she told him.

"You're sort of married?"

"We're living together, but we're going to get married in the fall. He works at Harrison Radiator, but he might get laid off."

"That's not what you really want to do, is it?"

"You mean get married?" Getting married would be fine. Getting knocked around was not. She had done nothing to him to justify Eddy's beating her.

"What's his name?"

"They call him Slow Eddie. It's a joke."

"Don't tell me your name," he cautioned her. "I'm going to give you your aura name. Even if you don't come with me, I want you to have your aura name. It's a present from me to you. From Flame to Cherokee."

But of course she went with him. She was twenty three and sad, and she left the cans half stacked. It was four o'clock and

Eddie worked afternoons, so she went to their apartment on High Street and took clothes and half the cash—three hundred dollars and change. Flame waited on the street, explaining that it was bad luck to step into the absent man's field of force. At the time she thought he was either lazy or afraid to go in. Much later she realized he had believed what he told her.

Flame travelled light, carrying only a leather backpack filled with what he needed to perform: the black top hat, a black silk cape, a Lone Ranger mask, and his magic paraphernalia. Thumbing and busing, they headed north while the weather was still good. She was happy enough to help him do his street magic, making a few bucks and seeing the country. Even diesel dirt and concrete were better than the Stop-N-Go. She never regretted running out on Slow Eddie, who was probably knocking around another woman within a month. And Flame was a better lover than she had ever expected to find, imaginative and not nearly as selfish as she suspected he really was. Lying in the grass and looking at the stars, she thanked herself for having left.

From the beginning, though, Cherokee had noticed that Flame's regular manner was very different from his show self. It wasn't that she expected him to entertain her when he wasn't working, nor was it just a question of charm. She knew he had to beguile his audiences, and she did not begrudge them the power of his green eyes or the spooky writhing of the snake on his hand or the words that came out like poems or stories or something else capable of transfixing dozens of people at once. But when the two of them were travelling he could go a hundred miles on a single word. He read and reread his magic books, silently practiced his tricks, burrowed into himself to collect his powers and his imagination leaving her entirely behind.

The first time Flame hit her, she forgave him. She was used to forgiving. Besides, even at his most sullen, Flame was nowhere near as bad as either her father or Slow Eddie. With Flame it was never regular, and sometimes two weeks would go by when he was as gentle with her as a movie star. She knew that there were men who didn't hit, and she figured she would find one eventually, but she had lived with much worse than Flame, plus he had the magic.

When the weather turned cold they went south, starting their tour in Raleigh, North Carolina, where she worried about the Ku Klux Klan; if they hated blacks and Jews and Catholics, they must surely hate magicians. But no one bothered them. After the southern tour, Flame told her to get a passport.

Just before they crossed the border into Mexico, Cherokee called Slow Eddie. She only said hello but he recognized her voice and began cursing her out. After a minute she dropped the receiver and let it dangle at the end of the jointed metal cord.

"Ex-fucking-zotic," Flame said as the bus creaked into La Paz.

"Maybe there's a revolution," Cherokee said.

"Nope," he told her confidently. "I read about this in a book. It's June 23rd, isn't it, the Night of San Juan. The Bolivians say it's the coldest night of the year."

To warm themselves, the townspeople had lit bonfires up and down the walls of the canyon, at the bottom of which lay the city. There were dozens, maybe hundreds of bonfires, around which people in ponchos sat drinking. By the time the bus arrived, the fires had been burning for hours, and the canyon valley was sealed in smoke. Rolling down the twisted road into the city made Cherokee dizzy. She knew there was a drop-off to the side though she couldn't see it. This was how it would be when the world burned up, she thought: just hanging smoke pocked with a thousand orange fires, and the world falling away as you went blindly down. "Ex-fucking-zotic," Flame said into her ear again.

Bolivia had always occupied a central place in Flame's theory of magic. In the old days, he told Cherokee, there was magic everywhere in the world. But after the Industrial Revolution the magic went away, and now it could only be found in places sufficiently far, like Bolivia, sufficiently poor, like Bolivia, sufficiently ex-fucking-zotic.

It was two days before the smoke cleared from the city. The first morning, the streets and walks were full of ashes from the bonfires, around which wove a few weary Bolivians. The spectacle made Cherokee nervous. In such a place, she thought, anything could happen. Flame took a more expansive view. "It's like burning away the illusions and the dross of Western rationalism."

"What's dross?"

"Dross is the trash you think is real and think you need, but it's not real and you don't need it. When the smoke clears, watch—we'll be able to see the magic. We're here, goddamn it." His excitement was contagious as a cold she didn't want to catch, but what choice was there?

While the smoke cleared they lay in the dark of a hovel of a hotel called the Palace of the Incas, letting their bodies adjust to the high altitude. Flame chain-smoked joints, swallowing the roaches for security, and Cherokee closed her eyes and remembered things. By now she had travelled far enough that everything that came to mind was worth recalling.

The afternoon of the second day the sky was clear, the mountain sun so bright her eyes hurt even behind sunglasses. She followed Flame to the old San Francisco Church, up Sagarnaga to the witches' street. Indian women in black skirts and striped fabric slings and cocked bowler hats owned the little hilly thoroughfare. Inside one-room adobe sanctuaries and out on the cobblestone street on upturned fruit crates, they sold their magic: dried llama fetuses, their empty eye sockets the shape of pathos; potions and herbs in packets, or heaped loose on mats; little plastic bags of colored rocks. Cherokee had no idea what they were for.

Flame was transfixed. He almost trembled. "We're here," he told her in a hushed voice. "But how do we get in? These women are just the guardians of the gates. I can sense that much. They're in on the magic, and their job is to keep out people who shouldn't get inside."

"Inside what?" she asked him.

Her question so irritated that she knew he'd have hit her had they been in their room.

They spent the afternoon on the witches' street. Flame bought nothing. It was too soon. In the women's presence he was reverent. He would not offend. The eye sockets of the llama fetuses followed Cherokee as she walked by. She hated Flame's excitement. In an unguarded moment she allowed herself to remember her pre-aura name.

That night Flame went into his shell without even a joint for company. The intensity of his brooding drove her out of the room, and she wandered the streets around Sagarnaga watching Indians and European backpackers hug inclines as steep as the Andes. Dross, she told herself, and the sound of that unnatural word in her mouth made her laugh. A man in an elaborate costume of beads and spangles and mirrors walked past, carrying an oversized devil's head mask under his arm. Maybe he's a messenger, she thought.

In the morning Flame explained his plan. It wasn't a question of knocking on doors in the right neighborhood asking where the magic men lived, he told her. What he had to do was to ascend to the necessary plane. Cherokee hated it when he talked like that; it meant he was excluding her. To get there, he'd have to fast. He could smoke joints, the more the better, but he could have no food, only fruit juice and water. No alcohol, not even ceremonially. Meanwhile he had to perform; the money from Lima wouldn't last long, even at the Palace of the Incas.

So they worked. Mornings they performed in the broad brick plaza before San Francisco Church. An Argentine fire eater and a Bolivian selling acne medicine and fundamentalist tracts were working the same space, but Flame was disdainful of what he called their "street shit." His own performance *was* superior, Cherokee acknowledged. He had picked up a little Spanish for his act, but most of what the Mystical Gringo did demanded only the eye's appreciation. In the afternoons they moved through the poor neighborhoods of the mountain city, and they made a little money. She hoped he had forgotten the fifty.

After several days Cherokee thought that Flame might be approaching the necessary plane of consciousness. Their life was intense. To keep up with him she smoked some joints herself and ate sparingly. In the thin air, colors happened, time bent around the crumbling adobe corners. Best, Flame's magic got better. It had always been good, smooth and confident. Now it began to seem almost supernatural. The smoke from the joints and the dry air burned their mouths, their throats, their lungs. They stopped talking, saved their voices for performing. Besides, talking only got in the way.

Once they made love, and Cherokee allowed herself to cry. After that, her dreams got loose and stayed with her when she was awake. One had the shape of an unborn llama with those miserable eyes. She disciplined herself to stay tough, to stay with Flame as he moved upward. Her true and only name, she repeated, was Cherokee.

But her doubts remained. Maybe she wasn't clearheaded enough or committed enough or discerning enough. She did not want to be left behind by Flame. Yet she worried, when her mind reminded her, about cause and effect. There were all kinds of causes, all sorts of effects. The effect of much dope and no food happened one night sometime during the second week. They were resting inside their cave of a room at the Palace of the Incas. She could see the dreams running around Flame's head and could have touched the colors, but they would have burned her hand. Then, without warning, he began to beat her. In perfect quiet, which she would not betray by screaming, she took it, expecting him to stop. But he beat her for a long while, and her body did the screaming her mouth would not. When he stopped for breath, collapsing face up on the bed, she took her backpack and ran.

In the street she bought a piece of bread and a bottle of Coca-Cola, a drink Flame disdained. It made her sick, but she kept it down. Her legs had begun to tremble, so she sat on a curbstone, planting her feet on separate cobbles. The night-time traffic of La Paz flowed past noisily. When the trembling stopped, she bought another piece of bread and a second bottle of Coke.

Flame would not come looking for her, she knew, because he would assume that she'd eventually come back to the hotel. She was a woman, he would decide, without options. She threw up on her third piece of bread.

One of the side streets off Sagarnaga was crowded with little shops selling musical instruments: drums and pipes and guitars and funny, fur-backed things that looked like hairy mandolins. On the stoop of one shop sat a Bolivian man in a striped poncho playing a long pipe. She stopped to listen. While wandering with Flame she'd seen the man before, but she refused to consider whether she'd looked purposely for him now.

"What do you want to buy from me?" he asked her finally. His cheekbones were high, his skin red dark, his voice singsong. He reminded her of a picture in a grade-school history book of an Indian filling a room with gold to appease a Spanish invader. His forehead wrinkled at her. He was handsome.

His name was Ernesto. He owned the music shop and he also had a band that played in a local club. He gave her a windowless room in his house. It was even smaller and darker still than the one at the Palace of the Incas, but no Flame either. Ernesto brought her food three times a day: hot soups, chewy bread, sweet, unrecognizable vegetables shaped like fingers and toes. She recovered slowly and tried to force her dreams back into her sleep where they belonged. The night Ernesto crawled into bed with her, she was not resigned, or resentful, or even particularly sad. Cause and effect, she explained to herself.

When she felt better she joined Ernesto's band. She had always been intrigued by the masked arrogance of musicians on stage, their cultivated distance, the way their mouths made fun. It pleased her to stand on a stage and look out into a faceless audience and be just as aloof as the guitarist with his proud, fast fingers. She played a tambourine, she refused to speak, and she sensed that she was popular with the crowd. She never saw Flame.

Cherokee knew she wouldn't remain here forever, but she had no wish to move on right away. Ernesto took her into his room, which had a window overlooking the sloping city. She scrubbed the glass in the window and put a small spider plant on the sill. She loved the soups and the strange vegetables, and it bothered her only occasionally that Ernesto gave her no money from the band's performances. In the toe of her extra sneaker in the bottom of her pack, she had taped the fifty, folded inside a sheet of paper. Ernesto would not even think to look. She was, after all, a welfare case, graceful, tranquil in her absolute dependence.

She had never been good at guessing when a man was going to hit her. Not with her father or Slow Eddie or Flame. Least of all with Ernesto, who had brought her food on a clean wicker tray. They were in the street. Her tambourine shivered lightly in her hand. Ernesto had been happy-drunk all night on stage, lover-of-the-world-in-all-its-weaknesses drunk. She told him she would meet him at home, that she wanted to walk a little. Would he take the tambourine with him? Suddenly, he punched her. The inside of her mouth bled. It was the moment she had not known she was waiting for. She took his arm to forgive him, but she saw him only from a distance. In an instant, without trying, she had reached her own necessary plane.

"Ok," she said in slow Spanish, "I'll go home with you."

"I'm sorry," he said sincerely. "I was just drunk. But I'm ok now. I'm sorry."

At home he was asleep in three minutes. Cherokee rose and dressed. She felt for the spider plant on the window sill and carefully pulled its roots from the dirt. She placed the naked plant on the bed at Ernesto's feet, picked up her pack, and left his house.

She wasn't tired, so she sat on the steps of San Francisco Church all night in the chafing, dry cold until oblique rays of light spilled down the canyon wall into the city. When people began to appear on the streets she changed her fifty for Bolivian currency. From a hardware store on Sagarnaga she bought a wooden case with a handle. On the witches' street she purchased a small llama fetus, a few vials and packets, a bag of dried coca leaves, and a bag of colored rocks. In the market she found a violet paisley kerchief and a gypsy gown decorated with colored whorls, and she changed in a public bath.

For luck, she began at San Francisco Plaza. She didn't see Flame there, and for the moment there were no hawkers. She sat on the ground, arranged her gown, and opened her case. In one corner of it she stood the llama fetus. She arranged the vials and packets in a way that pleased her eye and looked like art. She opened the bag of coca leaves on her lap so her nervous hands had something to play with. She propped up her sign, which said Fortune Telling in Spanish and English in attractive letters.

A tourist was her first customer. Not an American but a European, though she did not venture to ask which country. He spoke pretty good English.

"How much for my fortune?" he asked her politely. He was wooly, brown haired and brown bearded, like a civilized sheep.

"Two American dollars if you don't like it. Whatever you want to give me if you do like it," she told him impassively. A little group of Bolivians had gathered behind the tourist.

"Who are you?" he asked her.

"My parents were Americans," she explained. "They came down years ago as missionaries. They went into the jungle up north of Santa Cruz near the Brazilian border. I was born there, in the jungle."

"What's your name?"

She didn't want to give a name this soon; it would be bad luck. "Do you want your fortune told or not?"

"Do it, please."

"You have to believe in the magic. Only if you believe in the magic will the coca leaves tell me what they really think."

"Do your parents know what you're doing here?"

"My parents are dead. They were killed in the jungle looking for the magic men."

"What magic men?"

"I don't want to talk about them. After a few years in the jungle, my father began to see how the magic worked. He stopped believing in the Christian God, and then both he and Mother were killed looking for the magic."

It was not a lie, just the imaginative embroidering of certain original circumstances. The European tourist unharnessed himself from his backpack and set it on the ground. He hunkered before her, and she took his soft, white hand. She traced the lines with absorption, felt a tremor of response in his palm. Holding his weak, willing hand in hers reinforced Cherokee's sense of power and independence. After reading his hand, she consulted her coca leaves with the same concentration. She cradled the unborn llama, and she saw the man's actual future. She told it to him. Pleased, he gave her three dollars.

Bolstered but still nervous, she accepted a Bolivian customer, for whom she was sure she must be ex-fucking-zotic. The man looked hammered-down poor, his shoulders rounded, so she lowered her price for him. Holding his hard, brown, trusting hand to read the lines of his life, she knew that no man would ever hit her again.

The Bolivian left satisfied, knowing his intimate future like a warning, and Cherokee had a few free minutes in which to collect herself. She imagined Flame with the Andean magic men practicing their hustle, their quick tricks, and she felt forgiving. If Flame hadn't led her here to the mountains, she might be back in Lockport getting knocked around by Slow Eddie and stacking dog food. She tried to control her rapid breathing, felt dizzy because of the altitude, and closed her eyes against the flat bars of bright sunlight in the plaza. She was free. It was easy to put away her aura name for good and remember that she was Sarah.

The Book of Pain and Suffering

The only way I can think to put this makes it sound ridiculous: I went to Paraguay, I chewed on a magic weed, my life changed. But that doesn't come close to getting at what happened. When I do try to get close what comes out is rhetoric, a wall of words that hides what I would like to show, which is the reason and the color of my fear: I have been invaded.

It was supposed to be my idyll. I teach Comparative Literature at the University of Buffalo, with a willing weakness for Latin American fiction. For years I had been intrigued by Paraguay's one big-time writer, Augusto Roa Bastos, who had spent his life in exile, conquering and recreating in his imagination a *patria* maybe no one ever set foot in. I admired the stubborn aggression required to fuse memory with a powerful sense of place and come up with a country no one else could conceive. And then the dictator, General Stroessner, fell. After all those years outside, Roa Bastos could go home.

Sort of. His roots were in Toulouse, but he returned to Paraguay periodically. I wrote to him there, and he agreed to an interview for a book I wanted to do on exile and imagination. January was convenient for him, and after the kind of winter we had been having in Buffalo January was more than convenient for me. Go, Maggie, my wife, said. Get out of here, my children said. I went.

Asunción after 35 years of Stroessner has plenty of problems: crowding and unemployment and rickety infrastructure and untaxable contraband and beggars at congested intersections desperate to wash your windshield for pennies that won't solve their problems. But the city has not yet lost the charm of its past as a quiet colonial capital. I arrived early. There was more time than I needed to do the interview, which I hoped to stretch out and record, so before contacting Roa Bastos I took a few days to walk the city, languorous in the Southern Cone summer. Traffic was light, the streets quiet. Anyone who could afford to had left the country and the heat for the beaches in Uruguay and Brazil.

It was like stepping out of eternal winter into a pleasant dream of warmth. I went out even during the siesta hours, the hottest hours of the day, the sun on my back or in my face slowly boiling something ugly out of my system. Not particularly caring where I wound up, I explored neighborhood after placid neighborhood of houses that seemed like refuges, way stations on an exotic pilgrimage. Bright flowers spilled in dramatic cascades down high whitewashed walls behind which parrots actually jabbered. The orange-red tiles of long, low roofs were art and architecture, an eloquent human reshaping of the elemental mud. Ornamental iron gates, no two designs alike, peeled their paint in the sunlight, which flooded the city in bleaching white waves, leaving it in a trance I had no desire to disturb. All I wanted was to be there.

By the time I called Roa Bastos I was relaxed and ready for the interview, which went better than I could have hoped. He has aged well, grown into the lion status he acquired over the years of his success. His white hair suggests vigor more than age. A kind of down-turning sternness to his mouth and the lower part of his face is counterbalanced by the eyes, which are where the quick intelligence, the force of perception, gather. Through the course of the interview, which lasted four days, three hours a day, he was courteous, careful and precise. Some bitterness came through, of course; exile breeds it. And the combination of intelligent perception and artistic self-sufficiency made for a kind of supreme conviction that had its cruel side, especially when he talked about other writers. But he liked the idea of my book, and the central part his fiction would play in it, and he talked straight and brilliantly in twenty-minute stretches that I recorded, diligently making insurance copies at the end of each session. The only bad part was thinking about going back to Buffalo, where the snow was still falling.

So I didn't. The night of our third interview session, Roa Bastos invited me to a get-together at the Casa Viola, part of an impressive restoration project of colonial buildings financed by the Spanish government. He introduced me as Peter, his new friend from the snow-bound North. He was immediately overwhelmed with attention so I backed off, stood around with a glass of white wine on the brick-floored patio of an eighteenth-century building across the street from the presidential palace, in front of which black limos with polarized windows were parked waiting for the power brokers to finish the business of their day.

"The contrast is eloquent, is it not?" It was the first English I had heard since coming to Paraguay, and it startled me out of the abstraction into which I had fallen, replaying some of what Roa Bastos had said to me, testing it against the fiction, worrying the shape of my book.

Juan de la Cruz was a short man with a severe, dark face on which the goatee stood out like a symbol of protest. "You see it, do you not? In Paraguay, at any rate, art stands in opposition to power. The two are incompatible. We would all like to be able to tell a story with a happy ending, in which art finally vanquishes brute power, or power concedes some little sacred province to art, but we cannot. The struggle to the death continues. That's what charms me about this spot. It's like standing on the dividing line, with an architectural insight that defines the problem for you."

He was an architect and a gracious man who took the trouble to introduce me to people all of whom seemed to know Roa Bastos, or to want to. "You can divide the *Asuncenos* into three groups," he explained to me. "First are those, like myself, who believe he is a giant of a writer and deserves everything he gets. Then there are those who envy his success and spend an enormous amount of energy belittling everything he has written. Then there are those, the majority, who have no opinion because they are incapable of having one. They are the ones who flock to our Roa the way moths go to a light, simply because it shines."

Thanks to Juan de la Cruz I had a fine time at the reception, which Roa Bastos had not told me was in his honor. I drank several glasses of white wine, served efficiently by brown-faced men in white jackets who moved like civilized panthers through the well dressed crowd. I felt full, at peace, warmer than I remember being in a long time. A little breeze scudded across the patio, and the sun went down florid. Behind the presidential palace the Paraguay River went gradually black. When people asked about the purpose of my visit I was less reticent than I usually am. There was a particular pleasure, almost sensual, in talking in Spanish about the interview, my book project, the idea of imagination in exile.

"Roa's good," a round woman in a black dress said, nodding at me but talking as if out of the side of her mouth to the circle of people Juan de la Cruz had gathered around us. "Roa is very fine. But as long as he's come all this way maybe he ought to read The Book of Pain and Suffering."

A little nervous titter traveled the circle, and someone called our attention to the motorcade of black sedans moving in urgent state away from the palace.

"What is The Book of Pain and Suffering?" I asked.

A guitarist with club feet who had been imprisoned under Stroessner for making subversive music shook his head impatiently. "Nothing," he said. "It's a metaphor, it's nothing."

I understood that it was more than nothing, that I had brushed by chance against something local that mattered. The wine, the thaw, the successful interviews, and my book were all working on me. I realized I wanted something more from my trip to Paraguay than inspiration for a chapter. I felt a fierce, fast liking for these people who had suffered under a dictatorship I could scarcely imagine. I wanted to be touched.

"Asunción is a small town," Juan de la Cruz apologized. "We talk to ourselves too frequently, and we all know each other's jokes."

When the reception was over Roa Bastos waved once in my direction, then disappeared in a sleek gray Mercedes escorted by an elderly man with a patch on one eye. Juan de la Cruz offered me a ride to my hotel. I was staying in a modest, old-fashioned place away from the city center, camouflaged in a thicket of palm and banana trees in one of those residential neighborhoods whose sweet somnolence had caught me up when I arrived. "Listen," he said as I was leaving the car. "I'm sorry for putting you off the way we did at the reception."

"What is the Book of Pain and Suffering, Juan?"

He stared at his knuckles on the steering wheel of his Toyota Landcruiser. His strong hands were battered, the hands of a builder. "Asunción is a small town," he repeated.

I got back into the vehicle, and he drove downtown to an Italian restaurant with an outdoor patio far enough from the city lights to draw down the moonlight, which hallowed the trees and the plants that crowded the place. On the bricks of the patio floor the shadows of exotic leaves became dark spikes, sharp swords. The warm air was not particularly humid; it lay like silk on my skin, and I felt as though I had been led into some kind of middle sanctum.

Ordering a bottle of Chilean Cousino Macul, Juan de la Cruz decided to talk. "Against my better judgment. In the first place it's not a book. Not in the usual sense of the word."

What's good, I guess, is never good enough. My stay in Asunción had already brought me more than I had hoped to get. Roa Bastos took me seriously, treated me with respect, talked to me about his writing with interested precision as though I had been designated his personal recording angel. The doubled nastiness of academic politics and the Buffalo winter were equally distant. But I wanted more. I wanted to read The Book of Pain and Suffering

It was a collection of stories, Juan de la Cruz told me, written long hand and circulated among a select group of *Asuncenos* who agreed ahead of time to certain conditions. Anyone who read was required to keep the existence of the stories a secret. The stories could not be photocopied or reproduced in any way, and readers were obliged to keep them circulating. Any mention of publication would be considered betrayal and constitute grounds for expulsion from the circle. Those were the conditions laid down by the author, whom her readers called, behind her broad back, la Madre Tierra. Mother Earth.

"Mercedes Alcalá is a planet unto herself," Juan de la Cruz told me, "but she is hyper-sensitive, and she would not take kindly to the nickname if she knew."

"Why doesn't she want to be published?"

"She claims she isn't really an author, just a sort of dictating machine. She is the fountain up from which the holy water flows. That's part of it."

"But not all of it?"

He shook his head, waved a breadstick in my direction, drank some of the good red wine, which was sloshing around in my stomach with the white wine I had drunk at the reception creating an unusual, for me, receptivity. This was the way it was in the secret life I hadn't known I had.

"I think she's out of her mind," said Juan. "A kind of *idiot savant,* maybe, except that she writes. All that about being a recorder is just a pose she affects for reasons I can't guess at. The thing about the weed is nonsense."

"What weed?"

But he wouldn't say. He was more interested in trying to describe the stories to me. "Reading The Book of Pain and Suffering is like ... It's not like literature, it's not what you would call an aesthetic experience. It's more like ... It's like being inside a movie, maybe, if a movie were real."

"Will you show them to me? I'll agree to any conditions you want."

A gray striped cat with the moon in both eyes jumped from the low branch of a nearby tree and came up to our table. The branch quivered for a few seconds, the gentlest reminder of gravity. It sat on the mud-brown bricks of the patio switching its tail like a metronome. I thought if I listened hard enough I could hear the music. But Juan de la Cruz shook his head. "They're not my conditions. Mother Earth won't let anyone read she hasn't interviewed personally."

"Then ask her to interview me. Please."

"It's not that easy, Peter. One, you're a foreigner. And two, the rest of us have known Mercedes forever. We can put up with her. We understand her, sort of. She is part of us."

But the idea of the book that wasn't a book, and of the slightly terrible Madre Tierra herself, had taken hold in my imagination, which was floating loose in its own temporary exile. I am a person who refuses to push, who concedes to the first indication of force in others. Not out of timidity but as a tactic. I have found giving way to be the surest guarantee of maintaining the private space of autonomy I crave. So what I did was strange to me; I seemed to be observing someone not quite myself from under one of the spike-leafed trees of the patio.

I watched myself push hard against my new friend's reluctance, I refused to concede, and before the moon-eyed cat left us and we left the restaurant he promised to try to set up an interview with the author of The Book of Pain and Suffering.

"That's as much as I can do, and more than I should," he said, but it was enough.

The following day I spoke with Roa Bastos for the last time. I found him brooding and preoccupied, thrown off balance, perhaps, by the tremendous discordance between the country he had spent his life abroad imagining and the actual land to which he had returned. For the first time he looked his age to me, and the string of aphorisms he offered to be deciphered later, back in the Buffalo winter, seemed as forced as they were brilliant. I went away a little disappointed.

I knew without being told that I had to be patient, to wait for a call. There was time. My wife has found a second career training people in large companies how to work as though they were in small companies, and a new contract was taking her to Atlanta for a month. Our kids, in high school, were happy to be on their own for a little while and responsible enough not to go crazy. So I picked up again with my walks through the residential neighborhoods of Asunción, letting the city breathe its thick, narcotic spell on me; there was honey on that warm, wet breath, and anise, and orange. Something that grew as it rotted, rotted as it grew.

One siesta hour I lost track of time standing beneath a massive, splendid tree whose branches seemed to droop with the weight of thousands of orange flowers. Two people would have had difficulty joining hands around the base of the trunk, below which a wandering root had lifted and displaced the sidewalk. On the private side of a whitewashed brick wall a parrot nattered, a monkey griped, a maid absorbed in some domestic chore I couldn't see sang quietly in Guarani, the country's private language. My thoughts were more like dreams than words. I was on the outside of so much, but not, I thought, not forever.

"It would be a good idea to take something with you," Juan de la Cruz advised me when he finally called to say Mother Earth had consented to see me. "Flowers, candy, the most traditional thing you can imagine."

I took both, worrying that the chocolate would melt in the fierce heat. Have you ever let yourself go toward something you can't see or understand? It's the sweetest form of surrender, like recovering your state of grace. That was the condition I was in when I knocked on the door of the enormous old house in Manorá belonging to Mercedes Alcalá, author, if that was the right word, of The Book of Pain and Suffering.

Large does not convey any sense of the woman. Nor does fat. She was neither, she was both. She was massive. Broad and bulky, she filled up all the space in her vicinity, which meant any communication had to be, one way or another, long distance. She took the flowers from me, petted the petals, took the chocolate and looked accusingly at me. "They've melted."

"The heat," I apologized, but she was already calling for the maid to come get the candy and put it in the refrigerator.

She seemed to forget I was there, giving long instructions in Guarani about the box of chocolates to the woman, a frail woman whose thick black hair dangled in a shining tight plait, with dainty hands and feet. Next to her employer she was unnaturally tiny. While Mercedes spoke I watched her. Her neck and shoulders were powerful, the kind of build you saw on NFL linemen, except that the muscles were covered with an additional layer of fat. Not jelly-like fat. It was dense, hard, unshakable. It augmented the sensation of power she radiated. Her wide face was the palest brown, the eyebrows very thick, the outline of a mustache appearing and disappearing as she turned her head or twisted her face into stylized gestures of irritation or outrage. In every way she was what Juan de la Cruz had warned me: *formidable*.

The chocolates were taken away, the flowers clipped and put in a crystal vase in the foyer, and I was invited to sit in a long, low living room the walls of which were covered with some of the most tasteless, uninspired paintings I have ever seen. They went from floor to ceiling, leaving almost no white space, jostling against each so loudly that the walls seemed to shriek in pain. Ordering me to a slat-backed wooden chair, Mother Earth lowered her body with great care into a heavily padded chaise that had been reinforced to accommodate the weight. The little movement she had made since I came in appeared to have exhausted her, and she sucked in air in tremulous, rhythmic gulps that worried me.

"I wasn't going to talk to you," she admitted. The fingers of one hand toyed incessantly with a flat-faceted ruby ring on the other hand. "But Juan de la Cruz likes you, for some strange reason. He is one of the decent ones, though he's like all the rest when it comes to business. I wanted to get his help to invest a little money I have, but he was ready to trick me out of it. I saw that right away and told him no thank you."

I could think of nothing more preposterous than Juan de la Cruz cheating this curious, unlikable woman out of a little money, but the single cheap shot she took at him was nothing to the savagery she inflicted on the rest of the people I had met at the reception for Roa Bastos at Casa Viola. She spent a good half hour inventorying their foibles, their vices, their weaknesses and sins and crimes and chronic inadequacies. The subject elated her, filled her up with hot air that she exhaled at controlled intervals in sharp-bladed sentences that cut deep. These were the people, I realized, who were her fans, the faithful and enthusiastic readers of The Book of Pain and Suffering. Her venom appalled me. The art, I decided, would have to be awfully damn good to compensate for the artist.

When she tired of trashing her fans she remembered the chocolate, which the maid brought on a silver tray. Mercedes opened the box, lifted three or four pieces from the paper tray in which they sat, sniffed them individually as if to ascertain which was the poison one. "Where did you say you got these?"

I told her the name of the place, and she nodded vigorously, reassured, perhaps, that I had spent an appropriate amount on her sweets. I watched her eat half a dozen with slow gusto, savoring each piece as she nibbled at them in a way that reminded me of an animal picking at its dead prey. "Tell me one good reason I should let you read the stories," she demanded as she ate.

"Because you want someone outside your circle to look at them. You're curious to hear an outsider's opinion."

She shook her head angrily. "Dead wrong. You're presuming that I care about the stories the way writers care about their creations. But I don't. The stories are nothing but a burden to me. Five years ago—that's when they started coming to me—my life changed for the worse, and it hasn't gotten better. The stories, if that's what they are, are my cross. I don't write them, I'm just the pencil." Her empty hand groped for the chocolate box. Absently she tossed the empty paper shells to the floor. They landed on a hideous rose and purple carpet, a machine-made pseudo-Oriental.

Listening to her petulant rag, I began to think they were setting me up for an elaborate joke, at my expense, for unfathomable reasons of their own. There were no stories, and I would waste my days in Asunción chasing a phantom.

But she told me suddenly, "I'm going to show you the stories. Do you know why? Not because I care about what you might think, but because I feel better when I get rid of them. They make my head ache. When I pass one on to somebody the pain goes down, for a little while."

Bracing herself with her arms, with a tremendous effort she threw herself off the chaise and stood up. For an instant she tottered and I thought she was going to fall over, but she righted herself and ploughed across the room to a tall oak cabinet, from which she took a notebook. She opened the notebook, ripped out some pages, and waved them in my direction. "The usual rules apply," she told me. "I'm sure they've told you about the rules. This is the newest one. I dictated it yesterday."

"You can trust me," I assured her. At the time it wasn't a lie.

"Juan de la Cruz has charge of the rest of the stories. If you show him this one he'll know that it's ok for you to see the rest."

Mention of Juan de la Cruz reminded her again of how he had tried to swindle her out of the money her husband had left her when he died. I listened with pretended patience to the character assassination she carried out on her best friend and made my way to the front door. Even more than reading the stories, just then, I wanted to get away from la Madre Tierra.

"Listen," she told me, pinching the skin on my arm with remarkably strong fingers. "Reading these stories is not what you think it's going to be. It's not a pleasant aesthetic experience. There have been complaints. Look at the one I gave you. That should tell you whether your curiosity is worth the cost. My advice is that it's not."

"Thank you," I said, honestly enough.

"Don't forget," she repeated, closing the heavy wooden door in my face. "The usual rules apply."

When my eldest daughter turned five she asked me whether Jesus or the dinosaurs came first. I don't remember what I told her, but I do remember what the question taught me: What you do, what you say, is who you are. I didn't mind taking responsibility for a cosmology. But I have been troubled ever since by the closing up of possibility implied in being my daughter's father and a source, however fallible, of authority. I understand the need to develop a stable, functional identity; hard to establish a line of credit without one. It's like a quiet, protracted suicide, though, isn't it? What I didn't know I was looking for when I stubbornly insisted on finding out about The Book of Pain and Suffering was relief from the person I had become. Unfortunately, that's what I got.

The manuscript Mercedes Alcalá gave me was seventeen pages of plain bond paper, unlined, covered in a tight, schoolgirl's hand by someone who had been taught that neatness counted. I took the story with me downtown to the Plaza Uruguaya, sat on a bench in an oasis of shade while little boys with hoarse voices and tuber-shaped brown feet kicked a soccer ball that needed air, and pathetic young women in hideous tight dresses strutted trying unsuccessfully to hustle in the heat. Mercedes' handwriting was easy to read, but I read slowly. And my life changed.

What I had hoped to find was, at best, an authentic voice, an unusual point of view, a story that jarred. I was unprepared for what found me. It was not like reading; even the most active, involved reader maintains some kind of distance from the story on the page. The only halfway accurate way to describe what happened when I read Mercedes' story is to say that I disappeared. I ceased to be myself, a reader on a bench. I entered the story, the story entered me, and for as long as it took me to get through it I became the woman whose story it was.

She is a woman from the country whose husband has gone to Buenos Aires to work in construction. A dream convinces her that he is not coming back, because he has taken up with a young Bolivian girl working as a domestic servant in the house of a wealthy Argentine family. The Paraguayan woman has five young children, too young to be of much help in planting the cotton she needs to survive. She calculates her odds, takes a chance. She sells a portable radio her husband left behind, buys bus tickets for herself and her children, brings them to Asunción. She cajoles a family from home who are now living in the poor *barrio* by the river, la Chacarita, into watching her children while she looks for work. She finds none. Eventually she wears out her welcome at the house of the friendly family, who are having their own hard times. She pleads for a little more time. She becomes more aggressive, more insistent in her search for work, any kind of work. She finds none. One afternoon on a quiet street she finds an unlocked door. Inside a cabinet in the entry hall she finds enough money to buy either tickets for herself and her children back home, or else one ticket to take herself to Buenos Aires. She takes the money, walks back to la Chacarita wondering which she will do. There is a line, and she has one foot on either side of it.

It took me a while to return to myself after reading the story, and longer still before I could stand and walk. I felt as though I had ingested some sort of hallucinogen. I was reamed out, the cells of myself scrubbed clean and emptied. I felt violated, exhausted. I thought about reading the story through again but couldn't; there was nothing left of me to read. It faded, eventually, and I began to doubt what I remembered. Mercedes Alcalá, la Madre Tierra, was simply an exceptional writer with the power to draw a person inside her fiction.

"Nonsense," Juan de la Cruz told me when I tried to rationalize away the experience. I had stopped at his office on Calle Montevideo to surrender the story. "You're in the denial phase. We all went through it. You can't conceive of what happened; therefore it didn't happen. Look at me." He waved his arm to take in the work-a-day office, dominated by a drafting table and a computer with a large screen on which a CAD blueprint glowed. "I'm an architect. I live in a practical world of building materials and contract deadlines and labor problems."

"But you believe … "

"It's not a question of believing or not, or even of explaining. You were lucky. She decided to let you read. You're one of us now. The question to ask is whether you want to go on."

"I can't."

"Suit yourself," he shrugged. "Perhaps it's better that you don't."

"But you—the rest of you—you can't go on hiding her. You can't own her the way you think you do. She belongs to the world. She has to be published."

That made him angry. "I knew it was a mistake to let you in on the book. It's not meant for someone like you." Not for a gringo, he didn't say; didn't have to.

"Reading Mercedes Alcalá could change the world."

He shook his head. "She doesn't want to be published. She doesn't even know we've given the stories a name. If I told her what you just said she would forbid me to show you the rest. This is local, Peter, it's something that belongs to us."

We parted with mutual distrust. I told him I was going back home to Buffalo, and he wished me a pleasant trip, knowing no one could imagine or believe the truth even if I tried to describe it. But that same evening, from my hotel, I called him at his home.

He laughed easily when he answered, as though the suspicion and anger of the morning had passed between two other people.

"I knew you weren't going. It's like taking a drug, isn't it? You can stop any time you want to, but you don't want to."

"Did reading The Book of Pain and Suffering make you feel you were losing your mind?" I asked him. "All I can do is hunt for explanations of what happened to me."

"A little free *consejo*," he offered. "Learn from the mistakes the rest of us made. Stop trying to explain it. Read the book. That's all."

So I read the book. The following day the guitarist with club feet, whose name was Elixeno, brought the rest of the stories to my hotel room. We sat on the verandah drinking Campari and soda, and I slowly smoked a cigar he offered. To entertain his guests, the manager of the hotel had put a giant Paraguayan wild tiger, a *yaguarete*, in a cage at the far end of the patio under the trees. While we drank we watched a waiter in a white shirt and bolo tie unlock the cage, throw in a live duck, then lock the cage again and walk away whistling. The tiger, which had been sleeping, lifted its head once and stared at the duck but didn't move. The duck froze.

"Bad luck," said Elixeno. "I mean being a duck in a cage with a tiger knowing as soon as he gets hungry he's going to tear you to pieces."

"Is The Book of Pain and Suffering art? Is that what it is?"

He drummed his fingers on the table between us. "Art is what I do, Peter. Art is the music I make with my guitar. What Mercedes does is something else again."

"But what? What is it?"

He closed his eyes to a squint, smiled crookedly at me, drank his Campari and soda. By which I was made to understand that my mistake was in trying to understand what needn't be understood. So I stopped trying. When Elixeno left I took the sheaf of stories into my room, turned on the overhead fan, and read.

If sex is a cameo death, reading The Book of Pain and Suffering was a ritual suicide. In a real way, I ceased to be. I was overwhelmed. I stepped out of myself into the world of Mercedes' stories, into the people who inhabited that planet. I lived their terrors and tribulations, their ecstasies and humiliations and instants of insight, their brilliant accommodations and dull stubborn heroism, their inevitable, awesome loss. Not vicariously, not on the back of any metaphor, not by extension. I went there.

It was early evening when I stepped foot into The Book of Pain and Suffering. The sun was coming up over the city when I finally fell out again. I lay on my bed inert, incapacitated, undone. Cocks crowing hurt my ears. I lay without moving for several hours, and when I finally left the room my body was sore and stiff, as though I had been on a booze binge. My nerves were jangled, and I was more irritable than I remember being in my life.

Outside in the patio, in the cage with the *yaguarete*, there was no duck.

"You read them all at once, didn't you?" Juan de la Cruz told me when I handed over the stories at his office. "I can tell. You look like a man possessed."

"I have to talk to Mercedes."

"So go talk, if you can get a word in edgewise. Just don't believe her. She'll tell you about her weed, but it's a lie."

I remembered to take more candy and flowers, and that morning we went through the same odd ritual of possession and consumption that seemed to move the woman. The same slim servant woman appeared and disappeared like the spirit of goodness in light counterbalance to la Madre Tierra's grumpy bulk.

"Will you let me take the stories to the United States and be published there?"

"Not interested," she shook her head. Behind her on the wall hung a trite rendering of a country scene in which a giant flowering lapacho tree towered benignly over a farmer's thatch-roofed shack. "Tell me again where you picked up those flowers."

I told her. "Why won't you let me have the stories published?"

"Tell me what you think of me," she countered. "Honestly. Describe me the way you would to a third person."

Impossible, and she knew it. "I know what I am, and I know why. But I have my integrity, Señor Pedro. I refuse to take credit for something I am not responsible for. Come with me."

She heaved herself from the chaise and trundled back through the house into the back patio, a domestic refuge in the center of which stood an unpainted trellis covered with grape vines. Almost-ripe green grapes nestled in the thickness of leaves, which were mottled with sunlight. Behind the trellis grew some vegetables; half a dozen scrawny chickens made a lulling, self-satisfied sound as they foraged in the garden.

From the far side of the vegetables Mercedes pulled a leafy plant with a stalk that looked like rhubarb, except that the red was deeper, blood red. She put the stalk in my hands. "My husband was from the country," she told me. "His people were farmers. Years ago, when we built this house, he made a trip up north to Concepción and brought back some of this stuff. He never did anything with it, just let it grow. Five years ago, after he was long dead, I tried it. I thought I might put it in a salad."

"It's a drug," I said.

She shook her head. "I've had it analyzed in a laboratory in Sao Paolo."

"But it gives you the visions out of which your stories come."

But I had it wrong again. "You misunderstand the process," she told me. "You're still thinking of them as some sort of literary effort. I'm just the recorder, Señor Peter. I eat, I write. No one believes me, and that infuriates me. I've forced some of them to try the weed."

"And?"

"It seems to affect people differently. Most of them it doesn't affect at all. A few, yes. Juan de la Cruz became violently ill and threw up for three days."

"What about Elixeno, the guitarist?"

"Elixeno complained about powerful dreams, and for a week he was unable to play the guitar."

"I want to try it." I had made up my mind.

"Suit yourself. Pull up as much as you want. It grows like a weed. It *is* a weed, as far as I can tell. One thing, though."

"What's that?"

"The usual rules still apply."

I took three longish red stalks back to my hotel, where another bad-luck duck stood paralyzed in the cage while the *yaguarete* slept on its back, its feet up in the air like a kitten's. To ground myself, I called home. "I'm thinking about taking a year off from school," my daughter Alice informed me. Alice is in the twelfth grade, and universities across the land want her for her exceptional mathematics ability. "I'm going to buy a Harley and ride to New Mexico."

I asked her whether I could go with her and was satisfied when she said of course. She told me that the company in Atlanta had offered my wife a six-month contract, and our son Gerald was still undefeated in wrestling, continuing to pin every opponent who ventured onto the mat with him. I told her I was fine, too.

Afterward I sat on the verandah watching the day die in splendid colors. Newly showered guests came and went across the grass, waiters carried aluminum trays with drinks and ice buckets, and traffic on the street beyond the wall made a noise not quite like complaint. Without really making a conscious decision I chewed on one of the red stalks, which was fibrous like celery but with a slight peppery taste. Mercedes had told me the amount ingested would have no effect on anything. I ate the whole stalk.

When nothing happened I was more than disappointed, I was cast down and depressed. I waited, waited, and nothing. Waiting made me exhausted, and I slunk to bed before midnight.

What woke me was the dream, but the dream was not the vision, if vision is what I experienced. The dream was the antechamber, the room through which I stepped on my way. There was no story in the dream; a story requires a certain detachment. Nor was there a self conscious of observing; rather, it was as though I had been exploded into a million bits that fell apart, came together to make up a place—it had to be Paraguay—where something momentous was bound to happen.

And did. Awake, I threw the cover off and lay on my back staring at the ceiling fan, which rotated on low, the blades catching a little dull light from outside and throwing it off into the black air. I could not have written it down, the way Mercedes did. A woman of eighteen from a village in Amambay. She is standing in the shadow of the wall at the train station, near Plaza Uruguaya. The tight short dress she wears is the form of her aggression. She is sweating, and there is fire inside her mouth when a boy in a fancy car with polarized windows stops next to her and leers.

It wasn't a story, because a story is something you hear and imagine. Not a vision. A vision is something you see and imagine. The most accurate way to describe what happened is to say that I became that woman, for the duration of the experience. I understood completely what Mercedes meant when she said it had nothing to do with any literary enterprise.

The night was eclipsed. I have no recollection of time passing or not passing. In the morning things began to get crazy. I visited la Madre Tierra again and witnessed my experience vindicate her; *I told you so,* she didn't have to say. It dawned on me then that she resented deeply what had happened to her: Her life had ceased to be hers alone, become crowded with the clamor of strangers who hurt. And she had no place to which she could retreat, shut them all out. The world would stand up and applaud the fruit of her genius, if she let it, but she would not, because there was no genius, only its fruit, ripe and ready on a plate, like spontaneous generation. I appreciated her scrupled reluctance, and for the first time I admired her as a person, a little. I lobbied hard for her to let me take the stories back to the U.S., but she refused. The usual rules still applied.

It was time for me to go home. I had put it off as long as I reasonably could. And I didn't really want to stay in Paraguay, where I was an interloper. I missed my family, was disappointed not to have heard my wife's good news from her directly. I made a reservation for the following day.

My mistake, moral or tactical, was in letting the obsession grow in me. I wanted to go home, but I wanted to take the stories with me. What I did with them, if anything, would be determined later. For the moment, all that mattered was getting them.

The problem was Juan de la Cruz saw right through me. "You agreed to the same conditions the rest of us did," he told me. "Nothing has changed."

Except me. "All I want is one more look," I lied. "I'm going away, you know. The rest of you can keep reading forever. This is my last chance. Anyway it's selfish on your part not to share."

"I don't have them at the moment."

"Who does?"

"I'm sorry, Peter. I won't tell you."

We parted as friends in disagreement, and I thanked him for the trouble he had taken to introduce me to The Book of Pain and Suffering. Then I followed a hunch. I tracked down Elixeno through the owner of the bar where he was performing, went to the little house off Avenida Mariscal Lopez where I found him working on a piece by Agustín Barrios, the Paraguayan guitarist and composer.

"To make a living Barrios had to dress up as an Indian in feathers," Elixeno told me. "They billed him as the Paganini of the Paraguayan jungle. Can you imagine the humiliation?"

"I have to go home," I said. "Tomorrow. I wanted to have one more look at Mercedes' stories."

"Sure," he said. "Mercedes interviewed a new reader yesterday, a saxophone player friend of mine. But Tico won't mind waiting a day."

That easy. I took the stories, promised to return them the following day, took a taxi downtown and had them photocopied. The process took an agonizingly long time, and I was afraid of being caught in what I recognized was a reprehensible act. I won't attempt to explain away what I did except to say that it seemed short-sighted and small of my Paraguayan friends to keep their secret to themselves. It was like, I told myself, the decision to publish personal letters belonging to some great artist who, alive, had expressed the wish that they not be published. At a certain point, inexorably, such private property must become public.

That night, my last in Asunción, I was afraid to fall back into the stories. I read one page at random, felt myself teeter on a dangerous brink, put them away and slept. I woke once in the middle of the night, saw and stepped into a field of wet cotton, became the old man with a burlap sack tied to his waist who had to harvest that cotton, felt his arthritis shoot through my limbs in needles of pain. I was afraid.

But still obsessed. In the morning I returned the stories to Elixeno and went to the airport, arriving several hours before the plane was due to take off. I checked in, went through the security check, parked on a hard plastic seat and tried to sleep.

Coming out of a fitful doze, I guess I wasn't really surprised to see Juan de la Cruz coming toward me, Elixeno clumping along behind him. There was no small talk, not even any recrimination. Maybe they understood they would have done the same, in my position. "Give me the copies you made of the stories, Peter," Juan ordered me brusquely.

I opened my briefcase, handed them over. They were angry, of course, at my betrayal.

"I'm sorry."

"Is this the only copy, Peter?"

It was, and they believed me. They went away mad, and I went home to Buffalo.

It's been a rugged February. Snow every day. My beard freezes when I go out to shovel the walk. Maggie is away again on business. I am happy for her, proud of her success, but her absence in our house is loud. Alice is out a lot, busy with her friends dreaming the brilliant futures they are likely to realize. There's a prematurely elegiac quality to our relationship these days, a tender caution, as if our better, instinctual selves really understood that this is her last year at home. Gerry, thank god, likes to have his friends come over to our place to hang out. He is in the tenth grade this year, but with a little luck he will reach the state finals in wrestling.

Paraguay has seemed not so much a dream but a strange, compelling experience that happened to someone else, something overheard on a bus in the dark when you're half asleep. I don't think, just now, that I can write my book about Roa Bastos and imagination in exile. Last week I spent a full day replaying the tapes I had made of our conversation. He sounds as brilliant as he was in the act of speaking, but The Book of Pain and Suffering left me distant from my own desire. I packed the tapes in a box and put them away.

Tonight I went to watch Gerry pin his opponent in a minute and a half. He wears his triumph quietly and well, seems genuinely surprised by each new victory, and grateful for his luck. After the match I dropped him and a few friends at a place downtown they like to go for pizza and wings. He invited me to go with them, but I didn't want to be a drag on their conversation, so I drove home alone in yet another blizzard.

The streets were treacherous, on their way to impassable. Visibility was close to zero. In Black Rock I stopped at an intersection, sat staring through the windshield trying to see whether the way was clear. I didn't expect to see a person rise like an apparition in the snow, which blew sideways. A hand waving as if in distress made me panic. Without thinking, I ploughed through the intersection to get away.

But I couldn't keep driving. A waking version of the dream that had brought on the vision the night I ate Mercedes' weed jolted me hard, and I pulled over to the side of the road. I saw without seeing him the Salvadoran immigrant who had tried to flag down my car: His village near the Honduran border that had been shelled by government troops, then razed on a raid. His impossible trek out through Mexico. The garbage can he had lifted that evening at the restaurant in Buffalo where he worked, and the temporary hole the can made in the snow. The blue cold in his fingers, and the orange sun that inflamed his dream, and the guilt that made him sick to his stomach when he thought about people he had left behind.

Mercedes was right, and I understand her anger and resentment. It's not literature. And it's not a drug. It's an invasion, and the idea that it may go on indefinitely terrifies me. Whatever it was that happened passed, and I was able to collect myself and drive home, going slow over the black, snow-bound streets. The heat was off in the house, which chilled quickly. The idea, I guess, is to learn how to live this vulnerable.

Planting the Flag

Here's one that comes dangerously close to truth, and I hope it burns: There we are in the perennial sadness of Central America. Suddenly there are no more revolutionaries, no more counter-revolutionaries, no nothing. Where once hope crowed we now hear only pious horseshit homilies on balanced budgets and blind faith in the market economy, delivered by international bureaucrats making eighty grand a year, plus car and driver courtesy of the U.S. taxpayer. There we are sunstricken in the trellissed garden at don Pepe the exiled Catalonian's outdoor *parrillada* in the company of horny roosters and preening papagayos. Around us sprawls a seductive, green urban slum just like you always imagined south of the border, like some unexplored erogenous zone down below Uncle Sam's belt. The grill smokes, wafting the odor of salted meat through the garden. Around us range goats and donkeys and black pigs in free sunshine New Yorkers would kill for. There we are, a toothless tick on the buttocks of the great North American nation state. No one gives a shit, not coming not going.

Here we are, feces-faced at two thirty in the afternoon in this unending elegy service that we enact for the death of the Latin American Left.

Pepe has a restaurant to run, so he doesn't always grieve with us, the bastard. But some bug has infiltrated his ass today, and he is half blasted, so he recites some of Rigoberto's poetry. Rigoberto is the only one among us who has done something that will outlast himself. For a space of twenty years he wrote poems that are better than good, and people who understand how good they are have begun to translate them into foreign tongues. French especially. The French seem to think that by recognizing Rigo's anti-imperialist genius they are indirectly sticking it to the gringos.

To a man we are remorselessly romantic. Hearing some of Rigo's better poems recited in that exotic Catalonian accent puts us over an edge we have been inching toward since sitting down at noon. Rigo himself is an old man now. His hair and beard are silvered, his restless black eyes resemble those of a high-IQ hawk, and his tongue is caustic beyond caustic. But he cannot resist his own best lines any more than the rest of us can, and his eyes tear.

When don Pepe finishes I buy a round of beers for the table, and a round-shouldered waitress one of us will undoubtedly fall in love with shuffles to the icebox.

"At least have the honesty to admit that we lost, goddamn it," rages Mateo, slamming his empty beer bottle down on Pepe's wooden table. Mateo, who used to run guns and collect intelligence for groups of guerrillas who wanted to fix the world, is the single smartest person I have met in my life. He has read every book ever written in the Spanish language, plus a lot of translations. His memory is photographic. If he wanted to he could put Pepe to shame by reciting some serious Rigo. But even before the Pax Americana was firmly established he had given up activist politics. Now he's writing a history of Central America guaranteed to make all of us weep real salt tears. Mateo is as big as a tree, as violent as a storm pounding the Caribbean coast, as eloquent, drunk or sober, as Ralph Waldo Emerson on wacky weed.

What we lost—and I'm honored to be included, in Mateo's backhand way—is the revolution that was going to plant the flag of justice on Latin American soil. I don't want to get into any academic exercise about how come, and I have given up talking for a living to these eighty-grand bureaucrats who think they know. It's over. Period. Go forth, they are telling us, and balance your budgets. Pull in that ratty belt, Juan Q. Publico, and hump it toward the twenty-first century.

In the mood I'm in, I could cry thinking about haves and havenots, about the difference between tortillas-and-beans and notebook computers with mega-memory.

We drink our beer, Pepe disappears into the kitchen to articulate his loneliness to the new cook he has hired from Progreso, and Eduardo the best novelist who never made it anywhere leans his head back and sleeps in his chair. His mouth is open, his tongue is coated with a film of sickness, his teeth are yellow as a dog's. Don't let my tone mislead you; I have read Eduardo's almost novels, all of them, and there is a narrative power in them, a flashing passion, as good as anything on the continent in the past twenty years, which is saying a considerable amount. Eduardo, who is myopic and withdrawn the way your baser instincts lead you to hope a novelist will be, has probably the most serious drinking problem among us, commensurate with his serious talent. One of Mateo's projects is to collect Eduardo's manuscripts and stick them in his safe before the novelist has a chance to burn them, which I am sure he will do before too long.

The world has changed in a way that has distorted all of us, though maybe only Mateo has the intellectual honesty, the political smarts, to see that clearly.

I'm their token gringo. Through the '80s I covered the war in Central America and other sordid Latin sundries as a reporter for the *Miami Herald*. As far as I can judge I did a reasonably objective job in depicting the low comedy, the *campesino* tragedy, that U.S. policy produced in those years. I listened to anybody willing to talk, I sought balance, I worked to keep my personal passion out of the story. But the fact remains: I had been hoping, since Che Guevara got his in Bolivia in 1967, that the Latin American Left would amount to something. That it would plant that flag that didn't get planted. When it happened I wanted to be there, write the first best dispatch, dance on the mountain with them, share their wine of triumph.

In 1990 I quit the *Herald*. I'm coasting. I'm disappointed. These are my friends. Besides, I can't stand to be around gloating conservatives at home. They think they won a war they didn't even fight in.

Absent any definite destination, Rigo and Mateo and Eduardo and I are going to hell in a handbasket here. The Catalonian too, but he's making a little money on the way down, which resembles the way up in no regard.

At three o'clock Eduardo wakes, closes his mouth, opens it again to say "Ricardo is in jail up north. It hasn't made the papers."

Ricardo is a kind of success story. An archeologist by training, from one of the old-time landowning families, he joined the struggle to plant the flag when he was twenty four years old and has not stopped trying. He has just enough money to stay out of the sewer of corruption that flows beneath labor and the Left. He's an orator, and he looks the way Hollywood would like him to look if they cast him. His beard is always trimmed in a noblesse oblige sort of way. None of us can help loving Ricardo, who has made just enough mistakes in twenty years of activism to keep him human and permit us to sustain our admiration.

An ugly incident has happened on the north coast on one of the independent banana plantations, owned by a colonel who may or may not be retired. A handful of workers gathered at the plantation gates to protest non-payment of their wages were gunned down by men with submachine guns who may or may not have been wearing uniforms. There has been an upwelling of outrage across the nation, an investigation has been called for, and the outrage has subsided into stupor. *La memoria del pueblo,* Mateo is fond of saying, *es frágil.*

If Ricardo is in jail, and if it's not in the papers, that means ugliness. "It means," Mateo thunders, "that they are beating the living hell out of the man."

A shadow falls across our table. The round-shouldered waitress looks at us warily, then busies her hands with a piece of embroidery while she waits. Don Pepe's gravelly voice sounds distantly from the kitchen, where he pleads for understanding. Everything everywhere is suddenly irrelevant.

"The solution is obvious," Mateo decides. "We go to the papers. We get on the radio. We call the human rights groups in Europe."

"By the time we can build up enough pressure to do Ricardo any good," Eduardo says, "he's dead, and nobody ever heard of him."

"I can be on the air twenty minutes after I leave here," Mateo says. "Radio Testigo will give me all afternoon if I ask for it."

"So what? Nobody cares." Mouth closed and mind working, there is something disturbing about Eduardo, something slightly menacing. He reminds me of the kind of a guy you'd meet in a café in some European port city, with a story and a grudge and a plan for revenge. Plotting was never his weakness as a novelist.

Mateo doesn't like to be contradicted, even by his best friends, so he glowers and tears a piece of bread into shreds, which he rolls between thumb and forefinger into little white pellets. He throws the pellets one by one in the direction of don Pepe's livestock. The animals are grateful.

My head has begun to ache. I'm not in the same drinking league as my friends, when it comes down to it. I only drink from an empathetic impulse, from solidarity.

"It's not that no one cares," Mateo corrects Eduardo, "it's that a people on their back get a perverse pleasure in seeing that things are really as bad as their worst fears."

"If we had any balls to speak of, any of us," Rigoberto the poet says suddenly, "we'd go north and get him out of there ourselves."

This makes Mateo go hilarious. He steadies himself by clamping his two huge hands onto the edge of the table and roaring. "Blast him out," he says, and it's a self-indicting sneer. "We go north and shoot up all the bad guys and sneak Ricardo across the border until things cool off."

"If we had any balls," Rigo says suddenly. It's a challenge, and we know it. His hawk eyes scan all of ours like an attack of conscience, and I realize that here is the difference between poets and other human beings: Poets are not reasonable, nor can they be. Some of Rigo's finer poems are political excoriations of the Northern empire that go way beyond the reasonable. What he has said about my country is not fair, really, but in the making of his wonderful poems fairness does not matter.

"I'm game," Eduardo says quietly. He looks sober, but none of us believes him. Not even Rigo.

"You're both out of your goddamn minds," Mateo tells them, and he calls the waitress to attend our predictable needs. But a hole has been pricked in the gassy globe of our drinking afternoon, and we all know it. By three thirty it's over, when we should have gone on until dark, and then some. Mateo goes to his office; he can write even when he's drunk, plus he has hired his lover to be his secretary. Rigo and Eduardo have nothing to do but they disappear to do it together. Don Pepe has succeeded in capturing the affections of his cook, so he closes up. In that mid-afternoon trough of time and heat a languor like paralysis envelopes the little hilly city of green slums. I go to my hotel to sleep off the alcohol I can't handle.

When I wake, my head doesn't ache but the absolute darkness makes me woozy. There must have been a power outage across the entire city, which is as still as anything still alive can get. It's as though the whole place has been cancelled. From my window I can see the stars pulse in a display of that cosmic indifference that always makes me angry. I strike a match; it's 3:13 a.m. On the north coast Ricardo's jailors must have knocked off long ago, leaving him to sleep in his pool of pain. Only the truly arrogant or the truly ignorant would have had the nerve to touch someone as prominent as he. Though I am forty years old I cannot help being angry at Ronald Reagan. In my helplessness I go back to sleep.

At five, Mateo is in my room looking like death not yet warmed over. "We're going north to get Ricardo," he announces. He is haggard, sleepless, resolute. "We wanted you to know."

"I'll go with you," I tell him, sitting up scared.

Mateo reminds me of Poe's pessimistic raven, only bigger. "It's not your fight, Peter," he shakes his hed.

"If it's not, then I don't have one, do I?"

He thinks that one over for a minute, shrugs, and I get dressed in a hurry. In the car, the poet and the novelist are waiting with sweet hot black coffee and some hard rolls. They nod at me like co-conspirators. Now that there's democracy, we exit the capital openly, freely, confidently even at this suspicious hour. Now that there's democracy no one is likely to check the trunk and find the guns there. If anyone does, we can buy his indifference for twenty bucks.

Democracy notwithstanding, all of us feel conspicuous boating up the highway in Mateo's 1979 sky-blue Cadillac. Mateo inherited the car in 1985 from a Nicaraguan exile in a trade he refuses to talk about. He has spent enough on gas in the interval to have bought a fuel-efficient Toyota. But he is proud of his bondage and the quirky symbol, which shows a little of his complexity and makes me respect him.

The highway north is potholed and dangerous. The truckers are generally men of reason, but the bus drivers seem to want to take revenge for their underpaid, undersatisfied existence by courting a spectacular accident at every poorly banked curve, every blind spot on every hill. Not willing to talk, we slump back in the comfy Caddy seats and watch the landscape of rural poverty go by us hill by rugged hill. These shacks of mud and thatch, these distended bellies, this haunting stupor were all supposed to have been erradicated by now. Their unremitting presence puts a clot of sadness near my heart.

If you say it enough times, tortillas and beans become a mantra illuminating the poverty that was supposed to go away but never did.

We know we're halfway there when the landscape changes. The hills are smaller and lower. The green life on them is brighter, spikier, more suggestively tropical. Cane grows thick in the long valleys, and pineapple plantations look lush. The air is hotter, stickier, and on the dusty road berm brown children with curled toes wave bags of sliced coconut at every passing motorist. Amen.

When Mateo stops for gas in a cane-choked valley we pile out to stretch our legs. As though there has been a signal, pitched so high our conscious minds couldn't catch it, the adventure suddenly seems real to all of us. After more coffee and some baked corn *rosquillas* we go north again, plenty awake now. My friends begin to talk, and I get a strong, almost an overwhelming, sense of who these men are.

They are all storytellers, and I am sucked in listening to exploits and reminiscences, inventions and soliloquies that shape and reshape the disappointment, the loss, the consolations that bind them together. Gun-running and thug-baiting and mistress worship. The romance of politics, and vice versa. Moody guitars that played in all the rainbow colors. Wordplay that struck sparks. And the hard-to-kill dream, overarching like a massive tree, of a Spanish-speaking America ripe in peace and plenty and justice. No way Jose.

Rigoberto, his body well past prime, his fierce nervous intelligence reduced to revising, editing, pruning himself for posterity, worries about money. He has none at all, and no expectations. Eduardo paces constantly through the dimly lit labyrinth inside himself aware of just how close he came to making art. He is obsessed, these days, with documenting his stupendous hangovers, and with an illiterate country woman he met at a bus stop who loves him for nothing that has to do with his spent promise. The woman has a withered arm and is jealous in a way that does Eduardo more good than multiple vitamins.

Then there's Mateo. Even in the big Yankee frigate he's piloting up the highway he manages to look giant-size. Of the three, he alone could be said to have something like a stake in the country he loves, the society he despises. Bankrolled by a big-time European social science foundation with an endowed conscience, he earns a comfortable living doing his research projects. But it was also Mateo who came closest to real involvement in the old days. He ran some guns, brokered deals that led to the delivery of weapons systems, collected intelligence in a systematic way and got paid for it. His anger, these days, is consuming his energetic self in binges that leave him flat on his back for days.

Plus me. I would say I'm along for the ride except it's more than that. I'm along because I, like my friends, am reduced to a gesture.

We have a plan, of course. Even a gesture requires a plan. Mostly our plan involves locating the place where the police are holding Ricardo. Beyond that, there are guns in Mateo's wide-body trunk. Curiously, not once in all those hours does anyone bring up the idea of backing down, and I know these men well enough to see that they will not.

We lose an hour and a half when the Caddy blows a tire and the spare is flat. But there is still plenty of light, buttery mellow, when we finally reach the north coast. We stop for a few minutes at an empty beach to watch sedate brakers brush the littered sand, and Rigoberto passes around a small silver flask of rum. In that yea-saying late Caribbean sunlight the poet looks old, statuesque. Around his eyes crow's feet wrinkle, and the features of his face look chiselled. He looks peacefully stern, better than I have seen him look in years.

"Hijos de puta," he says, sweeping his arm long and slow to take in the beach, the coast, the country, and we understand that he means to say they are bastards who would transform this paradise into the miserable excuse for a country that his has become. His indictment is an eerie echo of the challenge he made to us the day before at don Pepe's.

Half an hour later we drive into Matacán, a seedy city of ten thousand that grew up around the piers extending way out into the harbor, from which millions, maybe billions, of world-class bananas depart regularly in container ships to the United States. Except for a few cobbles most of the streets are of a fine reddish dust that hangs in the air day and night. The garifuna music is incessant, the smell of fish and of fresh things cooking in oil is pleasant. A Caribbean richness deepens people's voices; there is such a thing, after all, as sun-soaked. Bastards, I think.

When public reaction to the massacre of the banana workers welled up, the police and the military had a few of their own arrested to give the appearance of a serious inquiry. They are keeping them in the little blue adobe jailhouse downtown, which means that Ricardo will definitely be elsewhere. We cruise the dusty streets in Mateo's Cadillac conspicuous as sin in high heels. People stare. That should worry us. If we were smart we would have rented some anonymous sedan. But anybody who would have stopped, taken the time to rent an invisible car, would not be here in the first place.

"This isn't working," Rigoberto tells Mateo after we have driven aimlessly for half an hour. "Park somewhere and we'll split up. We have to talk to people." The poet is more purposeful, more composed, than I remember him being ever. It is as though he has taken command of our rescue party, and even Mateo, who normally yields nothing to anyone, is willing to let him direct. He parks the car.

Rigoberto and Mateo go in one direction, Eduardo and I stroll in another.

"Maybe you want to go on by yourself for a while," I suggest to the novelist when we have gone a few blocks in the direction of nowhere. "With a gringo in tow no one's likely to tell you anything."

But he looks at me with his suffering fools look, nods and says, "In here."

A bar, of course. Inside, a ceiling fan squeaks, a large black woman in a yellow shift dandles a baby and hums, two young men ignore us and play pool, sharing a cigarette. Their shirts are unbuttoned, their hairless bare chests identical: flat, bar-shaped muscles, long-torsos. Eduardo orders us both a Salva Vida from a short bald man whose eyebrows form bushy question marks. The beer is cold, but I can't enjoy it, thinking we should be out pounding the pavement for clues.

"Rigoberto will find out where they've got Ricardo," Eduardo tells me, as if reading my nervous thoughts. He sucks down his glass of beer the way a juicer will.

"You're sure ... "

Again the look that pities me for my thick-skulled gringo stupidity. "He has to. Don't you see what's happening here, Peter?"

I do not, but maybe I do.

"For Rigo, there is nothing left. He put his heart and his life into writing poems that would bring down the empire, if you know what I mean. Plus he can't pay his bills. The French love Rigo, but they're not going to give him a pension, are they."

"And now it looks like the empire isn't coming down."

Eduardo shrugged. "He thought—we all thought—that the communists were the good guys, and that the good guys were going to win, eventually. The job of people like us was to keep the faith, keep the fire burning, until they did. Roberto's work is like one long poem of praise and solidarity. He's like John the Baptist warming up the crowd, only now it looks like the savior we needed isn't coming. Rescuing Ricardo isn't the least he can do, it's the only thing, the way his mind is working these days. You have to be crazy to be a poet in a country like this one. You want another beer?"

I do not, but I watch him drain two more Salva Vidas like water. We leave the bar like fugitives, and suddenly the day is over. I have never become used to the speed of a tropical sunset. One minute the sky is bathed in light; the next, it's midnight dark. But the sticky heat lets up a little, and our walk back to the Cadillac is a short idyll despite the dust that hangs like a halo everywhere.

Mateo is sitting on the hood, Rigoberto paces in the dirt. "The colonel has an old warehouse outside the city, a couple of kilometers north," he tells us. "Usually it's deserted, but there have been people coming and going the last few days. Some of them have uniforms. No one here has the slightest interest in knowing what might be going on there."

For the first time I experience a real solid attack of fear, and I wonder if there is a way that I can back out of this expedition gracefully. In the dark our voices seem to carry, though off to one side of the street two dogs have begun to snap and snarl at each other, giving us a little helpful cover. Somewhere a steel drum sounds, inducing sleep. At a great distance a hysterical woman laughs.

"Once we're out of town we'll stop and get the guns from the trunk," Mateo says softly. In his voice sounds a hard quality of interested calculation that makes me think again. "Peter," he tells me. "There's no reason for you to go any farther, amigo. You don't have to prove anything to us, you know."

The problem is I do. If he hadn't made the offer, perhaps I could have stayed behind. There is no doubt that Ricardo is at the warehouse, no doubt communism is dead. We leave Matacán slowly, as if to avoid arousing suspicion. It's a good idea to avoid suspicion anytime you're one of four strangers driving a sky blue '79 Cadillac through a small coastal city in a banana republic.

Outside of town we pull off under some trees and Mateo hands out our weapons: automatic rifles for Rigoberto and Eduardo, and identical .38 pistols for himself and me. If there were a way not to be here, I would choose that way. We get back into the car, whose doors close with a soft thunk, and five minutes later, on the shore side of a blind curve, the warehouse is inevitably there.

The light from an early moon is enough to show that it's a cluster of long sheds, really, with roofs of corrugated tin. A sagging fence runs the length of the property along the road. The sheds are set back from the highway a couple hundred yards. From one of them only an orange light, as from a kerosene lantern, shines dully.

Mateo turns off the Cadillac's headlights, points the car south, and leaves the key in the ignition. Single file, Rigoberto in the lead and me last, we walk along the sagging fence until we find a broken section, through which we slip onto the colonel's property. My hands shake. It's good that there is enough moonlight to see with, but I feel like a target. Once, Rigoberto stops and whispers, "We're not fools or cowboys. If this can be done without hurting anyone, all the better." I find myself nodding sanctimoniously in the dark.

It's surprising how quietly four urban men can move across unknown country in the dark. No one trips, no one coughs, no one makes a stupid mistake. We move as though we have practiced this in commando school. Soon we are stopped, bunched, weapons clenched, watching a bullet-headed grunt doze sitting up, leaning forward on his rifle on the steps of the little shed from which the orange light streams. Rigoberto and the others must have done more planning than I knew about. While the rest of us wait, Mateo moves off in the brush making a wide arc around and behind the shed.

There is no human sound anywhere, just the normal night racket of insects and birds and invisible animals. For the first time things move slowly, the way they're supposed to in a nightmare, and anxiety wells up in me like a geyser. Fear distracts me so that I don't see Mateo come out of the brush next to the shed. But when Rigo points I watch the former intelligence broker overwhelm the guard suddenly, one massive hand around his mouth, the other driving the barrel of the pistol into his side. The guard nods once, slowly; he does not expect the knock on the head that fells him.

When the grunt hits the ground the rest of us move forward together. By the time we reach the steps Mateo has the boy trussed and gagged expertly. There is no hesitation now, nor could there be. Treading softly on the wood plank steps Rigoberto and Eduardo—they have the rifles—throw the door open in a hurry, so quickly that the two men inside the shed, wearing olive drab t-shirts and anonymous military fatigue-type pants and smoking cigarettes, throw up their hands in a reflex of surprise and terror.

In a moment we have guns at their heads, and Mateo and Eduardo begin to tie and gag them, while Rigoberto and I lift Ricardo from the shuck mattress on the floor where he is lying scarcely conscious. In the uncertain light from the kerosene lantern hanging from a low rafter it is easy to see that he has been beaten badly. His face is swollen out of shape; he does not look a bit like the dashing figure of permanent revolution he has always aimed to be. Even with help he cannot walk. He slumps against me like a tired lover.

While we are busy trying to revive Ricardo Mateo has clubbed the trussed men on the head. In my fog of fear I admire the dispatch with which the historian is able to accomplish practical matters. His gunrunning stories now seem less an embellishment of circumstances than they have sometimes seemed. At the same time I hope no permanent damage will be done to the men we have hit. As Rigoberto said, we are neither fools nor cowboys.

"Something to drink," Rigoberto says to me when Ricardo shows no sign of being able to walk. "I'll get him something to drink."

He moves forward toward a table on which a full bottle of rum sits next to a pitcher of water. That's why he is closest to the door, which is why he is the one in the way when two men with drawn pistols come through it. The speed with which Rigoberto reacts is amazing. He is sixty years old, and his mind thinks in couplets. But before any of the rest of us can move he has raised his pistol and screamed something angry and unintelligible at the invaders. That forces their attention on him as the most immediate threat, and before the poet can get a shot off he is dead.

His blood sprays, and I smell something burning and foul. His chest a mess, Rigoberto falls forward, giving the rest of us time to react and aim. In what seems like the same instant Mateo and Eduardo and I all shoot, and the soldiers, or police, or paramilitary thugs, whoever they were, go down together in a heap.

"Sweet Jesus," Eduardo says, lurching toward Rigoberto on the bare floor. In the poor light his blood looks black, and it continues to seep.

"Not now," Mateo tells him harshly. "Let's get them out of here." Shoving his pistol into his belt, he scoops and cradles Rigoberto. Like a baby he carries him outside and down the steps into the darkness. Eduardo and I remember Ricardo, whom the shooting has wakened a little. "They shot Rigoberto," he says over and over. "They shot Rigoberto." The shock showing on his purple, swollen face, he looks ghastly, like a bad caricature of himself. Eduardo and I get on either side of him and drag him forward. He moves with maddening reluctance. "They shot Rigoberto," he says again. "The bastards have shot Rigoberto."

On the way back to the waiting Cadillac we expect at every step to be shot at, but nothing happens, no one shows. We cross the field of dense brush quickly, shying instinctively away from the row of empty looming warehouse sheds. Ahead of us Mateo, stronger than he has ever been, is running with Rigoberto in his arms. I can hear his breath labor, but there is no panic there, which calms me, unreasonably . Dragging Ricardo we cannot keep up with him. "Sweet Jesus," Eduardo says once, more in frustration than in fear now.

At the car, Mateo gently places Rigoberto in the back seat. The dead body crumples, falls forward into a position like abnegation. Ricardo, suddenly mobile on his own volition, crawls in next to him. Eduardo, riding shotgun, gets into the front seat, and I sit down reluctantly next to Ricardo.

Mateo drives fast but not too fast. He is keeping his head. We all roll our windows down, and as we go south toward the border I have the sensation that we are standing helplessly rooted while the Caribbean night races past. The rushing air has a salt tang, a fish tang, a tang of sex and promise. The sound of the tires on the asphalt is deafening. We pass a billion crickets, their song half swallowed by our speed. The moonlight makes a jungle of criss-crossing shadows on the road ahead that tear apart in black shreds as we drive through them. In the back seat Ricardo is crying with the rhythmic intensity of a baby.

"Mateo," Eduardo calls, "what if his body freezes stiff the way he's bent now? What do we do then?"

"Shut up," Mateo tells him angrily. He tells me to find the bottle of rum in the glove compartment. I uncap and pass it, and its raw bite steadies us all a little.

"You know something," Eduardo says between Ricardo's sobs, "you know something? Rigo is the lucky one."

But that infuriates Mateo. "I don't want to hear any of that shit. Do you hear me? Nothing phony like that. I mean it." There is enough of a threat in his voice to quiet Eduardo, and Ricardo cries more quietly, as if to himself now. We are all in shock, I tell myself, and the Cadillac is a goddamn hearse.

For a long time—miles maybe, it must be miles and miles—my mind is stuck in a circular track. I ask myself over and over whether Rigoberto is the lucky one. I am thinking very slowly, my mind is exceedingly dull, and there is no room in it for anything except that one question, to which no answer comes. In all those miles no one says a word, maybe because the roar of our car and the blue black night intimidate us.

But when Eduardo asks how far it is to the border my mind comes unstuck. It jumps its track, skates and slides. "A hundred and forty, hundred and fifty kilometers," Mateo says in a reasonable voice, and I am thinking again. I know, suddenly, that we will make it to the border and across, that there are a hundred blind passes over hills and through woods, and one of them will take us over. That we will give Rigoberto an honorable burial suitable for a poet in exile. That the swelling in Ricardo's beaten face will come down. I know that there is something knotted in the shooting at the warehouse and our complicity that explains why the revolution in Latin America we wanted so badly did not come off. I know that, pulling the trigger on the .38 the depth of my own complicity finally became clear to me, and that I have wanted such complicity. I know that something essential buried deep inside us is over now and will not go away. And I know, finally, that I am free to weep. And it burns.

Deep Red

By the time Luis León Borge went around the bend I had already changed my mind and wanted to write his book for him. Too bad I was too late. I even had a title to suggest to him: *The Last Revolutionary*, which was what I thought he might actually be, at least in Central America. But when I hit town in April, the dry end of the dry season, and began to ask around for him, all I got were conflicting accounts of what one local paper had dubbed "the enigmatic incident." The man himself had vanished. It was unreasonable to feel that I had been abandoned, but I did. In fact I was the one who had done the original turning down. I didn't understand why, once he seemed to be gone for good, it was so important to find the hard-luck radical, but it was. I hung around hunting.

For days gritty sheets of dust blew nonstop across the parched, poor, hilly city where I camped in a downtown hotel room. Dirt accumulated everywhere, wind-scalloped like corn snow. Nowhere, nothing stayed clean. Except for scattered patches of pines that had not been logged off the hills, nothing in eyeshot was green. Even the sound of gritty wind slapping yellowed palm fronds was dry. Outside the city, dirt farmers slashed and burned. Defenseless stretches of forest crisped and flared and burned, dying proof of Nature's spendthrift ways. When the wind finally stopped, a dense cloud of gray smoke as big as the sky itself settled over the city and hung like permanence.

I'm a reporter; I know how to ask questions. It's my job to reconstruct events by interpreting the conflicting versions people tell me. So it bugged the hell out of me not to be able to reconstruct the enigmatic incident in a way that made sense. The only thing everyone agreed on was the motorcycle: One placid hot morning in February, Luis León Borge, the last real revolutionary in Central America, had appeared on the quaintly cobbled street in front of the presidential palace riding a motorcycle and waving a submachine gun, or an automatic rifle, or a .45 caliber pistol with an extra-long barrel. By some accounts he stopped the bike and brazenly fired off his weapon, whatever it was, in the air in front of the detachment of green-helmeted guards on duty. Others reported that he passed the palace without braking, screaming something fierce and passionate and politically pithy that no one caught because of the motorcycle's two-cycle screech. One eyewitness quoted in the papers said that he was shirtless, but I found that possibility as unlikely as it was disturbing. Borge was sixty five years old, an age at which riding bare-chested on a motorcycle looked pathetic in any light you chose to cast on the act.

Quite a number of persons agreed that a propaganda bomb exploded at the time of Borge's apparition, loosing a brief shower of communiqués in the bright, revealing air. Did that mean a clandestine confederate in the crowd? But not a single communiqué survived as evidence. Were the police for some reason extraordinarily diligent in scarfing up the scattered papers? Why was no insurance copy delivered to the newspapers, as was usually the case?

More than any single contradiction in the accounts of Borge's earnest wild ride, though, one uncontested fact drove me crazy speculating: He got away alive. In my years in Latin America covering failure, strife and misery for several newspapers, I saw proof enough that the ones with the guns shot first and asked questions later, if at all. I tried to picture the scene: a row of armed, badly fed soldiers guarding their president's place of business in the drowsy heat. They would be thinking the normal thoughts of sex and money and their lack. They would be young, probably illiterate, reluctant conscripts too poor to buy their way out of military service. And they let an old man on a motorcycle waving a weapon get by?

I took the easy way out, decided whatever had happened in front of the palace was Borge's enactment of a bitter death wish, an honorable leftist's moral response to the death of communism and his dream of justice. But they let him get by.

Borge had hunted me up at my hotel the previous November when I was in town for the Orlando *Bugle* doing a story on economic reform in the isthmus, a less than sexy subject after the compelling farce the Sandinistas and Contras put on in the '80s.

"I want you to write my book," Borge told me straight out. We were sitting by the hotel pool under umbrella shade. Behind us stretched a terrific view of the city disappearing into a thin, romanticizing haze, the kind of view that inspires tacky tourist art. It was too cool to swim; we had the pool to ourselves.

Despite his age Borge was still vigorously handsome. He could have played cowboy heroes in Mexican movies. His brown skin was weather-buffed to a healthy shine, and the flesh of his arms looked strong and supple. His hair had mellowed to an impressive silver of the sort one associated more with perma-pressed rich folks than with professional political exiles. When he leaned out of the shade into the harsh coagulated sunlight his gray eyes showed clouded purple streaks, tiny jags of vivid color.

"I can't write anybody's book," I excused myself. "The *Bugle* wouldn't give me the kind of time I'd need to do something serious like that." True enough. But the abrupt no I tossed him made me feel as calculatingly cold as the Central American man in the street thought gringos must all be. I signalled one of the underemployed waiters and ordered us both a cold Port Royal.

For a few minutes we talked politics, the national pastime. Borge was not the kind of man to expose himself asking twice. He had returned home the month before after a decade of exile in

Nicaragua and parts east, one beneficiary of a bigger deal negotiated with the government that also brought home the head of the communist party. Borge had been the functional godhead of a respected splinter of his country's long-fractured Left. The Radical Revolutionary Left (IRR) had been known for a certain bullheaded ideological purity and for the impassioned reason of its call to arms; it blurred the line between radical politicking and armed resistance. Writing Borge's book would have meant walking backward along that line asking the right questions carefully. I knew that, and the idea, for some reason, disturbed me.

"What made you accept the government's deal?" I asked him, knowing it was unfair to ask interview questions when I had no intention of writing his book.

"I wanted to smell the pines before I died," he told me with a smile that only pretended to make fun of the words. He gestured behind us to the bare dry hills of the city in the thin haze. There were no more pines to speak of. Deforestation seemed too bloodless a word to describe the violated nakedness of those hills. "It's my country, is it not?"

It was that.

"Let me tell you an anecdote," he asked politely, and I ordered two more beers. "Back in September, the government and the military guaranteed us safe conduct to come discuss the terms of our return."

"And you trusted them?"

"We trusted some people who said we could trust them. At any rate a meeting was set up. In a neutral house here in town, in Lomas de Catarro where the rich people live. I was left on the street in front of the house to guide some of our people in. I arrived early. I was as keyed up as I remember being in my life. It was early afternoon, hot in a pleasant way that made me remember being young and apolitical in this city, back when we still had trees.'

"Anyway, waiting in the street, something happened to me that I cannot explain. This was before the dry season of course.

The trees were green. I was standing in the shade. I looked off across the hills toward the big cathedral in the valley. Between me and the cathedral was nothing but green, and it was splendid. But the strange thing was this: The beauty of what I was seeing made me sick. I mean physically sick. For a moment I came close to vomiting. I had to close my eyes to protect myself. From the poignancy of it, I mean. I was embarrassed because I knew some blockhead from C2 would be surveilling me. But I knew if I opened my eyes I would heave."

"Sounds like a political vision to me, Luis León. You had a vision of what you gave up when you became a revolutionary ..."

He shook his head emphatically, scratched at the soggy label on his beer bottle with the flat nail of one thumb. "What I saw had nothing to do with politics," he insisted, the purple streaks in his odd, intense eyes standing out like threats.

"Why do you want to have a book?"

"I need money. It's a straightforward capitalist transaction. I recognize that."

"Why me?"

"Your reporting on the Contra War was respected. I thought you would know enough to ask the correct questions."

I did. But he did not ask twice. Then two things happened to change my mind. An editor acquaintance I ran into in New York started pumping me about the changes in the Latin American Left post-Berlin Wall. He had been a Peace Corps volunteer in Paraguay and imagined himself a sympathizer with political remedies for social injustice. I told him about my conversation with Borge and the book proposal, and he offered me a contract. Then when I went home to Orlando my wife told me she was leaving me.

There's a connection. Angela had this theory, according to which my long-time fascination with the Latin American Left was the sign of a fundamental emotional immaturity in me. She wanted me to grow up, cover something different—the auto industry, maybe—and admit there would never be justice in the world. I'm not being fair to her, of course, but I grant myself this one cheap shot. Anyway she's too far away to feel the blow. She escaped to Maine and got a job, as though to put maximum distance between herself and anything Latin. And me. My editor at the *Bugle* said take as much time as I needed to recover.

I believed that Borge was still in the country. Whatever else his vision in Lomas de Catarro had meant, I thought it unlikely he would abandon the country he had wanted to liberate for an old man's exile on the dole in Cuba or Libya. I began looking in the obvious places.

Borge's son Ruben Darío was a successful architect; his firm had designed quite a number of the flashy new houses in Lomas that went up during the flush days of American assistance. The impatience with which he received me at his red-tiled suburban office guaranteed I would get nothing from him. But if I was going to write his father's book talking to the architect was a necessary evil.

"I have an appointment in thirty minutes," he warned me. "I can give you twenty five."

Ruben Darío Borge was as squarely handsome as his father, but his looks were subordinated to the lowest common denominator of a prosperous Central American man of business. I smelled arrogance on him like a cologne used too freely. I wondered how his father would evaluate the gold Rolex on his son's muscular hairy wrist.

"I have no idea where the old man is, and I have no interest in finding out," he told me as he handed me a perfunctory cup of sweet strong coffee.

"But you have seen him since he returned from exile."

"Once or twice, here in the office. We're not close."

"What do you think happened down in front of the presidential palace?"

He made a tent of his fingers into which he exhaled slowly, with evident irritation. "My advice is don't look too deep. What happened at the palace is simple: An irrelevant old man who is too pigheaded to realize his war is over made a public fool of himself. Nothing more, nothing less."

I used up my twenty five minutes but got nothing more than a confirmation of Borge's son's long-playing anger at his famous father. He walked me to the street as if to be sure I was really leaving. "Listen," he told me brusquely at the curb, taking my elbow and shaking it, "if you do find my father, ask him if what he's done was worth it."

"Worth what?"

"Years ago, when we were living up north, my father went out to a meeting. He was always going to meetings. Apparently the shit-for-brains police spy on guard that night missed him going out the door on his way to draft the blueprints for the international workers' paradise. Who knows why there was a screwup? But that was the night the security forces chose to firebomb our house. They didn't get my father, because he was out. But they got my mother."

It was a detail I was embarrassed not to have known.

"If he answers that one," Ruben Darío ordered me, "ask the old bastard whether it was worth it to have his son surveilled and harassed and threatened and beaten up by goddamn security apes for the first thirty years of his life."

For a moment I had the sense that the architect was not going to let me leave, that he would extort a promise from me to get him his answers. But he turned away impatiently and went back inside to draw blueprints for profitable houses for upper-middle class clients who invested their money conservatively in the United States. Maybe Angela is right, and I am basically immature about these things.

In my years covering the Contra capers I had developed a comfortable friendship with the editor of one of the local papers. Julio Cesar Barahona was a bona fide knee-jerk anti-American. His paper was predictably shrill, but the platform he made of it from which to publicize the military's horrific human rights abuses had won him in Europe a well deserved reputation as a brave crusader. We had a long slow lunch in a restaurant in a converted hacienda outside the city limits. Smoke from the grill blew through the open patio where we drank red wine surrounded by overeager, underpaid waiters dressed unconvincingly as Texas cowboys. In the bad old days the place had been lousy with ambitious spooks and hotdogging soldiers of fortune, American embassy drones and nouveau riche Nicaraguan guerrillas. I felt their lack, and the lack had something to do with finding Borge.

Barahona was obsessed with the fall of the Left. "It's money," he insisted to me twice, three times before our food arrived. Disappointment had aged him. His face was almost as red as the wine, his gray hair gone listless. The brown intelligent eyes let me know he knew he was talking to a reporter. "It came down to money, didn't it. When the Soviets and the East Bloc began to have serious problems they stopped financing liberation movements. Bam, like that. Then people in the Middle East who might have chipped in didn't. The exiles came home because they had nothing to live on abroad anymore. Castro's broke. The Mexicans are working on their budget deficit. Renouncing the armed struggled turned out to be the only thing these people had left to bargain away."

"And Borge fell into the same trap?"

Julio Cesar swirled his wine glass, drew a tiny wedge of cork from the red surface and flicked it onto the brick floor. A cowboy waiter with a red-plaid bandana around his throat hovered just out of earshot ready to apologize if necessary. Grill smoke wafted. Folkloric music heavy with regret played on somebody's radio.

"Luis León was with Fidel way back when, before the Granma sailed. He lived off Soviet money, they all did."

"But?"

"Two views of the world that conflict outrageously with one another can coexist in a single person, can they not?"

"Like a bank account in Miami and insurance contributions to the radical unions?"

The editor shrugged. I was not ordinarily that impolitic in an interview. I really didn't care what Barahona did with his own money.

"You think I'm bitter," he told me. "If I am, it's because there's no chance to put things right now. Not for another hundred years.

We are destined to remain your government's pawns long after you and I are dead. After my children are dead. We will continue to produce inexpensive, high-quality bananas for your grandchildren's breakfast tables."

"And Borge knew that? That's why he attacked the palace?"

"He didn't attack the palace. He made a gesture."

Barahona's interpretation fit too conveniently with my own. I thought we must both be wrong, and his gloom seemed uncomfortably like my post-Angela depression. I got away from him as soon as I was sure he had no idea where Borge was.

I spent a week, then two more, talking to people who might be expected to know something about Borge. Everyone had an opinion, no one had any information. The dry season hung on longer than it should have, the gritty dust blew, the haze of forest fire smoke above the city dissipated and was replenished day by day. May the third came—the Day of the Cross, when country people hung crosses in their homes and prayed hard for rain—but no relief. As often as I showered I felt as if a permanent skin of dirt had grown on my body. I spent my free time fantasizing sex with Angela, then long post-coital dialogues in which she convinced me that my search for Borge was the final phase of my political adolescence. What came after, she whispered into my imagining ear, would be much better than what had come before.

Straws. The leader of a small syndicate in a medium-sized wooden furniture factory who had tried in the 1970s to forge a practical worker-guerrilla alliance and lived to tell about it sent me to an old man who claimed to have gone to grade school with Borge. Pedro Avila may have been the same age as Borge but he looked half a life older. Cataracts covered both his eyes, his teeth had gone black and punky, and his liver-spotted hands shook in spooky syncopation with his words. I found him at his daughter's house in the Colonia Kennedy neighborhood playing the harmonica for a herd of grandchildren who didn't want to listen. By his second sentence he let met know he had seen Borge after the palace incident.

"Just once, you understand. Just the one time."

"What did he want?"

"Who said he wanted anything?"

"What made him look you up, don Pedro?"

"He wanted to get hold of Noche Clara."

"Who's Noche Clara?"

"We went to school with him." He shook his blind head at a memory he did not divulge, and his grandchildren took advantage of the slipped moment to escape the patio behind the house where the old man's chair was parked under a mango tree.

"I'm the only one who didn't get famous," Avila told me. "Not that that ever bothered me."

I believed him. "What is Noche Clara famous for?"

"Only a stranger could ask such a question."

"I'm a stranger."

"He runs the most successful cock fighting establishment in the history of this city."

But Noche Clara was a moving target. Avila explained to me that the man had a chronic cash-flow problem. Apparently the serious money he won promoting his legendary cockfights he gambled away in casinos across the Caribbean. In his mid-sixties, he lived out of hotel rooms like a restless twenty-year old. The only way to talk to him was to nab him at a Saturday night fight.

Noche Clara's famous cockfights, it turned out, had something to salve or satisfy most of the common human vices. I showed up about halfway through the evening's matches when the watchers and the betters on their concrete slabs were drunk enough, absorbed enough by the spectacle that they scarcely noticed the arrival of a gringo with no good reason to be there. In the ring a shirtless man with a gold chain and medallion swinging on his thin brown chest was intently sucking blood from the mouth of a wounded bird so that the animal would not choke to death. He spat out a thick red spray and placed the once-white bird gently back into the ring, its bloody damaged wings stiff and upright, propped like crutches to keep it in the fight. When the second bird, gold-feathered and bright as money, moved in and aimed its half-inch knife blades again at the wounded white cock, the noise of the people in the stands was euphoria cut with anger.

There was gambling, there was guaro whiskey and beer in long-necked brown bottles, there were tight-skirted prostitutes studied and aimless and cynical in the shadows behind the stands. There was sweat on everybody's money, and blood and feathers like abstract designs in the hard-packed dirt. There were dead birds and caged birds that might be dead before people got tired of seeing them die. There was Noche Clara with a metal cash box and a bodyguard whose M-16 might originally have been bought by the U.S. government to bump off communists.

I thought I might have to wait for business to close down, but Noche Clara was ready enough to tune out the fight in progress and hear what I had to ask. Short, small-boned, and sweating like a wrestler, he looked closer to fifty than sixty five. When I wouldn't take a cigarette he waved his hand with a finger pointing toward heaven and two cold beers appeared, like proof of spontaneous generation. Fastidiously he wrapped a paper napkin around one of the bottles and handed it to me. There was nothing dissolute about the man, just a portable energy you wouldn't have expected to find in someone his age.

"How come you want to find Luis León?"

"When I was here a few months ago he asked me to write a book for him. I came back to tell him I want to write the book."

"What kind of book?"

"I'm a newspaper reporter."

"What's to say you're not a CIA agent?"

"Those guys don't hunt down communists anymore. It's not worth the trouble. Besides, they won, didn't they?"

Noche Clara grinned, and the angry euphoric crowd moaned in one communal sound of happy complicity. The breast of the wounded white bird had been torn open, and no invention or ingenuity on the part of his desperate handler could keep it alive any longer. Some of the prostitutes flocked closer to watch the kill, which seemed to happen in an instant.

"Why did Borge ride a motorcycle to the presidential palace?" I asked.

"Luis León is an actor. Politics is acting, isn't it? An actor has to have an act. That was his."

"Has he come to see you?"

The gambling promoter looked calmly at me as if calculating some odds I couldn't see. His finger jammed up toward heaven and two more beers appeared. "He came."

"The book means money to him. Not a fortune, but real money."

"I gave him some money."

"To do what?"

"To buy a boat."

So I knew I had him. It took longer than I wanted it to take. I witnessed the frantic ritualized death of two more sleek and beautiful fighting cocks, both of whom went slowly. I drank more of Noche Clara's spontaneously generated cold beer. But I had him.

In the morning I took a slow bus to the north coast, the exotic and untouristed Caribbean shore. As the bus dropped out of the dry dusty hills into the greener landscape of pineapples and bananas and wart-shaped coconuts I was sluggish but not hung over. My brain was working fine. In slow rotation I thought about Angela, about Borge rampant on a two-stroke bike, about what I should do with my life now, since the revolution didn't pan out. I wondered whether what Noe Durón had said about Borge might be true of me as well.

Durón had come back under the same deal that brought Borge. Two days later he had set up a new political party. It was as though he had been touring abroad and come back refreshed just in time to shine as spokesman for the reasonable Left. "Luis León is not adaptable," he told me when I interviewed him at party headquarters, a stucco house in a tranquil suburb shaded by orange flowering acacias from which dry pods hung like shrivelled knives. "Politically speaking, he's a dinosaur. We love him. But he's a dinosaur."

Victoria de la Cruz was like Africa in Spanish. I didn't get there until the morning of the second day out of the capital. The hike in from the highway was hot and long enough that the back of my neck was burned tender by the time I got close enough to smell the water. A village of sand and thatch on the lip of the undeveloped blue Caribbean, Victoria had been founded by Africans escaping slavery. Rather than migrate inland, they had stayed. They fished. They traded. They plaited thatch. Sometimes they did day labor for wages in nearby towns. They stayed. And their village sat somnolent on the edge of the mesmerizing sea as if to challenge the notion that things must change.

I took off my shoes and followed the network of sandy paths hoping I did not immediately run into Borge. I didn't. Mid-village on the beach someone had built a sun shelter of water-weathered poles and bleached thatch. A strikingly tall, slim black woman with an austere face sat in the sand under the dappled shade of the shelter brushing her daughter's hair slowly. The child sprawled from her mother's lap onto the warm sand, her eyes closing and opening in a rhythm like the waves'.

"Shade's free," the woman offered. Her hair was almost hidden in a red kerchief. The effect doubled the impression of calm severity she radiated. I sat next to her and stared squinting out across the bright water. A few wind-flattened clouds cast shadows that rippled on its surface.

"I'm looking for someone," I told her after a few minutes of companionable silence during which her child drifted to sleep. The mother continued combing.

No secret about Luis León Borge. In Victoria de la Cruz they had heard something of him in the years during which the famous revolutionary had been out of the country engineering its liberation. People assumed his coming to Victoria was a forced banishment. He had showed up, rented a house from a widow who had two, bought a boat and begun to fish.

"Luis León is not a drunk," the woman clarified for me. Victoria de la Cruz, she explained, drew exiles. From everywhere: from Europe, from the United States, from Argentina. Once a

Japanese. Usually just one at a time, but few years passed without someone showing up as Borge had. Almost all of them drank seriously, or drugged seriously, rusted apart seriously in the course of their stay. That was the difference with this one. He had no evident consuming vice. He took his fishing seriously.

"Even though he's been tapped on the shoulder," she said.

"Tapped by whom?"

Finally she stopped combing her sleeping daughter's hair. Her hand rested lightly on the crown of the girl's head as it to ensure only healthy dreams got through. "That's what our old people say when God has marked somebody out."

"Marked for what?"

She smiled, shrugged, offered to find me something to eat. I accepted, wishing that someone, one time in my life, would comb my hair like that for six months or so.

I slept the afternoon off in a hammock behind the serious, hospitable woman's little shack, in a tangle of banana and grapefruit trees, thick-stemmed yucca plants, and massive bushy poinsettias. Once I woke and saw her daughter standing patiently in the tangle with a glass of water for me. It was not the way I had imagined things to be at the edge of the world.

So I was fresh and rested when Borge brought his boat, *La Victoria*, to shore that evening. As the sun sank loudly, like a punctured ball leaking purple ink across the sky, I watched him hop out and drag the boat high onto the sand. He stretched his net, which was badly tangled, took up his small catch of fish on a rope stringer, and lit a cigarette before he noticed me. He waved a hand at me to say get lost. I called his name.

"Too late," he told me. He shook his head and took off walking toward the village with his stringer of silver fish swinging.

"I want to write your book," I told him. "I'm free now. I left the paper."

Uninvited, I went with him to the house he had rented from the widow. Like the serious woman's shack, this one had one room, a pointed roof of thatch, a tangled yardful of plants and bushes. Borge sat on a three-legged stool in the yard and cleaned the fish on a low table. There was no second seat, so I sat on the ground. When the fish were cleaned a stoop-shouldered woman in an apron appeared, took away the fish, and put a plate of something fried, and something fresh and green, on the little table. Borge gestured that he would share, so we split the plateful, nothing on which I recognized by taste, smell, or texture. When we finished we rinsed our hands and faces, and Borge brought out a bottle of rum. He was more passive than I remembered him being, almost drained, as if the village had bled something strong and noxious from his pipes.

"I can cut it with Coca Cola if you want," he offered. But I didn't mind the idea of drinking straight warm rum. It was already dark, not cool but the air made tolerable by a fitful breeze rolling off the back of the black sea.

"I have a contract for your book," I told him. "It means money. Not a million dollars, but some money."

"Too late."

"What changed your mind, Luis León?"

"Just drink," he told me curtly.

I drank. Stars came out like bright white acne on the dark face of heaven. The breeze soothed. Someone in Victoria began to play a drum, and people laughed in little eruptions of bliss that spread in waves like gossip. The warm rum rubbed the inside of my skin. Mid-way through the second glass I told him about Angela.

"If she didn't have the courage to stay, you're better off."

"It's no good at the paper, either. All we cover is money stuff: privatization, foreign debt, liberalization."

"So that's why you changed your mind about the book."

"It's more than that," I told him, but I still couldn't say what.

We were three-quarters drunk before I worked up the nerve to ask him the sixty-four-dollar question. The drumming had stopped, replaced by a low-fidelity recording of some popular merengue songs. Somewhere in Victoria de la Cruz there was a party, in the ebb of which we could hear Caribbean waves stipple the shore softly. "What happened at the palace, Luis León? Even if you don't want the book I need to know."

"It's over," he told me. "The Sandinistas threw away the best chance for justice anybody ever had in these countries."

We were both standing, wobbly and blurred with the rum. I grabbed his arm, which felt rubbery and weak—he was too old, after all, to be starting a second career as a peasant fisherman—and shook him until he rattled.

"What happened at the palace?" I yelled into his face. He was docile, drunk, an old man with great political acuity and legendary organizational skills. I shook him hard; he rattled. But I knew that the moment for telling truth had gone past without my even seeing it. We sat down again on the sandy dirt of his rented back yard and finished the little that was left in his bottle.

I'm not much of a drinker. The hangovers destroy me. I slept hard on the ground at Borge's until an unidentified insect bit my leg, drawing blood and leaving a tiny welt that itched. When I realized Borge was gone I panicked. He tricked me, I thought. First he abandoned me and now he tricked me. Who says anything ever has to be reasonable?

My body creaking and complaining, I ran toward the beach where Borge had left his boat the night before. I was sure I was too late, but he was there, bent over the net he had stretched on the sand. He was having a hard time with the net, which didn't want to untangle. Coming close I saw his hands shake as he wrestled with the unwieldy brown mass, caked with sea junk and stiff drying seaweed. His baleful bloodshot eyes would have scared off anybody but a journalist accustomed to hounding people.

"You're too old to be a fisherman, Luis León," I told him. "Let me write your book. If not for you then for me. I need it."

He told me to go to the devil, kept working with no success at the net. His frustration, his inability to make his hands work, made me pity him. There was no one else in sight on the beach. The place was pristine, undefiled the way it was when Columbus stepped off his boat. The panicked sense of loss I felt seemed out of place in such scenic peace.

"You're not a fisherman," I said, "you're a revolutionary. Tell me what happened at the palace."

He glared at me, stood up and began to bundle the still tangled net. A stiff-armed starfish fell to the ground and Borge crunched it with his foot. When the net was compact enough to lift he heaved it into the boat, took hold of the gunwale and shoved *La Victoria* toward the water. The keel grated raw on the gritty sand. As soon as the boat was in deep enough to float he waded into the water, jumped aboard.

"You bastard," I called.

Oars in hand, he looked at me impassively, shoulders slightly rounded, and for just a moment I could have believed he was the sea-salt fisherman he pretended to be. "Too late," he told me.

"Tell me anyway."

He shook his head, began to pull on the oars. I told him he couldn't fish with his net screwed up the way it was. In response he closed his red, swollen eyes, pulled harder. Not the time to think. I waded into the water after him.

When Borge saw me coming he began to row harder, and I dove forward into the warm, salty water. I'm not much of a swimmer, but Borge in his old age wasn't much of a rower, either. I caught him easily, clung to the side of the boat making it list slightly to my side. The salt burned my eyes; they teared. When I opened them there was Borge hefting an oar ready to smash down on my curled fingers.

"Tell me," I told him. We were out just far enough that the water was over my head. My hungover body was weak; I was a gringo barnacle on the side of his boat.

The time he took to decide was the length of my life plus another uncalculated chunk I borrowed. I fixed on the oar, on his hands wrapped around it, on the smell of fish and salt and sweet slow rot that filled the proximate world. On Borge's slow-fast pulse in a thick blue vein in his wrist. "It's all an invention," he said to me.

"What's an invention?" My voice was not my own; it belonged to someone less desperate.

"People invent, especially the losers. That's what losers do best. They call it rectifying history, but it's really just invention, because that's what consoles."

"What happened at the palace?"

He looked at me angrily, shifted his position, and I thought he was going to break my fingers with his oar. But I had him. "I thought one of two things might happen," he told me. "Either I got shot by the soldaditos, or someone would become interested in writing my book. I needed money. I never put any away, though some did. The Sandinistas should have been bankers, they made a haul. Anyway I thought we'd be in power by now. And look where we are ... " He gestured with the dripping oar, taking in the sea, the sky, the defiled, unfree green continent.

"When it happened, I was surprised no one shot me. Three blocks from the palace I ditched the motorcycle and walked away like nothing ever happened, because nothing did. People invent, especially the losers. For a while I felt great. It was like surviving combat. But the exultation went away, and I realized I didn't want any book. The main thing was, we lost. Nothing else counts. Let the losers invent what they want to. We lost."

"The book is important," I tried to convince him. I was tiring of hanging on, even though the salt water buoyed my tired body.

"Go back to shore," Borge told me. "Leave me alone."

"You're not a fisherman. Let's write your book."

He lifted the oar higher in the air, and the way he held it told me he would not hesitate, now, to smash my hands. I let go of the boat, which rocked gently. I swam in to where I could stand. The water up to my neck, I watched Borge row steadily out on the flat and listless Caribbean. He was not a fisherman.

I waited two days, a third day, sleeping in Borge's rented shack, taking my meals with the family of the serious woman I had met when I arrived. Each night she told me the famous revolutionary would not be coming back. She looked at me sure I was auditioning for the part of Victoria de la Cruz's newest exile.

I waited a fourth day, a fifth. On the morning of the sixth day I washed my face and hands in an enamel basin of brackish water and walked away from the village.

Because of the heat, which came down like rain, I walked slowly. My feet kicked up little jets of dust. I was thirsty after a quarter mile. But there was plenty of time to fondle like beads on a string the little bits of things I knew. I knew that Borge was right, that they had lost, and that getting used to losing was a form of treason. I knew I would not write his book. And I understood, for the first time, that Borge's loss was also mine. I was not and had never been an objective journalist. I had wanted to see the good guys win, and they did not. Or else there were none. I knew that for me, there was nothing left to cover.

Before reaching the highway I lost sight of the Caribbean. Invisible insects twanged like saws. Free-ranging cattle chomped dry grass in an unfenced field split by the sandy track I was walking. There was no more revolution. My feet, always my most articulate body part, expressed their disappointment. It had to do with losing. And it had to do, I finally knew, with a power of invention.

Sixto in Harvest

In the dream sent to Sixto by his benefactor devil it was like dancing: the touching and letting go, with dignity in your feet and something fine and snaky coming out in the woman despite the best intentions of her prayers. In the dream also it was like a certain kind of sex: on dry grass in an open field at night with the moonlight papery over your head, the moonlight jumping up at you from out of the woman's eyes while she said nothing and you felt the wind find a line of sweat along the hollow of your back. Waking up with the momentum of the dream, Sixto knew that the decision was made.

In Paraguay there were no bullfights. But in the Mexican magazine his cousin Alejandro had bought in Pueblo Santo there was a bullfight story, with pictures.

Sixto sat up on his pallet and kicked away the sheet that had tangled around his legs. Little Bird and the boys still slept. Through the half-open door the last of the night air came in cool. Standing up, he felt for a half-smoked cigarette he had left above the door jamb. He lit a match, watched it flame, then blew it out and put the cigarette back on the flat ledge above the jamb. He stepped into the patio on cool, damp sand.

The black cock worried in its sleep on the barrel head. The hens slept on the low branches of trees. His one-winged duck had climbed onto the three-legged stool and stayed there as though it were safe. Over the eastern woods the illusion of light skittered in the black sky. At the head of the still, perfect hour Sixto cursed quietly, lathed in a feeling resembling contentment. He built a small fire.

When Little Bird, frowsy with sleep, came out of the house she was wary. "What are you doing up?"

In fairness to her he would waste no time.

"Where's that money your father gave you?"

"What money?"

He took her wrist and twisted it lovingly. "No games, Little Bird. I heard the boys talking."

"He gave it to me to make a down payment on the sewing machine."

"Get it for me."

He released her wrist. Her boyish face, made singular by a widow's peak that cut low into her forehead, appealed to the lover in him. It woke up his imagination. When she pursed her very thin lips it was as though her mouth had disappeared completely.

"You can hit me, Sixto, if you like. I'm not going to get the money for you." She slumped her body heavily, turning away her face. More than ever she seemed slight, capable of being hurt and loved.

Sixto said nothing. In the eastern vagueness the first cock crowed, and his own black beauty stirred and stretched. Dawn began to seep like quiet water into the basin of blackness. He had no impulse to hit Little Bird. He understood perfectly her reluctance to hand over the money. Better than hitting, an inspiration came.

Inside the house, in a small pocket she had sewn into the bodice of her better dress, he found the money he needed.

"Please," she said, but the mist of hope in her voice burned off immediately. She knew she had lost. She thought she had lost. If she could only understand how much she would win …

"With this," he lectured her a little, waving the wad of soiled bills, "you can buy part of a sewing machine. That's nothing. But

I can take it and do magic with it. I can triple it, I can make it into ten times this. You'll get your machine. I promise you. Not just part of it, either. The whole thing."

He slid open the top pole of the patio gate.

"Where are you going?"

"To make some magic, Little Bird."

Though it was early, by the time he had followed the path out to the road along both sides of which the village of Potrero straggled, a truck from one of the villages along the river was aggravating the dust. Under its weight of fresh wet cotton the truck groaned like a woman in labor, but to Sixto the sound suggested not pain but money. It was the money time of year.

Unfortunately, Sixto had had to sell his seed cotton. Still more unfortunately, the money he got for it had run through his hands. He detested working cotton. Still more, though, he detested picking another man's cotton by the day. Until his dream delivered him, it had been the only thing for him to do. Standing under the heat of a sun that grew hotter as it grew paler, he felt frustration, an odd desire with no object, plus a little excitement at the idea of money: its heft and smell, the odd way something so solid could run like water.

He hopped the low fence into the patio of don Hilario. That round fat man sat on a straight-backed chair, every other moment taking the mate cup his wife served him. The man's two ugly dogs lay at his feet as if they would protect him from something: thieves, death, or just the heat.

"Sorry, Sixto," Hilario sang out falsely, warding him off automatically. "I'm picked clean until next week at the earliest. Maybe five days if we get a little rain."

"I didn't come to pick cotton, don Hilario. I have a proposition for you."

"Save your proposition. You want breakfast?"

Sixto shook his head. He accepted the gourd and drank the strong, hot tea through the metal straw.

"What do you plan to do with that yellow bull of yours, Hilario? The one with the bad horn."

Patient, Sixto expected no answer. Hilario took the mate cup, which his wife had refilled with hot water. Sixto approached his problem from another angle. "How strong are the walls around Juan de la Cruz's dance *pista*, would you say?"

"Go back to bed, Sixto."

"I want to fight your bull there. Inside the *pista*."

The fat man's round body jiggled as Hilario laughed. "You a Mexican now, Sixto? Or a Spaniard, or what?"

"I'm serious. Close up the two of us inside the dance *pista*. Let people watch, and I'll fight him. If you want, you and Juan de la Cruz can charge people to watch."

"The Mexicans breed a special kind of bull, Sixto. My yellow bull is no fighter."

"But he's plenty ornery, and we can make him a fighter. Lock him inside the *pista* today and let him get mean hungry. Then tomorrow, we prick him a little and he gets meaner. You know, the way *los picadores* do."

Now Hilario's wife Aida laughed, wounding Sixto just slightly. In his dream, in no dream, did a woman resemble the slovenly Aida.

"I'll make it worth your while," he said, taking the wad of Little Bird's money from his pocket.

"How?" Hilario's eyes locked onto the bills.

"We bet this. If I win, all I get is your money. But you get the meat from the bull I kill. You can sell it easy. People have the taste for meat now that the money is coming."

"What about if you lose?"

"If I lose, you get this money plus I'll pick free for you for a week."

"I don't believe you," Hilario said. But Sixto could see that he had him. It took only diplomacy, a little time, and the visible wad. Hilario agreed to talk to don Juan de la Cruz about using the *pista*.

By the time Sixto left Hilario's place the sun was up and brooding, leaking heat like an oven with a broken door. Two more loaded lumbering trucks from up by the river had rolled through Potrero. The Potrero people were out in their fields picking, smelling money in the dust and the cotton fruit and their own sweat. Sixto knew where don Emiliano, the Chaco War veteran, was picking.

"You come to pick, Sixto? I could use the help." As he straightened up, the nearly full bag of cotton tied around Emiliano's waist seemed to pull him to the ground, like an unnaturally heavy belly. His wife and granddaughters went on picking on the far side of the field. Sixto heard one of them giggle once, and he remembered that she liked him. But the sound that came to his ears was more like money than sex.

"Can't pick with you today, Grandfather," Sixto told the veteran. "I came to make you an offer."

"Don't need any offer, Sixto. Need some help getting this cotton picked. Manuel was going to pick with me, but he went to Buenos Aires. Got a job in construction."

"You know that bull with the bad horn, belongs to Hilario?"

"Tawny colored. Kind of big. Bad temper when he gets riled."

"I'm fighting that bull tomorrow, Mexican style. With *picadores* and everything. Once that old yellow bull gets pricked a few times and smells his own blood, he'll be hopping and jumping and dying to kill me."

"I might stop by to see that, son. You're a senseless man, Sixto. You have a family."

"I know that, Grandfather. That's why I went to bet you on the outcome of the fight."

"How's that?"

Damp from sweat now, Little Bird's sewing machine money appeared in Sixto's hand as though he had conjured it. "Like this: If I kill the bull, you give me ten thousand. If the bull gets me, or even if I can't kill him, I'll pay you."

"You're not just senseless, Sixto, you're a fool. What if the bull kills you? Who takes care of your family?"

"Got to make a living, don Emiliano. Hilario will hold the money. You can trust him, can't you?"

Don Emiliano had gone through a desert war. The experience had left him coated with something tough and repellant, like an extra layer of skin you couldn't and wouldn't want to see. That was why Sixto had started with him, while his enthusiasm was fresh. As he knew he would, though, Sixto had his way. After the veteran, the rest of his day was easy.

When the evening had cooled a little and the last overladen cotton truck sailed through Potrero, Sixto walked home satisfied. As he expected, Little Bird and the boys were gone. They would be at her father's place. His father-in-law would be carping about Sixto's shortcomings. Little Bird would be defending him without words. The boys would be watching the argument go back and forth wondering whose side they should take. No matter. When he gave her back the money he had borrowed she would relent and admire him.

Scrupulously he made a list on the back of an envelope of the men with whom he had made a bet. He could win, he calculated, as much as he would have made on the cotton if he hadn't sold his seed. The prospect soothed him. As the sun ruptured over the west woods and blood color soaked the sky, he smoked the half cigarette from over the door. It was better, after all, to be alone for a while.

It would have been good to bring back the dream, but Sixto did not get the chance. He was awakened when he had hardly slept by the sound of voices in the patio. Sitting up quickly, he reached for his knife and tucked it into the waist of his pants.

"Sixto, come on out!"

As he opened the door to his mud-and-pole shack, their flashlights in his face confused him. "It's late, neighbors," he told them slowly as soon as he was able to make out the silhouettes of six or seven men.

"Let's see your money, Sixto," his wife's cousin's husband called. Sixto chuckled to himself at the threat in the man's voice.

All bluster. They were swelled up like frogs with it. This was the easy part.

"We figure you bet all of us with the same money, Sixto," another said.

"How could I do that, amigo?"

"Let's see your money then."

"I don't have it," Sixto admitted, drawing them in.

As though they were a single animal, a beast with one simple brain and too many legs, they moved menacingly toward his door, brandishing their flashlights and machetes.

"What I have," Sixto said, "is a backer."

"Who?"

"He doesn't want me to say."

"You're lying."

"Why would I do that to myself? Go home, my friends. Don't worry. If the yellow bull drops me and cuts out my heart with his twisted horn the way you want him to, you'll get what's coming to you."

It took a few minutes of time he might have been sleeping through, but they went away like children. At the gate, his wife's relative stopped and turned back as if considering a brand new thought. "If the bull drops you and hurts you but he doesn't kill you, and you don't give us our money, we'll kill you ourselves, Sixto. That's fair, isn't it?"

"But I'm going to win. I'm going to win, neighbors, so it doesn't make any difference."

Like children.

In the morning, as he had expected, most of Potrero took time off from picking cotton and gathered at the dance *pista*, the brick walls of which were low enough to let a person look over. Boys hung in the trees like fruit. Bottles of cane whiskey went slowly around, and the smell of commercial cigarettes perfumed the luminous air.

Stepping forward, Sixto knew that they were against him. It was like a particular smell, stronger than sweat but still a human smell. He gulped it in. At the door to the *pista* he conferred with his *picadores*: his cousin Alejandro and the blonde German twins with green eyes. In their hands all three held bamboo poles, on the ends of which long-bladed knives were lashed with rawhide.

"All the commotion and no food has made the bull nasty, Sixto," Alejandro said. It was good to have one friend in the crowd.

Sixto wanted to look around for Little Bird but did not. Instead he asked the *picadores*, "You're not scared to get in there with him, are you?" All three shook their heads and rattled their bamboo swords. The German twins grinned.

"You say the word, Sixto," Alejandro said. "We're ready when you are. We'll get him riled up enough to make people happy."

To think about losing was bad luck.

Waiting, Sixto felt a sort of pride that was like power. The eyes of the Potrero people raked and scratched him. He accepted a small drink of whiskey without noticing who offered it.

"Let's go," he said quietly.

In the beginning it was like comedy. The German twins were fast; they could outrun anyone in the village. They danced around the bull jabbing with ginger strokes at the yellow hide. Alejandro, heavier on his feet but steadier, advanced on the flanks. Watching in a condition of unnatural calm through the cracked door, Sixto smoked a cigarette.

It took less time than anyone could have guessed to enrage the bull. The sweat on his hide drew the dust, which blanketed body, back, and legs. After the *picadores* made a few successful strikes, thin lines of red began to run.

Rather suddenly, Alejandro made one deep lancing stab, and the bull, instead of going for the man who had hurt him, stopped short, turned and lunged at one of the twins. All three *picadores*, exulted and afraid, ran to the door, which Hilario slammed shut when they were safe. It was Sixto's time.

His cape was a length of cloth, not red as it should have been but blue with large white checks. His knife was securely in his belt. He wondered again if Little Bird had come to see him. The noise was like the cheering at a soccer game, except that they were all cheering for the bull.

In the ring, aware of being encircled by hostile neighbors who were eager for him if not to die then at least to fail, Sixto learned quickly what he had been wondering about without knowing that he wondered. Being there, doing it, was not like the dream, precisely, but it had something the dream also had: a feeling, a sense of being awake in strange territory. It was like waking in the woods in the morning when you were going hunting but didn't know where you were going to wind up. The bull, sullen and mad, came at him directly.

There was no longer any comedy, but Sixto's first smooth sidestep was better still, if they wanted to go to the theater. Turning adroitly, he taunted the animal with the blue and white cape. Despite their bias, the crowd cheered. Not for him, but for what he had been able to do. Stopping just short of the door, the animal shook its head, and bright drops of blood flew in the air around it. It turned and came at Sixto again.

Three times it was good, and Sixto felt himself becoming more graceful with every frustrated charge the bleeding yellow bull made. The fourth run his timing was wrong; his legs didn't move the way they should have. The bull caught his cape with the twisted horn and ripped it hard. Taken by surprise, Sixto fell. He was unable to let go of the cape, which tore almost in half.

Sensing its advantage, the bull was back upon him as soon as it could stop and turn. Its straight horn tore into Sixto's leg as the twisted one had torn into the fabric of the cape. The bull raised its head then, thinking to lift and toss the body, but Sixto's weight was more than it expected. The horn wrenched free. Dancing off for a moment, the bull charged again as Sixto rolled away in the dust.

Theater was what his neighbors wanted. Not a comedy but a family tragedy. The pain was exquisite.

As the bull came at him, Sixto sat up like a victim. When the animal lunged again, turning its head to use a horn, Sixto saw one thick vein stretched taut amid the neck muscles, and he drove his knife there. When the blood came it soaked him.

The frantic breathy barking of the bull as it died was no different from the sound any old cow made as it was slaughtered. It was a shame the blood would be wasted, spilling over him and seeping into the sandy dirt. Racing, leaking blood and shuddering, the bull was more dangerous than it had been before. But in what seemed a short time it threw itself against the bricks of the south wall and collapsed. The screams of the women and the shouts of the men followed it down.

Not personal pride but the decorum associated naturally with the event made it impossible that Sixto faint away. His leg was badly gored. Standing up, he saw the door open and the *picadores* racing in to support him. The noise of the crowd—his neighbors—was awful, but he could not interpret what they meant or wanted. Allowing Alejandro and the Germans to help him finally, he left the ring. He was pretty sure Little Bird had not come to see him. Taking the money he had won from Hilario's unwilling hand, he fainted.

That night Sixto drank some cane whiskey as he lay on the pallet in his house. The drink threw off the pain in his leg a little, but not much. Little Bird and his boys had not come home, which surprised more than worried him. She would get her sewing machine, guaranteed. But she had to come home to forgive him first, and she did not.

Despite the muffled way his mind was working and his ears hearing, Sixto was aware of the sentiment against him and his victory in the village. Perhaps no one had believed he had had a backer. No one could understand, ever, that it made no difference. They were different, not like him.

He worried a little that some of the men whose money he had taken might come to get him or the money or both. Not until he began to dream again, however, did they happen by. In the new dream they carried torches instead of flashlights, and their faces were bronze with the look of petrified Indians. They put him in a circle with high walls and they waited, but the bull was dead.

Coolness woke Sixto, it must have been. The air around him was clear, black, and busy with the freight of night sounds. In the swamp the frogs made their dumb thunking songs, and the wings of a night bird thrummed overhead. The men with torches had disappeared with the dream.

The pain in his bandaged leg was duller, a monotonous feeling by now. He regretted that Little Bird had not come home, and he wondered what kind of stories his father-in-law would corrupt the boys with. As his thoughts blew by the evaporating dream and then his hurt leg and then his family, a creeping exultation made itself felt along the length of his body. He had done it, done something. The yellow bull was dead, the cotton was coming, and it was the money time of year. Under his head he felt the lump of money. Lying on his back on the pallet he thought again: It was, after all, a little like dancing. Like dancing in the money time of year.

Lover's Leap

Two things about Guadalupe. Her skin was the color of honey in a jar held up to the sun. Think of the sluggish sensual way the honey slides if you tip the jar. I was her boring Anglo boyfriend, Nathaniel the Nondescript. By contrast, my skin is the color of day-old mashed potatoes observed in the glow of a refrigerator light bulb. I knew from the beginning that I had done nothing to deserve Lupe. She happened to me the way weather happens. That didn't bother me. What worried me was hanging on.

The second thing was she jumped off bridges.

I saw her before she saw me. It was January. We were both seniors at Alma College, a Presbyterian haven of study in the flat wilds of mid-Michigan. From the perspective of a distant, worried parent, Alma was a prudent place to send a volatile Latin bridge jumper. Lupe arrived late and alone at a post-New Year's party in the house of one of our history professors, a woman who crusaded doggedly to remake for the '90s the teacher-student political solidarity she remembered from the '60s. Lupe accepted her enfolding embrace at the door but gave nothing back, held onto her coat as though sure she wouldn't stay. She was high on something that made her body quiver every few seconds, not the draft beer everyone else was placidly sucking down. The light behind her green eyes was constant as stress.

Not to say that I was passive. In the course of the party, as the beer and hot proximity blurred all sorts of distinctions, I moved close enough to her aura of exotic allure that she had to notice me. When she quivered, my own body shook a little. That scared me; ten minutes after we met and she had me shaking. Ten minutes more and she fell against my chest, let herself slump guessing I would catch her. I did. "Take me away from all of this," she vamped, but I wasn't that kind of hero.

I didn't learn about the bridges until spring, when the ice had melted into ragged, punky chunks in the Burl River, and last year's dead leaves, soggy or stiff depending on the hour, appeared patterned on the ground in the recovering woods. It had taken no time at all to learn that Lupe was volatile, that she battered her body with drugs as exotic as she, that an impulse of anger and fear was pushing her to a continuously disappearing edge. But she was mostly gentle with me; off duty, I guess. I was the one capable of listening for hours to her monologues on Keats and Shelley, whose brand of Romantic compulsion had converted her to an English major. Lupe's poet-inspired froth fascinated me. Her light shadow of accent was like the fur on a peach; once you tasted it, you craved. My own major was biology. I liked taking plants apart, liked the fact that they didn't talk back. Their only eloquence was design.

"I'll pick you up in ten minutes," she told me on the phone. I was lying in bed wondering when she would consent to make love with me. For a month or so we had sparred and squirmed a little under covers, but she told me she was too nervous for sex; I should look elsewhere to satisfy my needs, and she would not be offended. Her voice reminded me that she was still saying no.

"I have a class this morning," I told her.

"Skip it."

I skipped.

She drove predictably fast in her red Mazda out north of Alma to an unfenced stand of woods through which the Burl wound at its deepest and most bucolic. A white haze wrapped the flat early sky, and it was cold enough to see our breath jet. We're animals,

I thought. My feet felt like prehistoric hooves as we walked under high-branched trees toward the mucky bank of the river. We're a species, I thought. A cold, gusting wind made the trees' upper bodies twist and bend a little, as if to get a better look at the odd hoofed species tromping and crunching below.

"I don't want to talk," Lupe warned me. She hadn't said a word on the drive, just punched stereo buttons to play and replay Glen Miller's String of Pearls. We followed the Burl upriver to a bend where it sliced in two a one-lane dirt road. The bridge over the river was old and picturesque, a scarred steel structure that had adapted gracefully to its environment since CCC workers built it in the '30s. We went halfway across the bridge on big weathered planks that looked like they would last the life of the Republic. Below us the water swirled by with a brushing, percussive sound, deep and cold. Lupe leaned into me, hid her head in my chest so that I didn't understand what she began to say. But I didn't want to move; she seldom moved her body in my direction.

It had to do with things she was sure I would not understand: the unplumbed sewer of corrupt politics in Latin America. The premature heart attack suffered by the Latin Left when the Berlin Wall fell on top of them. The horror of witnessing for your whole life the stratified life-in-death between halves and never-will-haves in her own country, in all those unhappy, eking-out countries in her part of the world. She had a red sports car, she had credit cards and global mobility. She was a late flower blooming in played-out mercantile soil. She had read every book they wrote on Che Guevara, but there were no more revolutionary mountains into which right-thinking people could retreat and talk strategy. The violent Left exhibited a pathology that was as horrific, almost, as the pathology of the reactionary Right.

She was right: I probably didn't understand. Mostly I got the sense she was taking herself more seriously than any gringo biology major was likely ever to take himself. But none of that mattered to me. What mattered was holding onto her. My hooves stomped on the planks when I couldn't think of anything to say that did justice to my love and my desire.

For about half a second I thought she was unbuttoning herself to me. But the real reason for shucking her jacket, then her jeans and shirt was to jump unencumbered into the steel-colored Burl as it steamed quietly below us. She moved so fast I scarcely had time to ache over the vision of her brown and perfect body perched and straining on the guard rail of the old bridge. Scream splash scream. Then she was floating on her back in the cold water looking up at me with hostility.

"Jump," she called.

I heard nothing very playful in her furry, sexy voice; more like a summons to attend other new things I would not be able to understand. My ignorance of all things worth doing and knowing shamed me. But a person who had to stop and wonder whether the unmysterious river was deep enough at that particular spot to dive safely was not a person who would strip and leap when he could see his breath jetting in the cold.

"I can't swim," I lied. An odd sensation to lie while yelling, as if the louder you said it the more likely you were to get away with it.

Lupe lifted an impatient hand and struck out for the shore. I watched like a dolt, fixed on the thin white stripe of her bra across that beautiful brown back. I carried her clothes down to the bank where she climbed out, but she would not let me come near. She dressed angrily, holding my fear of jumping against me. "I'm tired of you," she told me in a matter-of-fact voice I was afraid to believe. On the drive back to campus Glen Miller was the only one who said anything worth remembering.

After that I expected Lupe would drop me for someone more interesting, either politically or romantically. But she did not. I accepted the double bind of frustration and infatuation into which she had me locked, and by the time we graduated we had become close, dependent on one another in a way that surprised everyone who knew us. Graduate school loomed like penance. I became restless and morose, while Lupe camped in my room and leafed through catalogs hour after hour. I was the envy, people told me, of every heterosexual male on campus.

Once—just once—Lupe let me make love to her. But when I finally got to where I wanted to be she wasn't there; it was as if to surrender her body she had to vacate it, so all I did was fuck a beautiful shell. With some frequency she jumped from a bridge or did something equally melodramatic and dangerous, usually when she was under a chemical influence she never invited me to share.

But she surprised me. "You're coming home with me," she announced the day we graduated. None of her family had come north to see her get her American degree, and she was embarrassed to admit that their absence bothered her. A middling herd of my own extended family had driven the three hours east to Alma the night before the ceremony. I was touched and a little surprised to see that the contrast between our families quietly galled her. She came to my room early in the morning of what was going to be a stunning, bucolic day in early summer, a day as bright and hope-ridden as commencement day in a movie.

"I have to work this summer or I can't go back to school in September." My reflex stall disappointed both of us.

I was sitting in my desk chair half dressed, dense, a nerd in repose. Prone on the unmade bed in a position resembling an army sniper's, Lupe looked at me, squinted, sighted along an imaginary barrel. "We'll make fireworks love," she said. Gotcha.

I went. South.

South. Guadalupe's country resembled perfectly the cliché-image I had of a small, poor Latin country in America's back yard. Not back yard, she corrected me. The Yankees lavished great care on their back yards, nourished them with lawn furniture and fertilizer and enjoyed comfortable, fulfilling lives in them. That was certainly not the case with the countries below the southern rim of the United States. More accurate to say that her country lay inert on its aching back in the overwhelming shadow of the imperial giant.

"Geographical bad luck," she told me; location was destiny.

The place even looked like a tropical fantasy: In San Pedro, her city near the north coast, a non-stop sun lit up masses of exotic bright flowers everywhere. Hummingbirds hung. Shade trees drooped. Oranges and grapefruits and bananas clustered thick on the branches of innumerable trees with waxy green leaves. Muttering parrots and brilliant, nervous macaws decorated the interior patios of the wealthy people's houses like local color. High white walls topped with spikes or shards of broken glass kept the acquired opulence in and the Latin lumpen out. Along the webwork of cobbled and cracked-asphalt streets that had neither signs nor numbers, silver BMWs and runty, khaki-colored donkeys moved in roughly equal numbers in the stupor-inducing heat.

Waiting, I thought, for fireworks love, we cruised the city in Lupe's mother's pearl gray Mercedes. And cruised. Whenever we stopped at a street-light, beggars appeared with cupped hands and a genuine needy wail in their voices that was a quick-fix substitute for political consciousness raising.

"Does it bother you?" Lupe asked me once as she downshifted and we left a band of beggars to eat exhaust with their cake.

"Of course it bothers me."

"It was a mistake for you to come. You should go home and forget you were ever here. None of this will ever change, Nathaniel. Not in ten lifetimes. My mistake,"

"How come it won't change, Guadalupe?"

Her answer came out glib but wasn't meant to be. "Che's dead. Fidel's a dinosaur. Socialism is ... It's a poem that came out wrong."

"So work on the problem a different way. Be a union organizer," I suggested. "Fight the good fight."

She shook her head and looked suspiciously at me wondering if I was making fun of her. How could people cruising in a Mercedes talk about revolution in any way that wasn't a joke? We had plans, we had careers, we had all kinds of interests vested in the world that was.

"Not here," Lupe lectured me. "This town's too small. This country's too small. The mercantilists will never give an inch. The door's closed and it's going to stay closed. If it comes down to killing, they'll kill to keep what they have."

She had worked herself up to a pitch of feeling past anything I could follow. "Lupe," I said, "what the hell are we talking about?"

Without warning she stopped the car on a street I didn't recognize, shut off the engine, which pinged once to tell me something important might be happening. Up and down both sides of the quaintly cobbled street twelve-foot whitewashed walls were camouflaged with flowering bushes that dripped loud tropical colors, reds and oranges and purples, abundant as mercantile money. Inside the expensive car, sleek as a metal otter, I felt marooned. We were stuck on our own thin-aired planet, and for the first time since we had met I had an impulse to run, to escape from her.

But she leaned close to lick my ear, ran her hand along the outside of my thigh. "I hate my life, Nathaniel," she told me. "I hate this city, I hate this country, I hate it all."

The engine pinged quietly again. From one of the walled-in yards an exotic bird cawed furiously. Then the street was quiet as an old man's nap. Lupe wrapped her hands around the steering wheel and arched her plucked, pointed eyebrows at her reflection in the mirror. She turned the key and the engine came quietly to life, an obsequious servant. "If you don't help me, you're a bastard," she said quietly, still looking in the mirror, and I nodded. She drove, and I wondered what it was I had agreed to do.

I stayed, because I couldn't go. In dramatic undertones Lupe's mother let me know I had a useful sedative effect on her; I was welcome in their home. Mornings we drank slow coffee and orange juice on the family's flagstone patio surrounded by exuberant greenery, washed in sunlight, spoiled by servants on quiet feet. Lupe worked hard to teach me some Spanish. Once a week my parents called and fretted a little in clipped, long-distance sentences that I might be throwing my future away. But I was marooned, obsessed watching the fire inside her burn up the woman who had promised me fireworks love, so whatever I told my parents must have disappointed them.

I stayed. My bedroom was in an empty wing on the second floor of the family manse, a high-ceilinged cave full of heavy, gloom-gathering furniture that must have come over on the boat with the Conquistadores. Distant from the life of the house, it was a perfect room in which to experience fireworks love. No such luck. Most nights after midnight Lupe came to my room, and sometimes she took off her clothes, and sometimes she battered my body with hers, and sometimes she traced the outline of my penis with restless hands, and sometimes she kissed me in important places. But it wasn't fireworks love. In fact it didn't seem much like love at all, more like nervous frustration spilling out on me because I happened to be there.

One night after about a month of that kind of torture she showed up in my room late looking like the ghost of Florence Nightingale. Her white robe trailed like a queen's, her hair fell loose down her shoulders, her face was flushed rose. "I want you to leave tomorrow, Nathaniel. I'm tired of you."

"It's your mother's dinner, isn't it." The family had invited people over to meet Guadalupe's gringo scientist boy friend. "I don't want to go home yet. I love you."

"I won't behave," she warned me.

"I don't care."

"Suit yourself," she snapped. She left me to ride out the night alone. The darkness hummed like an animal. I ran my hand over the sheets where she had lain a moment and felt a sense not so much of loss as of something going.

The dinner to domesticate Guadalupe turned out to be as bad as she had promised. Her mother, doña Mercedes, was as big and regal as a ship of the Spanish Armada. She had to be big to bear up under the weight of jewelry displayed across her heavy padded chest. Mostly diamonds, and mostly big. Since Lupe's father had died she managed the family's businesses, doling out money and responsibilities to her children in accordance with her judgement of their capacity. Lupe's two sisters, married to men with their own money, ran the television station and an import-export business of some kind. Neither husband appeared at the dinner. The sisters, mirror images of each other's brittle, buffed self, caressed the ropes of braided gold around their necks and quizzed me in perfect English. That much I could take, and I could take the stylized grilling by family friends who had come when doña Mercedes summoned. Harder to take was don Felipe.

Don Felipe was the family failure. Thin and unnaturally wizened at forty, he was his mother's hanging cross. He had brought to bankruptcy two family businesses and come close, before rescue, to ruining a third. He gambled, he drank, he chased low-life women who invariably liberated the money his mother rationed him. He gassed, he pontificated, he slurped his soup. At the foot of the long mahogany table he sat like their own court jester.

"Mark my words," he prophesied to me. "Beware the Left." Doña Mercedes was captivating the other end of the table with a story about Republican Cubans in Miami. Felipe pulled the hairs on my arm to press his point, and I couldn't help flinching. "You Americans think the Communists are dead, but it's only a strategic retreat. Let your guard down once—and you will—and they're at the gate."

While Felipe gassed on, white-jacketed waiters circulated filling glasses and lifting plates. I had a hard time breathing. The food was rich, the wine was good, the silver was real, the politics were post-reactionary. My brain blurred. Not until the lights went out did I understand what had triggered Felipe's rave.

A year earlier a soccer stadium had been built a block away from the mansion. I knew the date on which the first game had been played there, because about three times a week doña Mercedes expressed through tight lips her sense of outrage at such low proximity. The mayor who blessed the project had betrayed his class. All kinds of riffraff milled in the streets around the house any time there was a game. Until the lights went out the homey roar of the dinner party had overcome the sound of the crowd leaving the stadium in an unruly, lower-income wave.

A silence I wanted to interpret as nervous hit the party as the waiters fumbled for candles and matches in the big mahogany sideboard.

"The goddamn Left controls the electrical workers' union," Felipe educated me loudly. His voice had a coarse quality to it that grated. With a few drinks percolating in him he had begun to slur. "They kill the power like this on purpose. They like to show their strength. In the United States you wouldn't let them get away with it, would you? What we need in this country is a few tough Republicans."

"Felipe," doña Mercedes warned in a voice whose artificial sweetness did nothing to disguise the motherly menace.

"It's the truth," Felipe insisted, a child corrected before company, and people's love of a scandal kept everyone quiet. Outside, the soccer crowd had found its voice. "Why will none of you admit it? They want to suck our blood, I tell you, and the day is coming when they will."

"Let's talk about something besides vampires," one of Lupe's sisters suggested, which broke the spell. People laughed, and one generous soul remembered an outrageous story about a vampire bat that got the table talking again.

Half drunk and venomous, Felipe drained his glass. Behind us, glass doors opened onto an enormous yard around which ran walls that must have been fifteen feet high. The crowd surged behind them. A man with a mission, Felipe pushed his chair back and disappeared into the yard while the guests chatted patiently in the candled dark. I followed Lupe, who followed Felipe out.

We stood in the black shadow of a dwarf palm and watched as her brother went through an ugly metamorphosis. After a few moments of night blindness, the moon was bright enough that we could make him out pretty well: Facing the high wall with his back stiff, his arms bent at the elbows rigid as sticks, his head cocked to eleven o'clock, don Felipe ran clip after clip of hollow--

point shells through the air-machine gun that had overheated his imagination. The target of his impotent wrath was the invisible, innocent, noisy crowd on the the far side of the wall. In his mind he was deadly. The weapon's kick made his body twist and jerk. I thought of a teenager aping a heavy-metal artist. He was yelling bilingual filth at his enemies as he blasted them, but they could hear none of it because of the happy, home-team racket they were making. I made out just enough of his angry foaming to feel a physical disgust. My lover's brother was an obnoxious reptile.

When I tried to put an arm around Lupe she brushed me away angrily. It seemed like a long time that we stood watching Felipe kick and spew and blast air bullets at the soccer fans in the street. But we got tired of seeing before he got tired of shooting. When a clip was emptied he patiently reloaded. His tie and jacket lay in the grass beside an imaginary bunker. No more dinner party.

I followed Lupe into an enormous garage behind the house and jumped into the passenger seat of the Mercedes before she had a chance to leave me behind. It took an effort at self-control I didn't know she was capable of for Lupe to maneuver safely past the milling crowd, out of her walled neighborhood onto a two-lane highway going out of town. As we drove the lights came back on, and irregularly spaced orange globes lit the road ahead of us into the rural distance.

No music, no talk. The headlights tunnelled. The metal otter raced. I knew with a clarity that hurt that we were headed for a bridge.

The place we parked and walked was nothing like mid-Michigan in any season. The air was jungle hot, jungle wet. It hung on my back like a sweaty shirt. Disturbed birds made soundtrack noises that faded and returned as we hiked. The trees were low and hunched; they had a thousand grasping arms. After a while we went through a banana plantation; the trees went on in humanly inspired rows. In the unlit distance dogs hooted, out-of--sync roosters told their dreams out loud, and a stew of night noises I didn't recognize made me feel that we were walking like victims to the world's wildest edge. As we got closer, a big river made an articulate roar nothing at all like the sound of Alma's placid Burl.

The bridge was silver in the light of an almost-full moon floating like a detached retina. It blanched the sky, hid the stars. We came out of the banana plantation onto a hard-packed dirt road onto the bridge. In a pale-blue dinner dress the moon turned sheeny gray, Lupe stopped and took off her shoes, and I went after her. Mid-bridge she unhooked her lapus lazuli earrings and tossed them like pennies into the river. She turned to face me as though I were the enemy she had to conquer.

"I told you you should have gone home," she hissed. Her anger at me was real as the river.

"It's not your fault, Lupe."

"Shut up."

"Please don't jump this time. This one is too high."

She cocked her head a little to one side as though listening to something that wasn't me. The edge of a flat, star-shaped cloud obscured the cyanic moon for a minute, then evaporated like smoke. Lupe's shoulders shook. It was the first time I had seen her cry. I moved toward her but stopped when the anger gusted in her again. She began slowly to unbutton her dress.

"Don't jump, Lupe. Jesus, don't jump. It's too high. Let's go back to town. I'll drive."

"Take off your clothes, Nathaniel."

"I love you."

"Take them off."

I took off my shirt, my pants, my shoes. I felt naked enough for two. Lupe slipped out of her fancy dress, dropped her slip, and I saw what I had thought was everything in the world I would ever want. Ever. She climbed the railing on the bridge, and the sound of the river seemed to rise as she went. On the railing she checked herself, balanced for a moment. Her toes curled. She looked down at me in my K-Mart underwear. Then she jumped.

This time no scream, just a splash.

There was only one choice and that was no choice at all. I hoisted myself onto the bridge's cool metal lip and leaped without reflection. My body as it dropped was terrified.

I landed on my side and sank fast; my body stung at the smack. When I came up airless and listing Lupe was treading water next to me calm as philosophy. She had shucked her bra, and I wanted badly to cup her breasts. But my ragged entry had shaken me. I couldn't catch my breath, and one leg hurt like fire; it had twisted when I hit the water. I tried to tread water but the bad leg wouldn't work right. I went under swallowing the river.

When I came up she was right there, and I flailed toward her, but she put her strong hands on my shoulders and shoved me back below the black surface. She held me there; I held my breath. She made a fist and hit me on the head. I struggled free and came up for air, but she tried to force me under a second time. My lungs were empty. I was scared. I slapped her hard in the face with the flat of my hand, and she floated away like driftwood.

When she was far enough away that neither of us could do any more damage to the other she struck out for shore, angling with the current so that she was quickly out of the shadow of the bridge downstream. Shock made my body work again, and I followed, gaining on her a little. By the time she was crawling out over a heap of slippery rocks on shore I was close enough to grab her ankles. When I did, she kicked me in the teeth with her heel.

She stopped, stood still on a flat rock. I lay in the water and looked up at her moonlit magnificence.

"You can't fix it, you know," she told me. Her voice was both aggrieved and reconciled, and I knew she was right.

For a moment neither of us moved. She was right. I had jumped from the bridge but I couldn't fix it. Half in and half out of the boiling river, I saw myself as a half-evolved creature; I was still an idea. But several thoughts came to me like little bulbs bursting in the darkness behind. I knew that when I climbed out of the water Lupe and I were finally going to make our fireworks love. And I knew it would be the last and only time. I knew that I would never be able to forget the image of her, naked and prematurely desperate in the bland moonlight on the bridge, and that the image would make me suffer. I saw her in protected middle age armored in ropes of gold like her sisters. And I saw that there was such a thing as a pocket of aloneness that, once experienced, would stay inside you and change your shape.

The Murder of German Morales

The murder of German Morales confirmed everything Anthony O'Hara thought about Central America and the repressive, violent country to which he had come. He caught the news on the radio lying on his cot in the room he was renting in a poor house, in a poor neighborhood, from a poor family with discreet and honorable ties to the committed Left. It was early dark. Semi-cool air lapped through the open window drying his sweat. His room at the back of the house had no light bulb, but he did not light his evening candle. Bad news bonded him to the struggle.

In a voice that thrilled because she had seen the disfigured bloody body, a woman reporter on Radio Presente described how a lone gunman had run up behind the president of the trash haulers' union and blasted away his neck at close range. One shot, splat and splatter. Listening, the North American representative af the Democratic Initiative for Social Change felt a second-hand grief that was like solidarity. And he felt shortchanged. It was still his first week in town. The day before, he had called Morales to request a meeting. But Morales begged off, said he had to make an urgent trip to Guatemala. No explanation. Not that he owed one. Splat splatter. Lickety then split.

O'Hara switched off the radio and listened to the self-absorbed sounds of the house and the street around him. A child bleated with a goat's voice, outraged, then shut up fast when its mother cooed a clear threat. In the back yard outside the door chickens puttered, and a sleeping dog sighed. Farther away, scratchy mariachis on a record worked their way through the *ranchera* he had already begun to associate with the scruffy green city, *El Rencor del Debil,* whose maudlin lyrics and weepy fiddle he associated, for no intelligible reason, with structural under-employment.

He thought about calling the DISC office back in New York to alert them to the Morales murder, but that was not his place or purpose. DISC's local representative, a man whose great credibility was founded on the torture he had survived over many years at the hands of government goons, would likely cable New York in the morning. O'Hara's visit and intentions—and DISC's first commandment—presupposed non-intervention. A hundred and fifty years of imperialist meddling could not be amended or forgiven overnight. The line DISC drew itself to walk was thin as four-pound test, but there was no other way to go. His task was justifiable: gather data for DISC's yearly report on human rights. His mission was trickier: support without intervention. Instead of calling he took a walk, and the music of *El Rencor del Debil* spread like viscous syrup across the absorbent purple air.

German Morales had only lasted a year as president of the union that first became famous in the 1960s for standing up to the police with passive-resistance tactics that won them more respect than contract benefits. His two front teeth were gold: sporty replacements for what he once lost to a rifle butt. A labor celebrity, during interviews he quoted Pablo Neruda's polemical communist poems, he quoted Walt Whitman, he quoted his own *campesino* grandfather at inspired length. He made jokes about Latin machismo and seemed to understand what women's rights might be about. His funeral should have been a spectacle, a solidarity celebration, a place to give angry voice to some of what was wrong with things as they were. But it was none of that. The day after the murder Morales' parents claimed the body and held a secret service to which no one was invited. Although he appreciated their grief and their need for privacy, O'Hara thought that the parents did their son's cause, which was the cause of all right-thinking, oppression-opposing individuals, short shrift. A second time he felt shortchanged.

The afternoon of what should have been the funeral O'Hara checked in at the DISC office. Parked across the street was a jeep with Ray-Ban windows, no plates, motor running. Water from the air conditioner was puddled on the cobbled street; they had been there a while. Surveillance still made O'Hara nervous. In California working with migrant laborers he had never felt the threat as something you could touch, hate so close it was casual. It had a shape: water pooled on dusty cobbles, polarized windows like a mask, new tires, unflecked paint on a vehicle that paid no taxes. No plates; nothing to trace. At the door he hesitated for a moment, looked at the jeep. The anger was a natural buzz; for a moment he felt rinsed clean, scoured.

"Standard operating procedure," Juan Ramon Velazquez told O'Hara inside the office. They sat on wooden chairs under leafy shade in the building's interior patio. Exuberant plants in crumbling pots climbed poles then drooped their heavy flowers. Dense, tiny-leaved ivy burdened a trellis that needed paint. Bottle-green flies languished in the heat, and Velazquez' hands trembled, the permanent consequence of a temporary technique applied to his body years before by one of the many goon squads that considered him a threat and a communist and squashable.

"I like that English word, goons," he told O'Hara. His English was precise, though he preferred to speak Spanish. "Certain words express their idea in one language better than they do in another. In English, goon is one of your better words."

Suffering had made Velazquez ugly. His body, anyway. The scars from brute-inflicted cigarette burns wound around his hands and arms like grisly daisy chains. In the bad old days before prime-time television and human rights advocacy groups the goons didn't care whether they left visible marks after an interrogation. His limbs trembled incessantly, he wore a patch over an eye that had been taken from him, and he walked with a cane because his legs were bad.

"It wouldn't do much good, would it, if DISC in New York put out a statement saying the security forces are harassing you again." O'Hara could think of no effective way to express fellow feeling with the man, who commanded his respect.

Velazquez shrugged, leaned forward over his little pot belly, raised his cane in the air as if to defend himself. He spat on the patio bricks and they rested a while watching the yellow web of saliva evaporate slowly. A Siamese cat appeared, hopped into the lap of the nation's premier witness to state-sponsored torture.

"Their intentions are good in New York," Velazquez told O'Hara, who felt rebuked.

"Joe Morgan knows the limits of what DISC can do for you, Juan Ramon. DISC people are pretty careful. They know there are limits to what they can know, maybe even to what they can feel. About this, I mean. About you, the things that have happened to you."

"The problem is they want it both ways, Antonio."

O'Hara waited, but he had to ask for the explanation he needed. A woman making coffee stirred in the kitchen shed behind them, and glass clattered quietly. He wanted to get up and peek through the front window to see if the unmarked jeep was still in the street but didn't. Looking at Velazquez' body, martyred alive, brought back the anger buzz. He was scoured.

"They want to see clean, just development happen," Velazquez finally explained, "and that's ok. They wish to be helpful. But they think it can happen like magic, like this." He snapped quivering fingers irritably. "Out of discontented lumpen they think there can somehow be produced responsible citizens who vote like Swedes and make their own high standard of living."

"They know their solidarity only goes so far, Juan Ramon."

"Solidarity! They also want to play politics, do they not? They want to make their political stand and bring down the bad guys. But that's a dirty business. It's not as neat and clean as development."

"Did you talk to Morgan in New York today?"

Looking like a battered professor whose academic probity had been questioned, Velazquez squinted, tossed the cat onto the brown patio bricks. "About what?" The cat disappeared into a miniature thicket of flowering bushes at the end of the yard, and the cook in the kitchen let out a loud hissing noise like steam escaping. O'Hara felt nervous sweat leak down his back, his chest, under his arms.

"About the Morales murder," he said hesitantly. Velazquez had begun to make him feel guilty, as though his real intentions had everything to do with interventionism, as though he were a predictable gringo meddler whose näiveté were a punishable offense.

"Did you see my statement in the papers this morning, Antonio?"

O'Hara nodded enthusiastically. What he wanted was some common ground he could stand on with the man. If not with then at least next to. "I wanted to ask you about that, Juan Ramon."

"Ask what?"

"I was just surprised a little, that's all. By the tone of the statement."

"Surprised?"

"I thought you went kind of easy on the government. At least that's the way it looked to me. From an outsider's perspective, I mean."

"How would you have done it?"

O'Hara found no adequate response. He shrugged, felt foolish.

"This is a war, Antonio," Velazquez lectured him, puffing a little with a preacher's on-call conviction. "And in war one calculates like a soldier: There is such a thing as strategy, as tactics, resources. One tries to choose his battles intelligently."

"A murder is a murder, isn't it, Juan Ramon?" A mistake, maybe a serious mistake. But he would not unsay it. He assumed there was nothing admirable about his stubbornness.

"Does the idea of cold calculation offend you?"

That road led only to an impasse barricaded before the fact by Velazquez, so O'Hara quit walking it. He left the banged up, crippled survivor of permanent protest to meditate alone in the shade of the patio, a human rights general consumed with his calculations. The goon squad jeep was gone.

O'Hara didn't have a lot of money to waste, but he decided to call DISC in New York from a public phone rather than Velazquez'. They hadn't heard about German Morales. But Joe Morgan was a development purist. In the '60s he had harvested sugar cane during the *zafra* in Cuba, and he had been with DISC from the golden beginning in 1969 when Che was only two years dead and needing to be avenged. Morgan had no patience for even the best-intentioned intervention.

"What are you trying to get at, Tony? Quit beating around the goddamn bush."

"It just seems strange is all. First that there was no public funeral. And then that Velazquez didn't try to mobilize you all plus the people in Europe. Right away, I mean. He could get a lot of mileage from the murder."

"You're fantasizing, Tony. Don't start getting on Juan Ramon's case. Let him run with it the way he wants to run. You're supposed to be offering a little solidarity, a little public support from us is all. What we want from you is material for the yearly. Sounds like you're coming down with a case of enthusiasm. You're itching to tell Juan Ramon how to do his job, which from all available reports he's managed to do pretty goddamn well without you up 'til now. Or do you have a better idea?"

O'Hara hung the receiver in its dusty cradle, which was the way conversations usually ended with Joe Morgan. The impotence, the irrelevance, of the American Left had rubbed Morgan raw in a tender spot during his political coming of age in the mid-60s, and the wound never quite healed. O'Hara got the message.

He wasted the rest of the day. He took a few notes, read a fat clippings file of reported abuses he had borrowed from the DISC office. The family who rented him their spare room were out for the evening. The sudden solitude was a luxury to be savored. He heated beans and tortillas and rice on the gas ring, then poured hot sauce indiscriminately over his heaped plate. At the empty dinner table he ate slowly, dousing the hot-sauce burn with a half-cold Salva Vida beer. He was Gumby-headed tired. The same woman who had reported the murder was halfway through a follow-up story on Radio Presente before he began to pay attention.

Something there. He had the impression she was saying, or wanting to say, more than the words themselves would permit. It was like listening to code. She reported Velazquez' mild condemnation, the government's and the armed forces' ritual denials of involvement, and a carefully phrased reaction from the Catholic Church, which wanted no enemies. She mentioned the family's unexpected secret funeral service. The reporter's name was Luz Garcia, and O'Hara admired the thoroughness with which she put together her story. But he could not crack her code, if there was one.

Maybe he was imagining something where nothing existed; fantasizing, Joe Morgan would have griped. He drank a second Salva Vida thinking about the anonymous goon squad jeep that had staked out Velazquez. Along with the beer, a rapid spasm of anger made him feel blurred and righteous. Someday there would be no more masked, unmarked cars, no more goons getting pathological kicks from inflicting hurt. To get to such a day, in a country like this one, they needed DISC and international outrage. They needed ball-bearing witnesses like Juan Ramon Velazquez.

They needed solidarity without intervention. Therefore Anthony O'Hara, collecting material for the yearly country report. He listened to the stylized, melodramatic lament of *El Rencor del Debil,* live this time, a few blocks away. He felt the greenness of his good intentions like a painful insight. A murder was a murder.

Luz Garcia turned out to be a compulsive. She met him at a small, artsy café decorated with pseudo-Mayan pottery and primitivist oil paintings depicting a country that only existed in the minds of tourists. She chain-smoked unfiltered cigarettes, her left hand holding the weed close to her mouth at an odd angle when she wasn't inhaling. She drained half a dozen of the little painted porcelain cups of coffee the waiter brought her. She was round, slightly overweight, and her face was haggard. He envied her the compulsions. She turned him immediately on.

"I admired the way you covered the murder of German Morales," he told her.

"That's what you want to talk about? How come?"

"Did you find it strange, the way things happened?"

She shrugged, sucked down smoke as if suffering from a hyperactive cancer wish. He liked the skeptical way she looked at him. "What is it to you?"

"I'm here working on DISC's yearly report. I'm interested, that's all."

"What does Juan Ramon say?"

"Juan Ramon is speaking in parables."

All he got from her was the address of German Morales' parents, which he could have gotten from anybody. She insisted on paying for their coffee. He left her convinced that she did indeed have a code of her own, that maybe there was something more to know about the murder than he could know. And that she would not help him.

Bothering the Morales family was the height of insensitivity. He bothered them. The parents of the dead president of the trash haulers' famous union lived in a neighborhood struggling to look permanent on the city's dusty northern haunch. They had electricity but no running water. The houses were uniformly modest, but most were painted, and some had gardens and fences. Animals wandered freely, but a few beat-up trucks and cars were also parked on the short streets. Life in Linda Vista was a quantifiable improvement over the objectless poverty of life in the country from which its residents had fled.

Mrs. Morales offered O'Hara a glass of orange soda with a lump of white ice. Despite the heat they sat inside the house, stiffly on lumpy upholstered furniture from which a daughter stripped dust covers as they entered the front room. They were polite to him the way poor people are in the presence of someone who might hurt them. But he got nowhere. When fifteen minutes had passed old man Morales, who drove a taxi, walked O'Hara to the gate.

"I'm sorry, Señor Morales."

Thin arms, bony hands, tough scarred brown skin. "Stay out of it, is my advice."

"Stay out of what?"

"Just stay out of it. There's no good can come out of it now."

"I don't understand."

The man looked at him suspiciously, and O'Hara's face flushed; he shook the hand of the murdered man's father and walked quickly away.

Joe Morgan liked to tell anecdotes about the European leftists who went to Latin America to cut the chains of dependency looped about the necks of noble savages. He was particularly hard on the priests, harder still on the Jesuits, whose cosmopolitan political fantasy prevented them from seeing what Morgan called on-the-ground reality. On the bus ride back to the city O'Hara wondered whether he himself was inventing a story where none existed. There was no reason to doubt Velazquez' way of handling the Morales murder; the man saw around corners O'Hara didn't imagine could exist.

And in the days that followed he laughed at himself. He talked to labor leaders, to journalists, to government hacks and armed forces p.r. flacks and underemployed diplomats from half a dozen countries. Except from the official apologists the answers he elicited did not vary: The military, or the police who reported to them, killed German Morales. Was it part of a systematic pattern of human rights abuses? The Americans blamed ignorance and bad habits; training would ameliorate all evils. An Argentine from the UNDP spoke with contempt of a culture of victims and victimizers bonded in a loving act of violence. German Morales loved to goad the police; in one way or another he asked for it. High theater? Long strategy? A low visceral drive? It made no difference. He got it.

Luz Garcia would only see him if he didn't talk local politics. He promised. They had dinner in an inexpensive, leafy-bowered restaurant listening to piece-rate mariachis. They went to see a Spanish thriller in a theater rank with urine. They went back to the artsy café and watched a Mexican movie about Frida Kahlo. Luz cooked dinner in the three-room house she owned in a neighborhood like Linda Vista. They talked about magical realism and French painters and George Orwell in the Spanish Civil War and Nadine Gordimer's politics, and they told each other their secret family histories.

The fourth night she invited him to stay, and they made love in a blue haze of cigarette smoke in her minuscule gray-walled bedroom. The sex was like articulation, like forming surprising, pleasure-producing thoughts with his body, which had been stupid for a long time. He tolerated and then craved the smell of smoke on her. He watched the haggardness disappear from her face while she slept as though it were a mask peeled away and what showed through was the one thing that really mattered but could not be named. But she would not talk about what was going on around her.

"It's my work," she tried to make him understand. "And all the news is always bad and won't get any better as long as I live. So if it becomes my life then my life will be nothing but bad news."

After three weeks he had absorbed all he needed for the human rights report. DISC didn't believe in blowing its budget on solidarity junkets. He was out of cash, which was the way it was supposed to be. The only solution was for Luz to go with him to New York. She was stymied at the radio, treading water. Unable to accommodate to a system of half-free journalism, she was atrophying into an attitude, a reflex of unvoiceable criticism. She was on the way to becoming her own cliché, and she knew it.

"No."

They lay in her bed. His body was beat, a shell through which sensation moved slowly. In candlelight the pouches under Luz's eyes sagged deep: dark receptacles for a load of knowing O'Hara could not carry. He rubbed a circle on her forehead, found the brushed indentations of worry lines there. "I knew you'd say no the first time."

"They don't let people smoke in New York."

"You can stay in my apartment and study English for a while. I'm not saying we do anything drastic. You need a change, that's all."

"What do you need?"

"Just you."

"I don't trust romantic declarations."

He wasn't discouraged, but there wasn't much time. "I'm confirming my flight in the morning. I'm out of money. I have to go back."

"I can't go, Antonio."

He pressed her forehead with the ball of his finger. Still such distance between skin and skin, him and her. Nothing metaphysical there, just a fact of one of those sciences that explained everything except what he wanted to know. "I'm going," he told her when she blew out the candle and put a pillow over her head.

Too late to catch a bus back to his room. He hailed an old red Toyota four-door taxi. The chassis quaked, the steering wheel trembled. The shocks were gone, and the dash lights went out at every pothole. The driver, sallow and angular, with the aggressive pout of an unhappy drunk, pounded the dash angrily to bring them back.

"You have any idea what a new car costs in this country? Not in a hundred years." He ran a red light at a deserted intersection.

"Take a guess how much it would cost me to get this one fixed up."

O'Hara wouldn't guess.

"Too bad the communists lost over in Russia. They had the right idea. They went at it backwards, but they had the right idea. Right here is where we need a revolution. A real one, not a goddamn circus like the Sandinistas put on in Nicaragua. In a real revolution they'd bring down the price of automobiles to the point that the common man could afford to run a taxi. But you're a gringo."

"I'm a gringo," O'Hara admitted.

The *taxista* threw up his hands, letting the wheel shake wildly. "You people will never let that happen, will you?"

They were there.

"I'm sorry," O'Hara told him, handing over a small wad of bright, worthless bills. He wanted to say something to bridge their gap. To say that he had some small sense of what it must be to stalk fares in the city late at night half drunk and full angry trying to make enough money to stay ahead, just far enough ahead to sleep two nights running without a wolf-at-the-door dream. But the story of DISC's two decades in Latin America—support without intervention—didn't quite cut it. He saw as if forever the man's belligerent face glowing juicer red in the pale dome light as he counted the bills.

In the clumped shadows on the street before his rented room O'Hara sensed movement, thought surveillance. He wanted to duck and run, but his fingers fumbled at the gate latch. The voice that called his name had no police-goon overtones. Just enough light to pick out the young man in jeans and t-shirt approaching with his hand out. "I am the brother of German Morales."

"Let's go inside. We can talk there."

"Don't worry. There's nobody watching. Anyway what I have to tell you won't take long."

"What's your first name?"

"Juan Pablo. Like the Pope, except he's a conservative. Listen, it wasn't the military or the police or the death squad that killed my brother."

"Then who?"

"My parents say stay out of it. They don't know I came. It's my own decision. My parents are old now, plus they think any bad publicity will only help the government."

"What bad publicity?"

"It's not fair. I hate the military as much as German did. They've killed plenty. But it's not fair that the ones who killed my brother get off like heroes. That's all. My brother was the hero, not them."

"Who killed German, Juan Pablo?"

A teetering moment; it crashed quietly. "The Movement. People in the Movement had him shot. There was a split. Over strategy, they said, but it was really over money. German was involved."

A band stretched inside O'Hara, then snapped. He felt the sag. "Who inside the Movement?"

The boy shook his head.

"You've only told me half of what I need to know." O'Hara took the boy by the arm and squeezed hard. He was as angry as the *taxista* had been.

"That's as far as I can go," the boy said. He shook himself free and ran back into the clumped shadows, and O'Hara went to his room knowing he would not sleep.

"What did you expect, saints?" Luz' question caused O'Hara to picture a line of robed applicants to the Unified Revolutionary Front. The MRU was serious Left.

"I need a yes or a no, Luz. Is it possible that MRU people killed Morales?"

"I don't want to talk about it, Antonio. Respect that."

So he called Morgan in New York. "I have a lead on who killed him. I want to stay."

"I can't send you much cash, Tony."

"I have a place to stay."

"What's her name?"

"Luz Garcia."

"I'll wire you a few bucks. Meantime, keep your head down. I'm assuming you don't want to get into this on the phone."

"I just need a little time."

"Don't make a move without consulting Velazquez. Play it his way."

Yes, Velazquez. O'Hara found him in the patio at DISC asleep in his chair with the Siamese cat on his gently heaving chest. Asleep, he looked like a heretic roughed up by medieval thought police. The cat glared, gave no ground.

"I want to talk about German Morales," O'Hara told him when he woke.

"Then talk. But first sit."

"I have something solid."

The morning sunlight was a wall of painful brightness. The torture victim blinked slowly and his eyes teared. Was that also the consequence of an interrogation technique?

O'Hara picked his words with care. "I think there is a chance that someone in the MRU shot Morales."

"You know, I assume, that Morales himself was connected, in a way, with the MRU."

"I know."

"Morales was a cautious man, his public persona notwithstanding. He knew how to walk the line."

"What line?"

"The line between legal political opposition and ... whatever it is the MRU does. He gave the government no excuse to close down his union. That's a tribute to his skill."

Persecuted years earlier, the MRU had gone underground and stayed there. They had not given up on the idea of a class war and revolution. The death of communism had only served to heighten their suspicion about the nature of the conspiracy they opposed.

"My source is good," O'Hara said. "I think what I have is solid enough to push for an investigation into the murder."

"I can see the headlines: DISC director calls for investigation into murder of leftist by his own kind ... Shoot me with my own gun."

A murder, O'Hara didn't say, is a murder. "If it's true, Juan Ramon, an investigation could clean things up. And in the long run that can only help us."

"Us?"

"Your credibility would guarantee a serious investigation." O'Hara knew he was compounding his mistake but couldn't stop. "You're probably the only person in the country who could make it happen. Say the word and the French and the British will press the government. Maybe even the U.S."

"I figure that's my call, Antonio. Is this what Morgan said, come down and shit in my nest? Morgan said you were good."

"Morgan says play it your way. And I probably should. But I guess I can't, now. I'm going to stick around for a little while, and if I can confirm what I heard last night I'm going back to New York and push people there to pressure for a real investigation. Fair enough?"

Sitting up, Velazquez squinted hard. His eyes teared in a stream. He folded his scarred hands on his belly and rocked on the grainy brown, sun-speckled bricks below the trellis. The cat slid reluctantly from his chest to his lap, and the DISC director whistled breathily through his teeth. "Look up the word fellow traveller in your dictionary, Antonio."

A murder was a murder.

That evening Luz slapped his face when he took his duffel bag to her house. "Stupid child," she told him. "You're worse than stupid, you're dangerous."

"Fair is fair, Luz. I'm doing the opposite of what Morgan told me to do. Velazquez has the right to know that."

"Juan Ramon is very close to the MRU."

"That doesn't surprise me."

"You don't see it, do you?" She was stirring something in a pan on the stove. The look of recrimination she slammed him with was enough to wilt new love. Whatever she was cooking began to burn; a mushroom cloud of smoke the shape of disaster rose in the close kitchen air.

"Then help me see it, Luz."

"Look at the possibilities."

"Ok. Let's say it's a set-up. The police, or somebody else—maybe even somebody on the Left who doesn't like Juan Ramon—wants to use DISC to make him look bad. So they invent this story of the brother and hope I'll buy it. If I don't, no loss."

"But?"

"But that's not what it feels like to me. It's not the police, I can feel it. I wish you had been there when Morales' little brother talked to me."

"What else?"

"Your supper's burning."

"What else is possible, Antonio?"

"If it's not a set-up, then there is a genuine split inside the MRU."

"There is."

"And it sort of depends on which side of the split Juan Ramon stands on."

"Assume he supports the group that had German Morales killed."

"Then he wouldn't be too happy with me and my investigation, I guess."

That was when she slapped him. His face stung, and his eyes burned in the smoky kitchen. "It's not a game, Antonio. It's not an adventure story. Did you think they're saints? You were stupid. You gave yourself away to Velazquez like a baby. He could have you killed."

"He's not going after a high-visibility gringo."

"Wouldn't it be a wonderful thing to hang on the government? A gringo human rights crusader murdered in the midst of an investigation? It would prove their point, and everybody would believe it was the government. You're in over your head. You have to go back to New York."

"I want to be sure, then I'll go back. If I can be sure who killed Morales I'll hop the next plane."

"Tomorrow."

He shook his head. No brag, just obsession. He closed his eyes and saw the color of the walls of the DISC office in New York, saw how they would look if he went back without knowing.

"I'll go with you," Luz offered, but he would not rise even to that bait.

With the taste of burnt beans in his mouth they made love like sparring partners, then fell asleep fast and hard. Anxiety animals fretted across the black floor of O'Hara's dreams, causing him to wake. Too cool. No sheet on the bed. No Luz. Moonlight memorialized the private disarray of her bedroom; he was an interloper.

He found her in the fenced square of back yard, wrapped in the bed sheet smoking a slow cigarette and looking at the moon. "If you're not going back to New York in the morning," she told him, "think about the way Morales was killed."

"One shot, in the neck. From behind."

The moonlight made the flat cloud of cigarette smoke around her blue. In the draped, glowing sheet she looked her own idea of a queen. "It happened at noon," she said, "on a crowded street. The guy who did it ran away on foot."

"Which is not how the squads do business … "

"They work at night. Never alone. And they always have a car waiting."

"Where do I go to find out for sure, Luz?"

"I think," she admitted, still making up her mind, "I can get you to see Comandante Flecha."

In 1981, Comandante Flecha had founded the MRU out of the embattled chaos of the fractious Left. He was a giant. He was the architect of unity, the healer of wounds, true north on the only compass pointing to change. For the government, he was democracy's most dangerous enemy. O'Hara had assumed he was out of the country. If he was there, he was deep underground. According to the folklore, Flecha had been German Morales' political godfather. O'Hara was learning. He knew better than to say thank you. He shut up, let himself be wrapped for comfort in Luz Garcia's glowing sheet beneath the solicitous moon.

He clocked it. Getting to the safehouse took three hours, at night, during which time the car they were in did not leave the capital. If the idea was to confuse him, it worked. If the idea was to be sure they were not followed, it was worth three hours. Two mute men he didn't know eventually left him alone in a shuttered room in an anonymous house in a neighborhood he would not try to find a second time. *El Rencor del Debil* played somewhere, too far off to catch the words. Comandante Flecha came in like an efficient waiter.

O'Hara had not expected an old man, but Flecha was almost that. In the weak light of a low-watt bulb he appeared short and stooped, his long hair drooping in thick gray strings. He offered O'Hara a glass of water from a pitcher on a small table. His voice was low to the point of gone, a river playing out over rocks. "Throat cancer," he explained. "The Cubans operated on me last year. Saved my life, for what it's worth."

"Whatever you tell me," O'Hara felt obliged to reassure him, "if you tell me anything, stays with me."

"You wouldn't be here if I was worried."

"Who killed German Morales?"

The aging revolutionary sat in a splay-backed chair alongside the shuttered window and sipped absently from the glass of water he had been bringing to O'Hara. The room was musty; invisible dust motes clogged the air making it hard to breathe. What remained of Flecha's voice was labored, hard to catch. The story came out in clots, like something sick coughed up under pressure.

The split in the MRU meant collective suicide, meant going back to the bad old days before '81. Some of it was ideology. The

Ola Nueva faction wanted to talk about renouncing armed resistance, about a political opening. The *Duros* faction said capitulation was treason, and traitors would be treated as war criminals. But more than ideology it came down to money. When communism died the clandestine money they were used to dried up fast. The drought made the money from Europe's soft Left, the money funnelled to the unions and *campesino* organizations, that much more valuable. German Morales had sympathized with the *Ola Nueva* but worked with both factions to keep the MRU from self-destructing.

"German was a born balancer," Flecha said. "In a just society he would have been a mayor. But the *Duros* called his bluff. They told him he had to set me up. I only came back a couple months ago. Their idea was to get me arrested, then maybe killed by the squads."

"They thought you would be able to keep the two factions together, and they didn't want to see that happen."

The comandante shrugged, looped a string of gray hair around a bony finger. "What I might do mattered less than what they thought I could do. Setting me up was supposed to be Morales' ultimate test of loyalty. If he gave me up, the leadership of the whole MRU was his."

"But he wouldn't betray you ... "

"He was tempted. Who wouldn't be? He told them not to worry. But he came to see me. He cried. I don't want to go into that part. It's private. The only way around it, we decided, was for him to leave the country until things shook out."

"To Guatemala."

"But the *Duros* must have given him a deadline, and he missed it. Killing him sent a message to the *Ola Nueva*."

"What about Velazquez?"

"If you had gone through what he has, which side do you figure you'd take? Juan Ramon wants to win. We all want to win. Put it together." He got up from the chair and poured a second glass of water. O'Hara imagined he saw in him the small habits, the forced constrictions, of a man who had lived underground for a long time. "I'm tired of talking. Our friends are waiting for you at the end of the block."

"I appreciate it, Comandante."

But telling the story had riled Flecha. Suddenly hostile, he stared O'Hara out the door. In the street two different men, as close-mouthed as the first, drove him in a nondescript pickup into the center of the city, where he flagged a taxi and rode toward Luz' place.

She didn't let him get there. When the taxi stopped in front of her house she stepped out of the darkness, got in quickly and told the driver to keep moving. O'Hara's suitcase was on her lap. "You're a fool, Antonio. Velazquez has *Duro* people out looking for you. They came by an hour ago. An urgent call from New York, they said. I told them we had argued and you went to a hotel, but they didn't believe me. They'll be back."

"I need to talk to Velazquez. Nothing I've done will hurt the MRU. He has to know that."

"Are you dense? No matter what you tell him he'll think you're going public with something ugly enough to cut off his funding from abroad. And that would make him vulnerable to the government again. Without the internationals, he's naked."

In the rear-view mirror the driver started looking interested. They paid him off and got out of the taxi at a corner O'Hara didn't recognize. They were downtown, for the moment untraceable. He followed Luz into a coffee shop, shoved the suitcase under a table, and watched her hands shake. She drank her coffee like a true compulsive. In the midst of the fear growing up in him he felt a fierce affection for her and, for the first time, a hatred of the politics he breathed.

"You did this to yourself, Antonio."

"I'm sorry."

"You have to go to your embassy."

He shook his head. "That would be like going over to the enemy. Besides, all they'd tell me is contact the police."

"Then we'll stay out all night, and in the morning I'll take you to the airport.

"I cashed my ticket in this morning. I was waiting for Joe Morgan to send me some money from New York."

So it was down to a bus. At midnight they boarded a non-stop monster heading north to the border. The coffee overdose compounded bad nerves. Although the bus barrelled O'Hara had the sensation of standing still, his legs pumping going nowhere fast. Luz was rigid, kept her distance. He wanted to lean across the armrest and take her arm but was afraid of her rejection.

"I'll get you to the border," she told him once. "I have a few dollars you can take."

"Will you get a passport and go to New York?"

"Write me a letter and I'll answer it."

"If you don't go to New York I'll come back."

She shook her head. "You won't come back. Not after this."

"I'm still on the side of the good guys, Luz. Even after what's happened. It's still the same uneven fight it always was, and the bad guys have everything they need to keep it that way."

At San Marcos del Norte the bus stopped, dropped people, gassed up. They stayed in their seats, staring at the late-night crowd in the station, which was filled with people mostly waiting. O'Hara fixed on a blind man with a disfigured face shuffling and shaking his metal cup. A barefoot girl whose flat toes curled up awkwardly led him around by his free arm. The man's lip moved incessantly but O'Hara was too far away to hear his hard luck story.

"If there's nobody here," he said, "does that mean there won't be anybody at the border either?"

After a delay that tried his nerves the bus backed out of its slot and onto the street, but moving brought back the fear it should have relieved.

"The *Duros* are organized. No sense talking. We're doing what we have to do."

"Will you let me say something simple and romantic to you?"

"Say it. I need it."

"It drives me crazy to think about leaving this country without you."

She leaned into him, and they both slept. O'Hara experienced inhabited dreams. He tossed, leaned on Luz, smelled the permanent stink of stale cigarettes, felt heat radiate from her body. Then the night was gone and they were pulling into a dilapidated bus station on the edge of a city that must have been the border. A crowd moved around the station like cunning killers hiding their intentions in the grainy gray light of the damp morning. He distrusted their innocent bustle, their happy chatter. His throat was thick and raw. His head ached, a coffee hangover. His bones were tired.

"The crossing is a kilometer or so down that road," Luz pointed for him as they stepped down from the bus. "From here we have to take a taxi. It's a deal they have going with the bus company."

"I'll go by myself." He was thinking how quickly he could get the money to her to fly to New York, and how much she would be offended.

"Wait," she ordered, "I'll go find a taxi."

The amazing thing was how well his brain worked, if it was his brain that was doing the thinking. Maybe it was just some kind of self-defense antenna on his body. Good after all that Luz was out of the way. Out of the milling herd of potential assassins he sensed, then saw the real one. Only one. Just the way they went for German Morales. He dropped his suitcase and ran.

Enough people in the station that the *Duro* man following him didn't risk a shot across the crowd. As long as O'Hara didn't know where he was going it made no difference which way he went. Did it? Did it. Lickety he split. Thanks to the antenna he left the station out the back entrance with something of a head start, last night's caffeine kicking in as he ran, eclipsing his headache with a feeling of terror; idiot's exhilaration.

Cobble street, dirt street. Lucky, too, that it was a border town. People in the streets. Moving shields. He was wearing sneakers with good tread, he had a head start, and he was terrified. Cobble street dirt.

Head-on running wouldn't work forever. Sooner or later he would lag, lose his lead. The *Duro* man would pull up, aim, shoot him calmly in the back. Either inspiration or the same useful antenna made him detour into an open doorway. A grandma knitting, a mother nursing both screamed as he went through their house, then out the back door. The fence was low enough to jump. He jumped, stumbled, balanced, ran along the long side wall of what must have been a warehouse. Out across another vulnerable street, then a jag back toward the station, into a side yard. Only chickens there, foraging across the weedy dirt of the patio. He was pretty sure the *Duro* man had missed one of the turns. The back fence had a gate, which was open. But instead of passing through the gate he dove behind a wood pile and lay flat on the earth.

Trying to keep his breathing from going hysterical brought on vertigo, then nausea. Pain cut his chest in two. Sweat fell off his face and made interesting little craters in the dust. The craters fascinated, distracted him. Head to one side and lying flat, he saw with the eyes of a paralyzed fish. He listened for whatever give-away sound the *Duro* man might make as he approached. He realized he was lucky: He had acquired, without trying, the patience of a lump of coal.

No hit man.

Patient as coal, he thought slowly. He would wait out the day behind the woodpile. When it was dark, he would make his way to the border crossing block by block, be sure he could get close to a cop checking papers before moving into any light. He would get to New York and offer his input for the yearly report. He would write Luz Garcia a persuasive letter of love, and she would say some kind of yes. Amen.

No hit man.

Waiting, he thought about the testimony scars on Juan Ramon's abused body. About making love to a lonely reporter with the taste of burnt beans and hot sauce in both their mouths. He thought about the goon squad jeep, and Joe Morgan's absolutist politics, and the juicer *taxista* who wanted a real revolution. As though it were a single and continuous thought moving around a seamless track, he understood that the world of all of them was going to change much more slowly than he had imagined it might.

No hit man. Single-minded chickens nattered and picked around him in the dirt. The sun gradually rose high enough to bake him. That didn't matter. What mattered was he hadn't changed sides. He was hungry. He was patient as coal. What mattered was that all this unbelievable bad was going to change more slowly than he had imagined.

Jumping Jesus

The night the Catholic God died, the Evangelical Jesus who jumped on his grave took the shape of a joyful God, a larking God, a God who might make life happen a little better. But don Luis Martinez knew from experience that there were two different kinds of joy a person could sample in his life, and when it looked as though he could not resuscitate his comatose taxi he hungered hard for the second. His wife doña Isabela, had she been there, would have reproached him just as hard.

Don Luis was no mechanic. It appeared that his clutch had gone out on him, and what it would cost him to get it fixed was double at least what he had. The only way to get a little more was by driving fares, and driving fares was out, now. He had backed into the lot at the ENFE train station in La Paz. The train from Arica, Chile, was due in shortly, and he was sure of a fare then. The clutch had been worrying him for weeks, so after parking the car he had turned on the engine again, depressed the clutch pedal, and nothing. As if he had known. As if the jubilant Jesus of doña Isabela and her Amen friends had a mean streak like his dead father and wanted to see how far his newest convert could be pushed.

The ENFE station was painted gray, almost holy church gray. The low sweeping clouds, their bellies ripped open by steeple pricks and other high pointed objects in the city, came a lighter, fresher gray. The rain on the taxi windows was see-through gray, like little fallen sky flecks. When the Kennedy girls came into his mind—just the idea, a picture to savor—don Luis had no will to shove them back out. Two kinds of joy for sampling, and maybe it would have been easier on him had the rest of the members of his new church admitted that much aloud one time.

In don Luis' experience the death of the Catholic God had been like the death of a crusty, ugly-tempered old bully. The accident happened suddenly, fast as a human heart attack. Don Luis was climbing the mud hill to home on a Friday night, bachelors' night out in La Paz, three fourths of a bottle of Singani sloshing in his stomach so loud he could hear it over the storm ranting. The neighbors had gotten together weekends to cut step shapes into the hill in the hope of stone from the municipality. But the stone didn't come, and ran had rubbed away most of their work. Don Luis, more angry than drunk, lost his footing, fell up and forward, and hit his head on a boulder. The blow stunned him for a moment, after which interval he was flooded with white light, the light of the superior joy. Then the bully keeled over, the living Jesus jumped up in his place, and everything wrong in Luis' life was soothed for several sweet seconds. By the time he reached his house, he was able to move the tongue in his mouth to explain to Isabela that he had been saved.

Hammy knuckles rapped the driver's side window, and there was Pedro, who drove a glaringly new vehicle, one of those mini-vans that could haul fifteen people, on contract to an investor. Reluctantly Luis rolled down the window.

"Train's late, they said inside," Pedro told him.

No comment.

"Let's go get coffee, *compañero*."

"You go," Luis said. "I don't want any coffee."

"What's eating you?"

Pedro was political. Until the shoe factory he worked in went broke he had been the union representative there and won a trip to Havana once, for a full month, mostly on the strength of his gab. He had a real gift. Driving a taxi had made him fat, though.

Luis had noticed him slide into his seat once; he had to insert his belly behind the wheel with care. He looked a little like the martyred Indian Manco Kapac must have looked—romantic and proud, with black eyes that saw the world's sadness from the height of an Andes peak—only fat. For Pedro, being political meant being anti-religion. Once he had told Luis that if there had been any real gods ever, gods good for oppressed Bolivian Indians, they had been slaughtered by the Spaniards, who set up Jesus as a kind of slave master, master bleeder, a sucker of human marrow. Doña Isabela and Pedro had met twice. Both times she came away to pray for his salvation, that he be led onto the path of light and know the superior joy.

Luis told him nothing was wrong.

"You sick? You look sick."

Next week he had to have tuition money for the kids' school. Impossible.

"Will you lend me some money, Pedro?"

"Who's got money?"

"My clutch went out."

Pedro shook his head. "What I have I'm saving for the kids' tuition next week."

Luis tapped the steering wheel of the old eight-cylinder Dodge with the tips of his fingers. The wind through the window was cold and wet. The windshield was a blur.

"You know anybody who'll fix me the clutch on credit?"

"I'll think about it. Hey, do you want me to give you a ride somewhere, Luis?"

"No."

"You sure it's the clutch?"

Luis banged the dead pedal with his foot.

"I'm going for coffee, I guess." Pedro obviously did not want to contaminate his Saturday evening with the bad luck of Luis Martinez, which might be catching.

"What time do they say the train is coming?"

The ex-union man shrugged expansively, which meant it looked like it wouldn't make a damn bit of difference to Luis if it never came in. He backed away mumbling, and Luis rolled up the window against the weather.

He had begun attending services at the Evangelical Church with doña Isabela with some enthusiasm several months earlier, after the fall and the white light that came after it. In that sanctuary, rest as he might, breathe clean as he might, twist his tongue in Jesuspraise as he might, he had never been able to escape completely from the suspicion that what he had found inside was the poor man's consolation. Doña Isabela was no fool. She saw through him when he stood sideways and she said what's better, a gut full of liquor? No contest, after all. And there had been times, a few times anyway, when he felt, almost saw, the white light on his own private horizon. Focusing his vision on a string-like pattern of rain beads on his windshield, he tried to pray a little.

When he could not concentrate, he thought through his options. He owed his mechanic money; there would be no credit there and who could blame the bastard. Isabela's cousin had a garage in Obrajes, but the man was a reactionary Catholic. He had broken with his cousin when she converted, and the few times the families mixed there was only rancor. He could use the little money he had to try to get credit with a stranger, but that was unrealistic. He could ... He could not.

He put on his jacket, left the driver's seat, and took the windshield wiper blades off the arms. He tossed the blades under the seat, locked the car, and walked across the street to wait for the bus. He was surprised that he could not remember which bus he had to get to pass by the Plaza Kennedy, but when one came rattling by the train station he knew.

The ride was too short for him to reconsider. Guilt was not what he felt but a kind of resignation that wore the mask. Stepping down from the bus as it stopped at Plaza Kennedy, he immediately made the choice he had to make. She was considerably younger than he, maybe twenty. She wore bitter the way another might wear black. In the long coat she wore in the rain he could not imagine the shape of her body, but that did not deflect him. She was muffled, wet, a mound. He liked it that her black eyes did not try to hide how she looked down on him.

They almost ran to get to her room. The rain was like some sort of hard pellets that made a million separate explosions when they came into contact with something: his back, her hair, the muddy sidewalk. Stepping inside, he felt pseudo-domestic, a man come home to bask before an artificial fire. The sex they transacted was just about as grim as he had thought it might be. Undressed, she was bottom heavy, beautifully brown, long armed. Her plait of hair shimmered as it dried out.

He sawed, she hammered. They traded. She hammered, he sawed. More than anything he liked her anger, the way she sawed at him as if she realized she could not pay him back at all but still had to try her damndest. It was a question of friction. If the superior joy was like white light, this other, muddier kind was just friction in the dark, just bumping and sawing. He felt clean and dirty at the same time.

Neither one tried to make it last. She disappeared into a bathroom to perform a ritual in which he had no interest, and something don Luis later interpreted as inspired intuition lifted him from the sag-bottomed bed. He knew where to look but he did not know why he knew. It was like inventing his own dream. Against one wall stood a three-drawered chest. In the middle drawer buried at the bottom below her personal trash there was an envelope. In the envelope he felt money, in dollars. Behind the saw-woman's closed door the toilet sucked hoarsely, an exclamation. Don Luis put his pants on fast, his shirt, stepped into his shoes. He could not button the shirt or tie the shoes but he was able to grab his jacket. Out and down her squeaking steps.

It was dark enough, wet enough, that the streets were almost empty. Maybe no one saw him. But he heard her after him, running and screaming things that didn't sound much at all like human words. What came out of her mouth was more like bird cries, the cries of a particular bird of prey he could not name correctly. It was hard going trying not to trip on his flapping shoe laces, and the wind got inside his open shirt and chilled him like death itself. But he had enough of a jump on her and he knew he would win. Eventually, winded and wild-headed, he was able to stop running. She was as gone as she needed to be.

He jumped on a bus for home, took a back seat by himself, and counted the money carefully. Almost two hundred dollars there. He wondered how long it had taken her to put together that much. He wondered where she came from, who her family were, whether they knew what she was doing, what they thought about it. He wondered if it would be possible for her ever to fuck for love, then thought the question was degrading, somehow, or missed the mark.

Somewhere close to halfway home, a thought that was genuine heresy occurred to don Luis. He kept his hand clenched around the envelope in his pants pocket, after he had buttoned his shirt, tied his shoes, and zipped his thin fabric jacket. His thought unnerved him: Maybe it had been the jubilant Jesus himself, the jumping Jesus spreader and spiller of white light, who had given him the inspiration and then the time to get away with his crime. Don Luis had never been able to believe seriously in the Devil. Therefore ... How else to explain knowing which drawer to go to?

He would have to find two separate convincing reasons to explain the gift. One for doña Isabela and one for himself. In Villa Fatima don Luis climbed down from the bus, tired, climbed slowly up the mud hill to home in the rain-effaced step holes. No one would bother his taxi overnight at the train station. In the morning he would find someone to fix the clutch. There were two kinds of joy available for sampling. He understood that but not why. On a far periphery the taxi driver could not precisely locate, there came down white light and in its shadow the Evangelical Jesus jumped and cried. Amen.

Black Moon Rising

Dream chemistry transformed the violent sound of a stone breaking glass into a single-scene adventure dream in which Victor Mesón, Bolivian hero, escaped the danger threatening him by tearing down a dark passage that gave onto a contracting circle of white light. What he came out of the dream with was the rush: a sensation of exhilaration that joined body and mind in a burst of pleasurable fear. Awake, he inhaled hard to get back the breath he had lost. Cold sweat made his skin clammy in the dry air. Not for a long time had he experienced that sensation. Remembering to stay low, he rolled out of bed in the dark and felt with blind, clumsy hands across the floor for the stone. There would be a message. Before he found it, Laurel switched on the light.

"Don't get up," he told her.

"What's going on, Victor?" she demanded. Not knowing vexed her; it was her job to know.

His hand closed on the stone, to which a piece of coarse paper was tied with waxy red twine. He stood up. If the Black Moon had wanted to do him damage they would have lobbed in something more lethal than a message. This was what Julio called being reasonable.

"You've been holding back on me, haven't you?" the North American woman said quietly. "There's something going on, and you're involved."

He opened his mouth to deny it but said nothing. He felt hounded, on the run, and no safehouse in sight. After a lifetime of inconsequence Victor Mesón found himself, suddenly, being stalked and courted at the same time. They wanted to kill him, and they wanted to write a book about him. It irritated him that such serious attention flattered.

Laurel Romansky sat up straight against the headboard. There was something aggressive in the casual, unconscious way *gringa* women had with their nakedness. A *latina* woman could be just as casual, as comfortable, but she always managed to suggest that her comfort was a tribute to you; you were her shield and sustainer, the guardian of the private space in which she could be free. The few North American women Victor had known all rejected the guarantee, and the guarantor. Their independence fascinated him. It had something to do, he assumed, with having their own money.

He disciplined himself not to hurry to read the message from the Black Moon. That was a trick of self-control that had been useful in the dangerous old days. He took a moment to study Laurel, wanting to identify something recognizably Slavic in the features, finding it in her manifold roundnesses. It was as though she were genetically swollen, some force of self inside pushing out to make connections with the world that would not be denied. Her round, high cheekbones charmed him; traced in the dark with a finger, they could have been the cheekbones of an Altiplano woman, an Aymara or a Quechua. But not the hair, which was a dusty sort of blonde, not brown but smoky, as though each strand had been painstakingly held over a fire and coated with something fine that could not quite hide the golden yellow. She folded her arms across her round breasts so that they bulged, an unconsciously erotic gesture that weakened him with pleasure. She told him he was an unconvincing liar.

"Give me the paper," she told him. "I'll read it to you."

He handed over the stone.

"Traitor," read Laurel, her voice steady and sweet. She was on the job now, a reporter with the scent of an unexpected story in her nostrils. Victor watched her pulse beat in the tiny blue veins of her wrists, watched the yellow light from the overhead bulb fall onto her opaque white skin and be absorbed there. His private aesthetic demands were satisfied with what he saw; a slow glow of pleasure distracted him from the threatening rhetoric she gave voice to. "Your past actions against the oligarchy made you justifiably famous, earned you a place of honor in the history of our liberation. But somewhere along the way you sold out. You have become one of the enemy you formerly resisted. That much is certain, and not surprising. The road is long, *compañero*, and few have the stamina or the vision to follow it to the end. But do not make the mistake of actively resisting our inevitable triumph. Attempt to place a barrier in our path and you will die. Immediately and without honor. You would be better advised to go outside and look up into the sky, Victor Mesón. Go out, traitor, and watch the Black Moon rise."

"Turn out the light, please," Victor told her. She did, and he sank onto the bed. What exhausted him was not the fear, which was real enough, but the effort of staring continually into the face of a conundrum that would not resolve itself: He might well be murdered in the name of the justice he had spent his life defining, defending, even loving.

"What is the Black Moon, Victor?"

It cost him, these days, to give anything away, even information, even to the woman in his bed. "The best kept secret in Bolivia," he admitted reluctantly. "That's what scares me. Why don't you go ask for an interview in your embassy? Tell them you're doing a research project on the White Wolf and his influence on contemporary politics."

"This isn't your average warning note, is it? The handwriting is sloppy, but the grammar is good, and the sentences are clear and clean. An educated person dictated this. And you know who he is."

Her quick perception, her political smarts, doubled the attraction he felt for her, which was considerable. In the dark he felt for her, tried to embrace her and pull her toward him. But she left the bed, untouchable, sat naked and comfortable in a chair in the dark. She wanted an answer, not affection. Maybe she knew his need was hollow.

He owed her no answers, however. He didn't really care whether Laurel Romansky wrote the book on him she had come to La Paz to write. He knew exactly how her project would play out: a quality hard-cover production with serious reviews in the mainstream media. The paper book jacket would be politically suggestive. Earth tones, probably, behind a stylized image that conveyed to *Yanqui* readers the sensual romance of blood and politics, injustice under a hot sun, palm trees on a shiny horizon toward which people and donkeys slouched with their unbearable burdens. There would be a party in New York, where dry people with pursed mouths congratulated Laurel for engraving something that mattered on the public record. After Reagan's obsession with the Sandinistas Latin America had reverted to what it had always been: the garbage dump of the North American imagination. People really ought to know the story of Victor Mesón.

Victor admired Laurel's seriousness; it was part of her appeal. She had shown up with a contract in hand, and time, and the kind of writing discipline required to make a book worth reading. And those credentials. When an editor saw the story she forced on him, the Cleveland *Bugle-Dispatch* hired her out of college as a stringer to cover the dirty war in Argentina. They took her on as a foreign correspondent on salary just in time to reap the blessings of the Pulitzer she won. In Central America she won no prize, but she was there early on, changing papers when the *Bugle-Dispatch* lost interest in her subject, and she stayed through the demobilization of the *Contra* in Honduras. Among the herd of journalists and academics and dilettantes of all stripes who followed things Latin American Laurel was a respected shining star. Any erstwhile fighter for social justice—Victor took pains to avoid the word revolution or any its derivatives—might reasonably feel honored to have been chosen as the subject of her big book.

"The story isn't over, is it, Victor?" she told him from the chair, an uncrossable distance. "How can I write the book if you're not straight with me?" Her voice was slightly nasal, and she had developed to high-pitched art the reporter's assault tactic. She persisted, bored into her interviewee until he was worn down and admitted her right to know as first on the list of those inscribed somewhere in the universal constitution.

When Laurel Romanski showed up at his Centro de Documentación he had lied to her, told her he would cooperate fully. Not for himself but because the struggle was not sufficiently known, and the more clearly it was understood the more likely justice would be to prevail, ultimately. It was not clear to him whether she had believed him.

For a moment he lost track of what she was saying, giving into the pleasure of her voice, which sounded in the darkness like a silk cloth dragging softly over a hard surface. But he was not ready to concede her any power over him, least of all the power to touch him. He was a hunk of wood. This is what she had taught him: that you could get yourself into an affair with an interesting woman, lie in bed close enough to feel the heat radiating from her body while she slept, make eye-opening love and quote Neruda to her and still not be touched, not in the way you needed to be touched by somebody.

Impossible to sleep, and he knew her well enough to know she would not make love just then, not when she had work to do. There's no such thing as an objective, independent, totally uninvolved reporter, she told him the first night they slept together. Don't you think it's better to recognize your prejudices and work around them? Her certainty had made him feel doubly fucked: the critical and commercial success of her book would turn him into one more exploited object, one more salable commodity with which the empire and its recording angels would have their way, their final and conclusive say. And make him feel pretty good while it happened.

"Tell me what the Black Moon is," Laurel insisted.

Write my book, write my epitaph. He got out of bed again, moved in her direction.

"No," she said emphatically. She pulled on his white robe and followed him into the upstairs hall. Over the years he had dealt with enough North American reporters to know that figuring things out, putting the puzzle pieces together, meant as much as sexual ecstasy, as much as democracy and middle-class hegemony to them. It was a useful illusion, their certainty that everything could be known if only they lifted up enough hidden stones, drew enough lines connecting the right dots.

At the top of the stairs was his retreat, a small, round *sala* that was his alone. During the day a Spanish-style window out over the street, supported by massive weathered beams, collected light and dropped it on the bright rugs scattered across the floor. At night, in candle light, the antique weavings draped on the backs of the peg-and-leather chairs, hung artfully on the rough white adobe walls along with masks and feathers, showed that it was the room not of a collector but a cherisher. The polemicists were always talking about rescuing Bolivian cultural values, which conjured for Victor an image of a heap of folk artifacts sliding down a dark abyss. Maybe that was they meant.

From an ornately carved wooden chest, rescued by his Spanish grandfather from his *estancia* when it was taken over by liberated peasants in the revolution of '52, Victor took a bottle of Singani and two glasses.

"I can't drink in this altitude," Laurel warned him, but she took the glass he handed her, understanding the price of what she wanted. Which he wouldn't give, not just then, anyhow.

From a second drawer in the same chest he took a pistol, an ugly old Luger, lay it on the little round table next to the chair where the reporter his lover sat. This wasn't melodrama, it was finding the way to the words.

"Who do you want to kill with that?" Laurel asked him. Fastidious, she put her glass down. She had scarcely drunk from it, but he topped it off with Singani, straight up and clear as the light of heaven.

He wanted to say several simple things to her, without detours or irony. But at forty eight he was frozen up. Before deciding to reconstruct society from its foundations he had studied civil engineering in Lima; he had a practical mind that understood machines, understood how things went together. He imagined his emotional works to be like those inside a clock, except that they no longer turned when wound. When he talked, these days, what came out was rhetoric, or anecdotes, or a posture, which maybe explained why it was so hard to start.

He looked at the pistol, surprised himself by giving something away. "I'm not happy unless I'm on the verge of losing a beautiful, intelligent woman—someone like you, and I'm always on the verge because I don't treat them properly."

"This is complicated, Victor," she complained. "Are you sharing a psychological insight I should know about for the book, or is this a warning for my personal benefit?"

Oil from the barrel of the pistol had stained the white tablecloth. Outside, a car went by making a quiet rattle over the cobbles of the street. It did not slow down. He remembered what it was like to listen like that, convinced each time that this was the one, the vehicle bearing your death on rubber tires. For an instant he hated Laurel Romansky. "The gun belonged to a Bolivian major," he told her, "a counter-intelligence specialist. A friend and I took it from him in 1967. I was twenty two at the time."

"And Che Guevara was your hero, and Che was on the march in Bolivia ..."

"When I was four years old my parents died, and they sent me to live with my grandfather in Tarija. My grandfather was a transplanted Spaniard, a Catalan; he never got over his exile in the New World. He had a modest *estancia* but lost it in '52 because there was no clear way, in the confusion of the revolution, to distinguish guilty oligarchs from innocent farmers. He was old when I knew him, blind and bitter but still intellectually hungry. He brought in a tutor to teach me to read, and I spent the next years of my life reading to the old man. Everything, I read him everything, from Cervantes to Aristotle to a bad translation of Walt Whitman to the papers from Buenos Aires and pulp novels from Mexico. I had what you might call a prematurely developed political intelligence. I read *Kapital* when I was nineteen, most of it, anyway, and Lenin, and Fanon. Che Guevara was putting into practice what everyone else was only talking about."

"You wanted to join up with him."

"We weren't as green as you think. We had already been to Cuba, in 1966. We were in the middle of all that back-and-forthing between the Moscow faction and the Peking faction, and whether the *foco* was the way to go in Bolivia, and who was in charge of the revolution here. But we were too little, too late, thanks to your CIA. The Bolivian military would never have found Che on their own."

"Be specific, Victor. Who went with you?"

"We were in Vallegrande when we heard they killed him in La Higuera. We were carrying a message from the POR, and then there was no one to give it to. In the half a minute it took to hear the news, hope died. Not my hope, all hope. I don't know whether you can understand that." He gave her a minute to try. It seemed only fair to punish her for not having been there. She swallowed in silence.

"After it was over, the military brass cleared out of Vallegrande pretty fast. But there was one colonel, less an imbecile than the others though no less a political troglodyte. He stayed around town waiting, I think, to see whether someone like us just might show up, another thread he might unravel in the knot of sedition threatening to choke the *patria*."

"Who was with you?"

"Julio Quispe was my local hero. He was a couple years older than I, and he was wild and committed. He once left the severed head of an army colonel impaled on a pole in front of the presidential palace, with his signature in red on the note pinned to the beheaded colonel's hat. His father was a miner, killed in Oruro in a noble and unsuccessful strike nobody ever heard of. But the beautiful thing about Julio was the way he understood intelligence work. He had the gift. We had our own little service at the time, and thanks to Julio we knew something about this colonel. We knew he was a great admirer of the Nazis, for example. He had spent his formative years with the Argentine brass, who imbued him with his sense of mission. He was methodical, and cruel, and he could think strategically, which is to say more than a week into the future."

"You haven't said yes yet, you know, Victor. I mean yes you'll really cooperate on the book. You like the attention, a little, and you like a captive audience of one, don't you, but you're holding back on me. I can feel it."

He chose not to respond. What the North Americans never understood was that there was no such thing as inalienable right in the world, only advantage conceded under duress. He owed her nothing. "Some compulsively martial men make the mistake of being too methodical, too fixed in their ways. We were grieving the loss of Che, and the pain made us blind, but in my case anyway the pain also gave me the push I needed. The colonel stayed in town for several days. We watched him. We were in the house of a family we could trust. We noticed that every day near sundown the colonel took a walk out of town. Who knows?—maybe he had a sentimental side and enjoyed the sunset. The evening of the fourth day we were waiting for him."

Victor closed his eyes, rubbed them with the balls of both thumbs, reached absently for his glass of Singani. "I should have learned from what happened that peace on the planet is impossible. Because I enjoyed the pain we inflicted on the colonel, Laurel. I still enjoy the memory of it. We kept him conscious as long as we could, so that he understood who we were and why we were doing to him the ugly things we did. I myself hit him in the face and broke his nose with the butt of that pistol. Can you imagine the way the blood ran from his broken nose?"

"Julio Quispe is part of the Black Moon ..."

"This isn't for any book. Do you want to hear it?"

She stood up, went to the window and looked into the street. "Do you think the book is the only thing I care about?" she asked the blackened glass.

He did not trust her. She was capable, he presumed, of manipulating her feelings to get what really mattered to her, which was the book. "You made a mistake, Laurel. You shouldn't have let yourself start anything with me."

She breathed on the glass, drew a design of arching wings with her finger in the spot of moisture that collected there. "Tell me," she said.

There was virtue also in making mistakes. He made one. "They are Bolivians," he told her, "but they have links with the Shining Path in Peru. They take their name and inspiration from a movement at the turn of the century that terrorized the oligarchy for a little while. Haciendas were overrun, peasants were temporarily liberated, ruling-class throats were slit. They were led by a wild albino whose father was an overseer on one of the big estates. They called him El Lobo Blanco. The White Wolf had served in the military. That's what gave him his organizing and tactical experience. These days people like you would hunt him up to interview him. In your story you would call him a charismatic psychopath with an unconquerable sense of inferiority and a talent for making the rhetoric of revolution sound like ... like the message of the Bible. These days his grandchildren want to do to Bolivia what *Sendero* has done to Peru. I have some hard information on what they've been doing to finance themselves."

"It's cocaine, isn't it?"

"Not the finished product, just the coca paste. Even in drugs we are reduced to the status of raw-material suppliers. Somehow they got the idea that I was going to publish what I had. I pushed a source too hard, and he was the wrong source."

"So are you planning to publish what you have, Victor?"

"This is a documentation center, isn't it?"

"They threatened you."

"Julio sent someone, a self-righteous fool whose inferiority complex is more than justified. They are living clandestinely in the mountains, mostly. Out there they have a certain amount of support from *campesinos*. But they have a safe house in the city. Anyway I didn't handle our conversation well. We both got angry, and I made the mistake of saying I could cause them big-time grief if I let the world know where they were getting their money from. The message tonight is Julio's way of telling me I better not. It's a courtesy, I guess."

"I can help you get it published outside the country," she told him. "In the U.S. It can be done so that there's absolutely no way to connect you with what comes out."

Her *Yanqui* practicality, her impulse to solve problems, ticked him off, weakening his resistance to her. He wanted to want nothing from her, least of all help. "You don't get it, do you?"

"It can be done," she insisted, armored serene in her sense of capability. Her kind had put men on the moon, had they not?

"I want to go somewhere," he told her, but he could not bring out the rest of it. Where was a place, a conceivable space, a little lull of time in which politics did not enter or impinge. In which freedom meant not liberation of him or her or any oppressed other, just the lightness of air moving, and being there to feel it.

"Victor," she said, turning from the window. The little bit of Singani she had drunk tipped a balance in her. When her mouth opened the sound that came out at him was a chirp.

In the hunk of wood, possibly, beat a small green heart.

In the morning his forty-eight year old body hurt. The pain of reinsertion into an imperfect world cleared his head, though. Making coffee, he told himself he was free to choose. Not even Laurel would blame him if he did nothing. Brick by brick he had built the Centro as a fortress to defend human rights, not to gather intelligence. Julio was a fanatic, but he would not kill Victor unless his ex-comrade gave him a reason to. If Victor Mesón died the Centro de Documentación died along with him, and there would be no castle behind whose walls undefended people could shelter. If … then … Why did the thought of doing nothing seem like death?

They were crowding him. After breakfast Laurel hung around reading files, which put Graciela, his assistant, in an ugly humor. Victor had committed the tactical error of a short-lived affair with Graciela, who was studying to be a lawyer. She was a quiet, persistent woman, the daughter of a Supreme Court judge from Sucre. Some day she would be the human rights champion she needed to be. Their work relationship survived the sex, which had been a matter on both sides more of curiosity than desire, but Graciela would not forgive him his fascination with a *gringa*. She found the idea of his sleeping with Laurel politically repugnant. She smoldered.

The day's take of people with problems was also higher than normal. When people showed up at the Centro Victor was unable to say no, come back later, especially if they had traveled from the country. He listened to their stories, which invariably had to do with unfair, ugly and unfixable things done to them. He took notes, kept a good record of all the bad things, did what he could, which was little enough.

He happened to be in the little *antesala* full of benches where people collected when Ernesto came by. Watching his son step gingerly past the *campesinos* patiently waiting their turn to talk Victor realized, as if for the first time, that it wasn't Ernesto's political passivity that disappointed him. It was the unconsciousness, the ease with which the boy was able simply to count these people out of what mattered.

"I need to talk to you a minute, Papito. It's important."

Paternal pride, a pride of connection, swelled in Victor when Ernesto led him by the arm back into his office. The boy was as tall as he, with his mother's fineness of features: the softer eyes, and her pale brown skin, *café con leche* steaming on a cold morning.

Victor didn't mind that his son lived down below the city in Calacoto, the refuge of the rich, and that his friends all drove cars the cost of which would right considerable wrong in a considerable number of villages on the Altiplano. He didn't mind that Maria Dolores had raised the boy, after the divorce, to inherit the world that needed changing. Every time he saw his son, which was still pretty often, he felt an urge to fall at his feet and kiss them, to say an unconditioned Yes of simple praise. What bothered him was the blindness. Flesh of his flesh but without the eyes.

"I have it figured out, Papito."

For an instant Victor was tempted to tell him about Julio and the Black Moon, but the impulse to shield his son was stronger than the need to confide. He listened while Ernesto described his plan to study English in the U.S. and then get his Master degree in Business Administration.

"What does Maria Dolores say?"

"She's all for it, Papito. She says she'll get an apartment somewhere, just far enough away to leave me my privacy. She's going stir crazy in Calacoto."

"I don't have anywhere near enough money to help you, Ernesto."

The boy looked at him and laughed, as though the idea hadn't crossed his mind. Probably it hadn't. "She's got it covered. All I want from you is your blessing. I want you to think it's a great idea, Papito, that's all."

Victor despised the weakness in himself that equated his lack of cash with some sort of manly inadequacy. Fair enough to blame that one on Maria Dolores, because that was how she had made him feel after she inherited her father's pile. He made a gesture in the air that a short-sighted boy might interpret as a father's blessing, and Ernesto went away happy.

After he left Victor took a break. Closing out the misery collected in the *antesala,* he sat at his desk and closed his eyes. The alcohol-detritus pain rose to the surface of his consciousness and bobbed like a fishing float. He felt trapped, stepped on, invaded. Around him needy people were breathing all the available air, leaving him gasping. Foreigners were always making a big deal about the thin air of La Paz, and Victor was a big man; his body demanded a higher proportion of the planet's resources than most. Laurel had shown him a paragraph, once, from her manuscript draft: When she knocked on the door of the Centro de Documentación Boliviano for the first time the threshold was filled with Victor Mesón, a tree-sized man, towering, a physical aberration in this impossibly high mountain city. The man who looked down through thick, square glasses at her was a gatherer, she wrote, a hunter and sniffer out. He was a high-IQ squirrel disguised in the body of a bear. The black goatee, the long black hair, made his white skin look whiter. In jeans and an alpaca sweater he looked as little like the Aymara and Quechua Indians he defended as she did.

He had thought, when he began, not that telling people's stories would be enough to make justice happen, but that the telling could heal him. The Bolivian Documentation Center was established in a house that had belonged to a granddaughter of one of the tin magnates. In 1973, at twenty four, Nimia Patiño had published a book describing her moment of awakening on the Prado in La Paz, when she watched an out-of-work miner expire on cold paving stones at midnight. Intended as a kind of public confession, the book sold well, was translated into French and English, thrust her into a brief interlude of fame she found distasteful. She could do nothing, it seemed, that didn't result in profit from the tribulations of other Bolivians. Since that turning point in her life she had worked to expiate her inherited guilt by bankrolling projects she thought had a chance of setting her country's wrongs right.

During the Banzer days, while the MIR Party was underground, Victor met Nimia at a meeting of exiles in Paris. It was a serious gathering of the serious Left, called to coordinate the fall of Latin America's sundry tyrannies. Someone with a sense of humor dubbed it the Domino Encounter. Buzzing on the periphery of history, Nimia spent thirty six uninterrupted hours with Victor Mesón in the dump of an apartment he was sharing with Julio Quispe. When she walked out the door—her choice; he would have liked her to stay another thirty six, anyway—she told him to expect a letter from her lawyer. He thought she was joking. But three weeks later came a letter explaining that Victor Mesón was now the owner of a substantial stone house in the neighborhood of Sopocache in La Paz. Included in a sealed envelope was a handwritten note from Nimia.

... I watched you for a long time while you fell asleep in bed one time, the second night I think it was. When you're asleep the courage comes out on your face. Awake, your intelligence causes you to talk too much, so that you're just one more cock-of-the-walk exile in love with his own bravado. What I had always feared was confirmed for me in Paris. Even the most serious among them—among you?—suffer from an excess of swagger. And their self-love impairs their political judgment. Lucky for you I was there in your bed to see there is something more in you, *querido* Victor, and to tell you about it now. The cost of the house in Sopocache is this piece of advice: Don't die in a place like Paris waiting for the revolution to end all revolutions, and don't go looking for a bullet on top of anybody's barricade. Use your intelligence ...

The same night he got the letter from Nimia Victor experienced the defining dream of his adult life. In the dream was a mountain, and the sun reflecting off a white lake at the base of the mountain. He himself stood somewhere on the mountain, perhaps halfway up the slope. Below, on the edge of the lake, people were carrying stones, enormous boulders, really. Even from a distance he knew that they were in great distress, and a feeling of absolutely overpowering hopelessness invaded him. It was a relentlessly intense feeling, and he took it for a vision. When he got out of bed in the morning he had no clue to the dream's meaning, but the vision drove him out of Paris back to Bolivia, where he started the

Center in Nimia's house. The idea was simply to document abuses, to get it down on paper, all of it, so that there was a record.

And he was lucky. It worked. A Dutch group from the dogmatic soft Left adopted the center as its one Latin American cause. They gave money, and they made sure everyone knew they were watching, at just the right pitch that the bad guys assumed there was more trouble to be had in doing away with Victor Mesón than benefit in closing down his center and disappearing its instigator. The Centro de Documentación developed a reputation as a serious resource center for good information on bad things happening in Bolivia. Foreign journalists came, sometimes politicians on a visit. During the Garcia Meza days the *New York Times* did a feature story on the place, which also helped. Victor Mesón wore an invisible bullet-proof shield.

What he had to do, really, was close the circle, which had been drawn with Julio Quispe at a safe-house meeting in Villa Miseria in 1965. When he died at ninety, Victor's Spanish grandfather left him the house and a few hectares that had survived the events of 1952. But to Victor, his head and heart full of what he had read to the old man, his inheritance was a drag. When a neighbor made a deal with a local judge to get title to his land Victor didn't fight back. He used the crime committed against him, instead, as the final proof he didn't need to show that Bolivian society was corrupt and needed final fixing.

At the meeting in Villa Miseria each found in the other what he needed to complement himself. Julio had the practical talents required to collect intelligence, to plan strategically. He was an operational genius. But Victor had the words, the ideas they both needed to explain to themselves what they were doing. His passion was in his intelligence. The two men understood each other perfectly. They meshed. They motivated, they organized, they made things happen when others hung back. The high point came when they took revenge, however unsatisfactory, on the colonel who had been there when Che was assassinated.

But it was as though the death of Che really were the death of hope. For Victor, anyway, the dream acquired a slow leak. At the

Domino Encounter in Paris Julio told him Nimia Patiño is poison, she'll corrode you. Victor was tolerant. How would you expect the son of a man killed in a miners' strike to react to the granddaughter of the man who owned the mines? But the cord that bound the two men together in their idea was stretched. Nimia was just the pretext. Julio had shown up in the house in Sopocache that time, Victor realized now, to cut the cord through by proving what he already knew: In his heart Victor Mesón had only been waiting for the opportunity to sell out.

The door swung open, and a woman from an Altiplano village near the Peruvian border came in to tell him her husband had disappeared. Only a loss of that magnitude could have broken down her timidity to the point that she would come to the city and open without knocking the door of a man who might be able to help find him. Her husband was an unexceptional, inoffensive man, she told him. It was people with malice in their hearts and poison on their tongues who came up with the story that Rufo Mamani went over the border to join the guerrillas.

This was what Victor did best. He questioned the distressed woman with patience and tact, drawing out details, straightening the crooked parts, working his way to some reasonable sense of what might have happened. He made no promises, he was professionally pessimistic, but he could not keep her from going away happy, convinced that don Victor Mesón had the power to bring Rufo Mamani back.

The woman, a broad, squat *cholita* with the kind of striking, ruddy round face you saw on local-color postcards, left behind something like a smell except that it stimulated not just his nose but all his senses. It caused him to remember her village, which he had never seen: damp wool and stony earth, potatoes boiling over a small fire, a black pig stuporous in morning sunshine. Llamas on a dirt street, beer in a big green bottle. Inexplicable news in Spanish from the radio hung like a noxious cloud over the settlement of bricks and tiles and sun-dried mud where this woman, harder than a stone, worried about her missing husband, and the fever lingering in her daughter, and the lack of money and prospects and options that made her stubborn fatalism holy, a marvel to see if you had the eyes.

What scared him was how hollow his outrage felt. Not that the woman's plight meant any less than it had meant years ago, not that he cared less.

But there was a gap of feeling between the man who defended people like Rufo Mamani and another man, hungrier and harder to please, who inhabited Victor Mesón. He had made better than good on Nimia Patiño's investment. He was a human rights hero, and angels with bright blazing hair guarded his sleep. But success didn't satisfy, it only drove deeper the wedge between who he was and the hungry man, still full of holes that needed plugging.

He had to get out of the house. He asked Graciela to sit in for him with the rest of the morning's visitors, then sneaked upstairs evading Laurel to his grandfather's cabinet. He wiped the barrel of the Luger with a cloth and put it in the pocket of his jacket. It was like acting out a daydream: the world reduced to your stage.

In the street he felt naked, and there was nowhere to go. Knowing Julio, there would be a tail on him, and he would have a gun. The instructions of the man tailing him would be that if Victor Mesón—a man too big to mistake—walked toward the office, say, of *Presencia* newspaper ... Which was more destructive, the Black Moon's paranoia or his own?

It was December. White clouds trailing gray bellies softened the bright sky. The air was warm, not quite sticky but with the smell and the feel of rain. He took a taxi to Villa Miseria, then strolled with forced slowness downhill over cobblestones through the market. Aymara women in layered skirts and bowler hats bustled or sat on sidewalks selling mounds of oranges, flashlight batteries, soap, a hundred small items piled into small, neat pyramids over which flies cruised slowly. Out-of-work miners from Potosí wandered with their wives and daughters among the Aymara envying them their piles, hunting for work that did not exist, gaunt and greedy and hopeless in their gait. This was the Bolivia, stubbornly intractable, that made a joke of the rhetoric of democracy pushed so vigorously by the North Americans and their *criollo* sidekicks.

In a maze of sprawling market stalls, the smell of urine rising heavenward from a dozen individual streams, Victor watched a fancy four-wheel drive Jeep maneuver, bog down and then stop in the streaming gruel of petty commerce. When it stopped, a man with a fifty-kilo sack of flour on his bent back reached reflexively and pounded the side panel of the Jeep, making a satisfying thunking noise. A woman close by with a child on her back wrapped in a bright striped shawl kicked a tire and walked on.

It became an event. For several minutes people coming past approached the car and struck it with their fists, their feet, whatever they had in their hands. From where he stood Victor could not see the driver; he had to imagine the fear and anger building that finally resulted in his hitting the horn and pushing resolutely forward forcing hostile pedestrians out of the vehicle's way. The sea of people parted and the car disappeared down the crest of a hill toward the center of the city. When it was gone Victor looked but could see on no one's face an indication, a recognition, that something had happened.

Something like panic only slower rose in him, blurring his ability to think. He was unable to process what he had just seen, though it provoked the same sensation of hopelessness his dream in Paris had. He felt in his breast pocket for the pistol. Julio had wanted the Luger badly; if he had realized it at the time, Victor told himself, he would have given it to him. His holding onto the gun all these years seemed, in his vulnerability, like just one more indictable offense. He looked around to see whether he could pick out the tail. No way.

A *cholita* he remembered vaguely as having helped once at the Centro passed him on the street, nodded her head in guarded recognition, disappeared like an apparition. Behind her went a man, probably her husband, carrying under his arm an enormous devil's head mask decorated with beads and spangles and dozens of tiny round mirrors. For the moment, Victor's fear was simple: He did not wish to die.

He could choose to do nothing. Julio would watch, keep watching long enough to be satisfied that the traitor Mesón was not going to double his treachery. But eventually he would stop watching.

Unable to think connectedly, Victor understood one thing clearly: He could not do the nothing Julio demanded of him. The decision had little to do with any sense of civic responsibility, or even with the desire to prevent the prolonged nightmare of terror that the Black Moon would inflict on Bolivia in the name of revolution. It had to do, rather, with the hungry man, who was angry and unappeased. He wanted a showdown. He wanted to believe that revolution was still a sacrament, not to be defiled with drugs. He wanted his life to change. He wanted to begin feeling.

In the middle of the market, under the invisible eye of a Black Moon shadow, his decision was a resolution that delivered its own epiphany. He was going to tell the ugly secret he wished he didn't know. The air over the market smelled like rain. The clouds had packed tight in regular, furrowed rows that sealed in the noise and the smells of La Paz. Later, maybe the next day, there would be a downpour, the kind of rain that flooded the streets. Out of all possible places on the variegated Earth to be born, here. La Paz was his, and he loved it. He had to tell.

And then he didn't.

"You ran away," Laurel accused him. The hallway was dark except for a globed bulb behind her making a vague halo around her head. Standing in the doorway of his room in the Hotel Luxor she stood like conscience in the flesh, only rounder and worn, a little, with experience.

But it wasn't running away, it was lunging blind in the direction of something he couldn't quite see. It was muttering *I want this* and grasping for something that might not be there. He had packed a small bag, stuck in the Luger, disappeared. There would be a scandal, and much speculation.

Fear made him angry made him mean. "How did you find me?"

"Graciela wouldn't give me the time of day. But Ernesto said you used to come here after you and his mother fought. You named him after Che, didn't you? And now he wants his MBA from Harvard."

"Is the idea to kill me? They followed you."

"I had to see you, Victor."

He did what he always did to ensure that he lost the woman he wanted, he bullied. He pulled her into his cave, switched off the ceiling light. "Afraid the subject of your big book was going to give you the slip? How much of an advance did they give you for my story, Laurel?"

"That's not fair." She reached in the anonymous dark, which smelled of disinfectant, tried to hold his face in her hands. But he would accept nothing that might temper the anger.

"I was careful, Victor," she insisted. "Do you think I'm a child?"

He tried to recall a woman he hadn't become angry enough at to drive away. If there had been more time with Nimia Patiño in Paris, he probably wouldn't have the house in Sopocache. *You love rejecting me,* Maria Dolores had told him when she divorced him, but the accusations of embittered ex-spouses didn't count.

"Go away," he told Laurel. If she left, their relationship might survive a while.

"You knew you weren't going to show up," she said, guessing, probing. "You're setting yourself up for something, but I can't see yet for what."

Perversely, it produced pleasure to think of the scene he had created: He had called a press conference at the Centro, something he did infrequently enough to ensure a good turnout. The *antesala* and reading room would have been full of reporters from the local papers, the wire services, maybe the tv stations. They sat around smoking and speculating, waiting for a human rights story big enough to justify their coming out, big enough for Victor Mesón to publicize it. But no Victor Mesón. He set it up, then walked away. Left with the mess to clean up, Graciela must have been ticked.

"I was afraid," he said. Maybe that was the way to do it: talk to her as though to himself alone, in simple sentences. "I don't want to be shot in the back of the head when I step out of my car downtown."

"You were afraid before you called the press conference," she pointed out.

Talking about Julio cost him. It wasn't that he had buried the memory. Just the reverse: He had lived in it, replayed it, taken himself to court, convicted and sentenced and absolved himself so completely, so often, that the idea of involving someone else in his private anguish seemed like violation. But telling Laurel somehow worked to dilute the anger, making him feel unconscionably free, as if confession really were a sacrament. "The first few years of the Centro were bad. I'd get up in the morning wondering whether they were going to close it up, or haul me away, or burn down the building, or ... They had all the options. All I had was the idea, which came out of that dream in Paris.'

"One night I woke up and there was Julio, sitting in a chair in my bedroom smoking Marlboros in the dark. Cigarettes were the only element of gringo domination he ever accepted. I've seen him turn down smokes when he really needed one because it wasn't Virginia tobacco. He was supposed to be in Europe. The government had him on their top ten list, but he couldn't stay away. Plus he hated France, he said the French were racists who only tolerated us because they wanted to stick it to the *Yanquis*."

"He wanted something from you."

"When my eyes adjusted I could see that he was holding the Luger, caressing it the way you would pet an animal, maybe. He had rummaged around in the house until he found it. That gun was always something between us, I'm not sure what. What he wanted was a rest. He wanted to stay. And I said no. I was afraid if Julio hung around they would find him and use him as an excuse to shut me down. We had begun to have some successes by then. I explained that to him, showed him how his staying could hurt people who had no protection. But he didn't want to hear it. You're a coward, he told me. For him it was that simple."

"You did the reasonable thing, Victor. Ask one of those Altiplano women the Center has helped what she would have had you do."

"What does reason have to do with it? Maybe I was a coward. But there was something else, something I knew while we were in Paris: Julio was a fanatic. He lived in a world of simple absolutes that I wanted to enter but couldn't. I understood how things worked for him, and for a while I tried to make them work that way for me. You live inside a small circle, closed. It has the same convincing reality a dream has. And you learn to block out anything that threatens to open the circle. Your thoughts, your actions, everything takes on a level of high seriousness that makes you believe you are anointed. You're not on the periphery of history, you are history in the flesh. The revolution happens through you."

"He hasn't changed, has he? It's all there in the note he sent. For Julio, your faith just wasn't strong enough."

As they talked an invisible, weightless bird had settled on Victor's shoulder. He was less angry than he remembered being, and two things that had been blurred since Paris snapped into clear focus. The vision and the rhetoric of the Black Moon revolution still had a hook in him, but Julio was mad, in a political way that twisted him. And the successes of the Bolivian Documentation Center were not enough, never had been enough, to make of Victor Mesón the Bolivian hero he had needed to be.

He let Laurel lead him to the bed and gentle him onto it. She lay down next to him, wrapped one leg around his. He lay on his back in the dark, let himself be taken away with the sensation of comfort her hand rubbing his chest produced.

"It's not the book, Victor."

"I don't want any book. You write books about dead people. I'm still alive, in a way."

"What do you want, then?"

"I want to stop. Everything. I'm burnt out. That spoils the ending for you, doesn't it? No drama, just a burnt out man hiding in a hotel room. No revolution, no hero."

But she was strong enough not to let him keep beating. "My first lover was an Argentine," she told him, "much older than I. He was my professor at the university when I did a semester in Buenos Aires. He was a Jew and a sociologist, so he started out with two strikes against him. Plus he had no fear, he was one of the few who really don't. It has nothing to do with heroism, it's biology, maybe, I don't know what. Saul was disappeared when they heard he was publishing in American magazines under a pseudonym."

"You were the one who helped him get published."

"My father was an editor. I grew up knowing people in magazines. I thought I was helping him fight the good fight by using my connections. After he had been gone long enough for us to know he wasn't coming back I became an engine. Working twenty four hours a day, because Saul and the security goons who took him away and their dirty war got into my dreams. For a long time the pain and the anger powered the engine."

"But not forever."

"I have some money saved. Let's go to Honduras. We can rent an island off the north coast, a whole Caribbean island, for practically nothing."

"I want to be king of the island."

She crowned him. He stood up, went to the window and looked down into the pleasant round plaza called Isabel La Catolica. If someone from the Black Moon was out there he would not let himself be seen. For a few moments Victor watched a slight, frail-seeming woman from Potosí with a baby slung on her back standing motionless under a street lamp. Even her hat sagged. The woman stood rooted to the spot as though there were no place left in which to seek shelter and sustenance, and something for her child, and therefore no more reason on Earth left to move. What did it matter that he had the eyes to see her? The woman started once at the sound of a car horn, and he was released.

When he came back to the bed they undressed each other ceremonially, slowly, piling their clothes in a little mound on the floor. His jeans peeled, shirt off, the pleasure rose in Victor and blinded him. He felt it everywhere, in the tips of his fingers, even on the underside of his tongue. There was all the time in the world, which pulsed. The room was unheated, the night-time air of La Paz cool enough to prick the skin. Laurel threw down the bedcovers, and they lay on their sides and explored with their hands. Not as if for the first time, and not remembering any first times, but remembering that this was how it could be, this sweet and slow and forgetful. She smelled faintly of lemon, and when he kissed her between her legs the taste was salt and he felt nourished.

They fell asleep together, like tumbling head-first into a cave of comfort, and he thought they were chilled awake at the same instant. Laurel pulled the covers over them, wrapped her hand around his penis. "What time is it, Victor?"

"I'll go," he told her.

"Go where?"

"To the island in Honduras."

"It doesn't have to be forever. Call it taking a vacation."

If she wanted to soften something sharp in what he was telling her that was fine. "Graciela can run the Center," he thought it through. "She's tough, and organized, and they can't intimidate her. She'll do fine. I need to do one thing first, and then we can go."

"There's nothing you have to do, Victor. Just let it go."

"I have to talk to Julio. Face to face. I have to tell him I'm giving up. I want to tell him I won't give away what I know about the Black Moon. I won't stand in his way. Let them build their strength out in the mountains and imagine they will conquer the country, just like we all thought thirty years ago."

"You're still trying to set something up, Victor. What? You can't talk to a fanatic. There's nothing to prove, not to either of you. You're trying to carry on a dialogue with an idea."

But he would find Julio and talk to him. Laurel took her hand from his penis, wrapped her arms around him, said something in burred, quiet English that might have meant We'll talk it over in the morning. She slept, and Victor Mesón, crowned king of his own Caribbean island of escape, stayed awake to see what it felt like to be free.

He had always been susceptible to the weather, superstitious connecting the mood of the planet with his own private humors. Therefore the rain that pummeled and flooded La Paz meant release. The clouds bunched tighter, sealing in the city. The rain held off, kept on holding as if waiting for him to make up his mind. Then let go hard. In the morning after breakfast brought to their room he asked Laurel to stay in the hotel, ventured out alone in a downpour that had already made the streets impassable. Silver-topped torrents of dirty gray water covered the cobbles, stranded vehicles, carried trash and debris and a stiff-legged dead dog downhill toward the suburbs of the rich, whose serene removal from the life of the city was still, in the mind of Victor Mesón, a structural inequity requiring redress.

It took him an hour and a half to work his way on foot uphill to Villa Miseria where the Germans had set up Fe Ciega, a benevolent institution described in their brochures as dedicated to empowerment and the raising of consciousness through the development of literacy and artisan skills. Padre Wolfgang Webern would make it a point of honor to show up during the flood, though he knew that in such weather he would not find a single taker for the liberation remedies Fe Ciega peddled with earnest conviction.

"You," said the German, surprised to find the human rights hero at his door. Webern was blonde and beefy, red even at rest. He made Victor think of Bavaria: a stuffed and groaning barn holding the harvest from fields of plenty. "They told me you disappeared, Victor. What was all that about a press conference? Very mysterious."

The priest's Spanish was good. He spoke slowly and deliberately, never made a mistake in grammar. You could watch him change course halfway through a sentence to escape a construction more complicated than his resources would allow. The pronounced accent was like a slur. And his discomfort was obvious. Padre Wolfgang did not know quite how to take the founder of the Bolivian Documentation Center. So he bantered, letting Victor know he was not to be accorded the level of respect earned by those truly committed to the struggle. Fe Ciega did an adept job of maintaining supportive links with the hard Left, the ones with guns, for whom Victor Mesón was a sell out, part of the established order that still needed overthrowing.

"I need to get a message to Julio Quispe," Victor told him, accepting a mug of coffee in a chipped blue enamel mug that steamed. They sat in the priest's office, whose walls were covered with colorful posters espousing social change in several languages.

"Can't help you, Victor. If the Bolivian government thought Fe Ciega was in touch with a man like Quispe they'd take the political heat and close us out. They don't like us in the first place, you know that."

Victor took the hit without reacting. You're not trustworthy, the priest was telling him. You could be setting us up. A day before, before the flood, he would have lashed out in righteous outrage, pinned the sanctimonious German activist to the wall with the force of what he said. But he was free now, and patient, floating on a pool of calm.

"Julio will want to hear what I have to tell him," he said reasonably, putting Webern under the obligation to pass the message. It was that easy. "Tonight. Ten o'clock. At El Monticulo."

"Who even knows whether Quispe is around? I wouldn't know myself, but from what they say he's not a man to take unnecessary chances."

Webern wanted to spin out the conversation, to jab some more at Victor in order to demonstrate his moral superiority, the purity of his solidarity, his open-eyed understanding of Bolivian political reality. Victor would not have minded trading hits with him; his bull-headed certainty left him vulnerable to an attack from the flank. Instead he asked for a pencil and paper. Letting the priest watch him work, he drew a neat half moon in the middle of the paper, then shaded it in.

"What's that?"

"This is for Julio." He handed over the paper, finished his coffee, left the priest agitated and went back out into the rain, which had driven everyone off the streets.

When he returned to the hotel, soaked through and drained from having fought the weather, Laurel was working on her notebook computer.

"What chapter are you on?"

She shook her head. "This is a letter to my editor explaining that I'm going to return the advance because I can't write the book. Then I'm going to call a friend in Miami who can help us get set up in the Bay Islands. Do you want a boat?"

"Not a big boat," he decided. "A small boat. But it has to have a sail. I want to learn to sail."

"I made reservations to leave," she said, but he saw what she was doing.

"I'm going to meet Julio tonight."

Her anger was clear, clean, under control, a thing to be admired. "It's what you've been maneuvering to set up, isn't it? You're a fool to take the chance, Victor, or else more *machista* than I thought."

"I just want to tell him in person that I'm giving up."

"You're lying."

"All I'll do is say good-bye."

El Monticulo was a lookout kind of place, an urban park on a knoll in Sopocache with marble statues and eucalyptus trees and paths to stroll and, in the daytime, a knock-out view of the city and the mountains beyond. At night the lights of La Paz lay like bright flowers on a deep lake of darkness, and the wind never stopped blowing.

The rain had blown itself out. All that was left of the clouds were wispy gray strips that appeared to flap in slow motion as they dissipated, illuminated by a three-quarter moon that rose over the canyon up the sides of which the city straggled. After the storm the air was cold.

And Julio Quispe standing with his hands in his pocket, not out of a dream but out of the imagination. Hunched, in black, he was a grounded bat. An overhead light left his face in shadow, but there was enough diffused white light to see the stress of aging. The skin was stretched tight, the face looked battered. He looked like a man who had lived underground for a hundred years.

"You're looking good, Victor. Success has made you fat." His voice had also changed. It was full of the bitter stridency of a prophet who had spent too much time in the mountains as midwife for the necessary baby who would not be born.

"Julio!" The urgency that had driven Victor to El Monticulo was gone, instantly. In its place was a passionate tenderness, a sweetly debilitating affection for the man who stood in front of him like judgment deferred. What he wanted was to communicate his freedom to his *compañero*, to point a way out.

"The German was convinced you were setting me up for the police. You really threw him when you drew that black moon."

"What about you, Julio? Do you have sharpshooters in the trees?"

Julio waved impatiently. "A question of honor."

"It isn't going to happen the way we thought it would. The revolution we wanted, I mean."

"You were never tough, Victor. From the beginning I had my doubts. What you wanted was the idea of revolution, the fantasy of making one."

"Whose idea was it to finance the Black Moon with cocaine?"

"What we are doing is not for the squeamish. Does the notion of *Yanqui* adolescents addicted to drugs from the Southern Hemisphere distress you? Not to use the weapons we have at our disposal would be the real crime."

Victor had promised himself he would not get trapped into a go-nowhere argument. What he had to do was reassure Julio he would do nothing, and go away with his affection intact. He shook his head. "All I wanted to tell you is that you don't have to worry about me. I'm going away, I'm leaving Bolivia."

"With your blonde *gringuita*?" Such bitterness chastened Victor, but it had no power to make him feel guilty.

"Do you hear me, Julio? I'm not going to make any trouble for you."

"So I'm supposed to say What a relief! and let you walk away."

Late and reluctantly, Victor understood. A point of honor, Julio had said. No sharpshooters in the trees of El Monticulo.

"You're volatile, Victor, always were. You let the emotion of the moment pick you up and carry you away. You're changeable. The little incident of the press conference decided it for me. What were you thinking? Anyway you could change again tomorrow. The Black Moon is too big, too important, to let the whims of an emotional man put us in jeopardy. Publicity, at this point, could be fatal. The gringos are spooked by what they've seen in Peru. Bolivia is smaller, more manageable. They'll bring in their helicopters and soldiers and tell the world they're looking for drugs, and they'll wipe us out." He shook his head, rejecting the possibility.

"I'm giving you my word, Julio."

"Your word?" There was a crack in his laugh, something ugly under great pressure splitting open.

It was a question of timing. Things happened jerkily, out of sync, as if there were no connection between one thing and the next, as if half an instant could have made all the difference in the world. Julio was disgusted, irritated with something not apparent to Victor. He reached for something he didn't get to, and the gesture of helplessness Victor honestly felt was translated into the movement of a hand on the Luger in the pocket of his jacket. Which jumped. The conscious part was going for the shoulder. The shot stunned the leader of the Black Moon, and his shoulder ripped, giving Victor enough time to knock him down, out, unconscious.

He gathered up his friend, held the body close, went stumbling down the steps out of the park to the Brazilian Volkswagen Laurel had rented. She saw him coming, opened the back door, and Victor lay the body in on the seat. His jacket and jeans were sticky with blood.

"He was going to kill me," he told Laurel.

"He's alive. What are you going to do with him?"

"Drive," he told her, and directed her down through the city. The terror, the panic he felt had to do with getting Julio Quispe out of the car. All he really wanted was to change his clothes, to burn them and shower and scald his memory into forgetting. "He wanted to kill me," he repeated to Laurel. "He was acting honorably by doing it by himself, alone."

"So you should have let him do it?"

Victor reached for the pistol in Julio's pocket, found it, threw it out into the street at a dark corner. Laurel drove responsibly and well. Downhill and out of the city through Obrajes. On the near edge of Calacoto he had her turn right, and they began climbing again, up into the Valley of the Moon. The idea, the only idea, was to dump the body down the canyon.

Valle de la Luna was like a separate planet. The rugged landscape into which they drove the VW was littered with enormous, weird piles of white rock: caves and outcroppings, slab-like heaps and piles of bleached stones. In the moonlight the spiky cactus plants cast long, ribbed shadows. When Laurel parked the car, Victor dragged the body out of the back seat and across the moon-like surface to the lip of the canyon, at the bottom of which Julio's body might lie undiscovered for months.

"He was going to kill me," Victor explained again.

She knelt by the body, felt the pulse, looked at the ugly, torn shoulder. "He's going to wake up. His system is shocked, that's all. He's going to wake up and start hurting."

"Am I supposed to kill him before I dump him over? Is that the humane thing to do?"

She looked at him soberly, and the panic snapped. He identified the quietness of spirit, the self-sufficiency, that would make it possible for a person like him to live on an island with her. "I'm not judging anything you do, Victor. I don't want you dead. Do what you have to do."

He looked down at Julio's face, tranquil in sleep but with the tightly contracted conviction of something passionate still evident there. It was the face of a fanatic. The bloody shoulder was black in the white moonlight, and Victor's hands were hot.

He did what he had to do. He took the Luger from his pocket, threw it down the canyon. The noise it made bouncing on the rocks was small and tinny. He knelt by Julio's side, smoothed his coarse hair, which had become matted with blood. And he kissed him, the way a jilted lover would kiss. He walked away, and Laurel followed. Of the interesting things left to remember, probably the most interesting would be what it had been like to be free.

The Nature of Fiction

They drew the light of the sun and the eyes of passersby. Her teeth were more than a vision, they were a revelation. Perfect was no word to describe such brilliant symmetry. He watched her step out of the back seat of a teal-blue Mercedes into a lesser world. A gold rope hung from her neck like a fallen halo, smooth silk shifted on her shoulders. She crackled. He lusted to be close enough to smell the money on her breath. Then, in the dirty little chaos of the cobbled street, she smiled. And he hurt. From that moment on, he fell.

What the woman's teeth revealed to Angel Rojas was nothing: the nothing that he was, he had, the nothing that he counted for. He drained his sweet black coffee, tossed the plastic cup into the gutter, watched the woman disappear the way visions did, leaving a bitter taste of longing under his tongue, not for her but for what she was, which was something.

After the coffee stop he walked ten minutes to the office, the closest thing, in his cumbered existence, to freedom. He squandered it describing himself. His own teeth—twisted and stained, with craters of rot that periodically erupted in pain that made him sick to his stomach—were the least of it. What really hurt was the profile: a low-level functionary in the research department in the basement of the National Office of Investigations—the locus of insignificance. A forty-three-year-old cipher-citizen in one of the poorer countries in Central America—the locus of inconsequence. His face was concave, his complexion sallow unto sick. At night in bed, when Pilar stretched her hand to find him, he wasn't there. His wife held against him precisely the thing he was unable to change: a kind of negative presence more disturbing, closer to death, than simple absence.

He disciplined himself not to count the thirteen steps down into the basement. Machicado looked up from the mirror in his desk drawer into which he stared when he thought no one noticed. He sucked on his pencil, looked at Angel with the face of an injured plaintiff. "Diaz was here ten minutes ago. He was sweating, and he whistled under his breath. He wants to see you in his office."

Machicado was only thirty five, and his wife was twenty and pretty and still believed in her husband's prospects. Machicado's attitude of bemused superiority, watching his friend and co-worker slog toward a future with neither sun nor horizon, was intolerable.

Angel did not worry that he was in serious trouble; when he was angry, Diaz sent up smoke signals. Angel would have been more curious, but the lingering vision of the silk-and-gold woman's splendid teeth had tumbled him into a distracted funk.

"Refresh my memory," the head of research commanded gently from behind his massive wooden desk, the clean expanse of which was broken only by a telephone. Diaz believed in delegating. A retired major brought in to clean up a mysterious mess in the department the year before, he radiated high purpose. He continued to wear his hair close cropped, military fashion, and he was in pretty good shape for fifty plus. The man bristled, but Angel was inured to his enthusiasm. "You were the one who turned up that piece on Meza, weren't you?"

Eladio Meza was a human rights hero and one of the government's most credible critics. Angel felt a moment's apprehension. In a moment of bored pique he had invented a little episode for Meza's file, which needed fleshing out. It had to do with running guns to resurrected rebels in Nicaragua. On the wrong day, in a place like research, one mistake of idle invention like that could land him in the street.

"I'm sorry," he began. He stopped when he saw surprise wrinkle his supervisor's red ears, which reminded him of miniature satellite dishes, efficient collectors of useful intelligence. "You surprised me."

"Surprised?"

"That you remembered, that's all."

Diaz' big ears took that one in; Angel could hear the faint clink it made dropping onto the floor of one of his secret interior warehouses. "There is high-level interest in Meza at the moment. You've seen the remarks he made in Paris."

"That we are no closer to a real democracy now than we were under the military. The President is the colonels' puppet, the courts are corrupt, and the Congress is inept."

"There's more to this than appeared in the press, but I'm not at liberty to go into it with you. It has to do with international financing, and with our credibility. The point is, we would both be well served if you came up with something more on Meza's gun-running activities. There are leads to follow; follow them. Feel free to get out of the office. Be discreet, but produce. Put something solid together, Rojas, and you won't regret the effort. Am I being sufficiently clear?"

If not for the perfect woman's perfect teeth he might have confessed his error, risked some minor punishment, passed an uncomfortable week. But he did not want to confess. Besides, Meza was an alcoholic, and as good as a traitor in the way he ran down his country to gullible foreigners. Before he left Diaz' office Angel hated the human rights hero.

"So what are you going to do?" Machicado wanted to know. He was picking at his teeth with a mechanical pencil with a military camouflage barrel. Machicado considered himself fatally good looking, thought he could make it as an actor in Hollywood or Mexico City, given the chance. He could not conceive how repulsive he looked just then, like a dog on a dump scratching its private parts.

Angel took the Meza file from the cabinet, spread its contents on his desk, tuned out his co-worker and began to read. There was plenty of material, but almost all of it was press clippings, statements Meza had made, statements made about him, summaries and analyses of the studies and reports his office put out. Angel's modest invention seemed unconvincing in the mass of print detailing the virtue and the vision of Eladio Meza. ... *During a visit to Managua to attend a congress of sociologists, Meza was observed meeting with members of the MPL, an extreme radical group opposed to the democratization process. Meza was observed on a second occasion participating in the delivery of a truckload of M-16 rifles to a warehouse known to be a conduit to the MLP.*

"I'm going out for a while," Angel told Machicado. "If Diaz calls tell him I'm out doing research."

"Want some free advice?"

"No."

Gone. He gave himself the luxury of the morning walking around the city without thinking; his powers of reason contracted into his legs, which moved with a mind of their own. Passive, he followed. It was the green side of spring. The air smelled wet and loamy, with the undercurrent of something animal in it, the scent of some dangerous creature too enormous to visualize. Clouds with tangled manes of streaming hair dropped strange, floating shadows over the low hills and stony valleys of the capital. Angel took off his watch without looking at it, dumped it in his breast pocket. He walked. After a while, he noticed that he had begun to disappear.

A coolish wind came sidewise down the street he was walking, and he felt the cold air blow through his body, come out the other side. Pedestrians seemed not to see him; he stepped off the sidewalk into the street in order not to be knocked down by a woman in a hurry wielding a rapier-like umbrella. For the first time since he could remember, he stopped calculating, stopped dividing time into units of worry, stopped berating himself for having failed to achieve an identity of consequence. He became an eye.

With no lid. He tried to close the eye but couldn't. Curiously, the pain and clarity of seeing without thinking was like freedom itself. Away from the city center, on a broken-cobbled street going uphill, through an open gate he watched an old woman in a sagging yellow dress making tortillas. Her talented hands shaped the dough better than any machine. Fast, faster. Unfiltered sunlight fell on the grassy space in the yard in which the woman sat making her millionth tortilla, pooled there and covered the ground. Still working, shaping the dough with strong, brown, treadle fingers, she raised her eyes to the street once but did not see Angel Rojas. He wasn't there. In the space he vacated lurked something else. For a long, unfettered moment he listened to it breathe.

"You can prove all of this … "

Machicado, respectful in the presence of a superior who might someday promote him, watched the little drama play itself out. Diaz' purposeful intensity fatigued Angel, made it difficult for him to think connectedly, but he had anticipated the question and was able to answer.

"No, I can't prove it. I don't have enough information to prove anything. What I have is pieces of a puzzle. But they go together."

"Well keep doing what you're doing."

"I have to be out of the office."

"Of course," Diaz agreed impatiently. "Just stop by my office before you leave."

"You're digging your own grave," Machicado told him when Diaz left. "It's too clever by half. All they need to do is check out one detail, and you're dead."

"I've thought it through. They don't care whether the details are true. What they want is for me to confirm what they already believe."

"How much is Diaz giving you?"

No way would Angel fall into that trap. "I'm going out for a while."

"That's all you do these days is go out, Rojas. It's not fair. What do you do when you're not here?"

"Research, *mi compañero*. That's what they pay us to do."

"Yeah well it looks to me like you're researching yourself into a corner. They won't forgive you, you know."

"They don't have to."

But Angel had too little patience to waste it arguing with Machicado. He was enjoying being on top, for the first time, in his relationship with his co-worker. Machicado envied him his access to Diaz, the bonus money he was sure Angel was receiving, the relief from routine in their airless basement. Angel might have felt sympathy for Machicado but did not.

He had learned he needed a tranquil place to work in, had found it in a little *confiteria* that never seemed to attract any customers interested in its baked sweets and exotic coffees and quiet classical music. The waitress, a slight woman with a noble Mayan face, seemed to be waiting, not for him but for something momentous to happen, something that would justify the ordeal of waiting she was evidently undergoing. She served him a Colombian coffee and left him in peace. He wished he had enough knowledge to know which German genius had written the music that burbled and cascaded in the air. He opened his notebook.

What he hadn't expected was the deep, sweet satisfaction that came when he put together an alternate life for Eladio Meza. Now, after two weeks of intensive work, it was difficult, and sometimes it seemed silly, to draw legalistic distinctions between what the world knew about Meza and what Angel intuited.

It turned out that Meza had forged an alliance with the MPL in Nicaragua with the goal of overthrowing both governments in a mini-domino movement that would result in the hard left's coming to power when people least expected such a development, least of all Uncle Sam, who was currently dozing. Meza's principal contact in Nicaragua was a pseudo-sociologist by the name of Borges who had succeeded in maintaining a productive working relationship with the Sandinistas, principally the Ortega brothers, at the same time that he represented serious elements among the serious left, who had no intention of letting the currents of neo-liberalism and sham democracy sweep them downstream to irrelevance. The genius of Borges was to have maintained respectable cover as a social scientist.

Borges was Angel's master stroke. His researcher's instincts were sound. He had understood from the outset that he could not stray too far from what he knew about what was happening in Nicaragua. He had come across an interview in *Barricada* with the polemical, wooden-tongued sociologist, decided the poor man deserved a fuller life than the humble one he displayed to the world. So Angel created it for him. The Meza-Borges connection was the pivot on which turned a genuine understanding of events.

He could have done more, and done it well. But he restrained the impulse. Apart from the Nicaraguan media, his source was a disaffected Sandinista living underground in fear of retribution for his role in the assassination of a *comandante* who had been using government helicopters to haul precious woods out of the jungle. What did in the *comandante*, in Angel's opinion, was his refusal to cut in a rival officer. At any rate, he assured Diaz that the source was content with the modest gratuities the research department was able to funnel his way. But the question of credibility asserted itself every time Angel sat down to work: How much could the man be expected to know?

Two days earlier, Meza had announced a trip to the U.S. He was going to visit the executive director of Americas Watch. What he didn't say was what everyone understood: He was going to denounce something big enough that he had to do so from a distance. Angel knew he had to fill in the backdrop to the trip, but that required cultivation of a new source, and he could not move precipitately. As badly as his superiors wanted good dope on a bad guy, Diaz was no fool. Angel closed his notebook, capped his pen, paid for his coffee. One misstep would be fatal. The waitress with the Mayan face brought him his change as though bearing a message from her dead ancestors, something that needed heeding.

And then he was in his own home, without thought or volition. He could not remember having come home in the middle of a work day; neither did Pilar. He found her sitting in the dark watching a lottery game on television. The screen was filled with numbered balls rattling in a hopper like popcorn, while a woman with telegenic cleavage and a vacant smile twisted the handle.

"Nothing's wrong," he told his wife. The kids were at school. Alone with Pilar as he was, without the buffer of children and domestic confusion, he felt a sensation like embarrassment.

"I don't think I want you here in the daytime," she told him. She stirred her coffee with a spoon, stared at the lottery balls on the screen.

The fine thing about what had been happening to Angel was the freshness of vision it gave him. A silver comb holding up her long dark hair, Pilar did not look like the discouraged wife of an invisible man. She was the daughter, at the moment, of a Spanish spy run afoul of his own government. The father had died in penniless exile, abandoning her to oblivion. Her pale skin looked unhealthy, as though she pined, and pronounced black half moons gave more depth to her black eyes than was really there. He felt guilt, pity, and a rising wave of tenderness so unfamiliar it took a moment for him to recognize. He crossed the room, found a bottle of rum in a cabinet, poured some into her coffee cup and offered it to her.

"You've changed, Angelito," she said. "You've been having another woman, and now you feel bad and want to make it up to me."

He shook his head. "Drink," he told her, and the remarkable thing was she believed him. She drank, passed him the cup. He tasted more rum than coffee.

"Tell me what you want, Angel."

"I want to make love." Saying it, he realized it was true.

She shook her head hard, as if he had insulted her. But she was as ready as he was to escape the lethargy that was their life, and with some coaxing that was itself a pleasure she surrendered her distrust in their living room. They undressed each other slowly, as slowly as though they had all the time they needed. No telephone would ring, no child's face would appear in the doorway, no clock would go off in their heads reminding them of duty and logistics and how much groceries cost. It was like climbing blindfolded into a high-sided boat to travel up an unexplored river. Pilar was ordinarily a silent lover, and Angel sometimes spoiled the love for himself imagining the reproaches she was quietly formulating. But this time she made noises like a bird's self-absorbed chirping, and when she reached climax she laughed long and deep in a way that restored his sense of accomplishment.

"I've been having a dream," she told him. They lay on their backs on the floor, sharing what was left of the rum and coffee. "Three times now. I'm a bird, a black bird with tremendous long wings. I'm flying, but it hurts. I don't know why it hurts until I realize my claws are wrapped around a big boulder. So I let the boulder drop."

He didn't want to hear more. "I have to go back to work."

"What's happening to you, Angel?"

"Work is going well, that's the difference."

"You're like a different person." No judgment, just comment.

He rose and dressed. He fished for an envelope in the pocket of his pants. It was still sealed. It pleased him not to know how much Diaz had given him, and therefore how much he left lying on Pilar's breast. "Things are looking up," he told her.

"Angel," she said as he crossed the room. It occurred to him that she might lie there like that all day, which possibility delighted him. He imagined finding her serenely drunk by evening, chirping and dreaming while the kids danced around her body, which became a domestic bonfire of good feeling.

He stopped.

"We made good love," she said, and he was released.

"You wouldn't be enjoying this half as much if I wasn't here to watch," Machicado told him. The future star of Mexican *cine* helped himself to the delicate, flaky pastries on a tray Angel had brought to the office to enliven their coffee break.

"Tell me one thing: Is Meza a patriot?"

"You tell me something, Rojas: Where is this going? You can't keep inventing forever. One morning Diaz will wake up and tell himself it's too good to be true."

Angel had found his source on the inside: Meza's secretary, angry at her employer because he had cut off the affair he was having with her but still kept her on the payroll. It was an unbearable humiliation for the woman, who had three quarters of a college degree and abundant plans for her future. He admitted he had been lucky: Meza had in fact recently terminated his affair with the secretary; it was common knowledge and easily corroborated. Diaz was happy to provide the small amount of cash she demanded; her primary motive, Angel reported, was revenge. As important as luck was knowing how to take advantage of what came your way.

So it turned out that Meza's trip to the U.S. was going to be the stage from which he denounced the military's cover-up of an investigation into the brutal murder of striking workers at a banana plantation. The grisly details of the incident had consumed the country for a week, and both civilian and military authorities promised that this time—this time—the perpetrators would not go unpunished. Meza's strategy was to use the case as a hammer to bang away at the social evils he had long been reporting: weak civilian administration, military impunity, disregard for legitimate labor rights.

"What's going to happen if they take Meza to court, Rojas? Let's say there's a trial, and the government is forced to use this stuff you've been inventing. What happens then?"

"There won't be a trial," Angel told him. He believed that. He understood that the affair could not go on forever, that he was risking his livelihood, his retirement, his honor. But he was a cool-headed man; he knew how to calculate. And he calculated he could push it for just a little longer, maybe until Meza returned from the U.S. Several times since his first foray into recreating the past he had been awakened at night by dread. His body twisted in the bed, he sweated, his head was inflamed with colored visions of discovery and shame and judgment. But he also calculated the odds of something lasting developing out of what was, after all, an experiment. The job of Diaz' deputy might become vacant in a few months. Angel Rojas, reinvigorated and receiving a respectable salary, could handle that job.

"How do you know there won't be a trial?"

"The government would be putting itself on trial if they went after Meza. He's a fox. He'd see it for the public relations opportunity it was. All I'm doing is feeding a small fire in the brains of a few military officers who need fuel to keep going."

"You're good at this, I admit that, Rojas. Everything you've produced has seemed real to me. Sometimes I go home thinking that what you wrote is Meza's real life, and when I see him on television or read about him in the papers I interpret it all in the light of what's in that folder. But you could still get hurt, you could be very badly hurt. And I don't want them thinking I was in on it."

"I've been careful, Machicado. If anything goes wrong, I promise you, you won't get hurt." He saw that his co-worker continued to be troubled by the thought of all the extra money Angel was receiving. "Look, let's go celebrate something tonight, the four of us. Call Primi and tell her the Rojas want to take her out. I'm going out for the afternoon, but you can call me at home later and we'll figure out where to meet."

"You're going out again?"

"Research, my friend. It's research."

"I don't want to go out tonight."

"Suit yourself," Angel told him. "If you change your mind give me a call."

Machicado loved going out, and so did his wife Primi. It was what they lived for, in a way. Machicado liked to tell jokes and clown and gather the praise for his entertaining ways, and Primi loved basking in his glow. So Angel wasn't surprised when the phone rang early that evening. He had already told Pilar they were going out. With the money from Diaz' envelope she had bought herself a new outfit: a blue affair with a black shawl that made him remember she was the abandoned daughter of an Old World spy, and that he owed her a certain amount of chivalry, and respect.

"Did you hear yet?" Machicado asked Angel. Angel recognized the timber in his voice: it was dread, once removed, the same dread that had awakened him at night. In an instant he envisioned himself in Diaz' office explaining away what he had done. It could be done. He sucked in air; it felt like his last breath of freedom.

"What?"

"Turn on your radio."

"What is it, Machicado? Damn it, tell me."

"Turn on your radio."

Machicado hung up. In her wonderful blue dress, her eyes made up with something new, Pilar looked at him and knew immediately it was over. "Liar," she said to him quietly over the heads of the children, who were absorbed in a cartoon on the television.

Nothing to say. Before he could read the lines of the news bulletin appearing on the bottom of the TV screen Angel was out the door.

With nowhere to go, which was where he went. He walked, taking care to avoid any place in which he might hear a radio playing. He realized that he was in pretty good shape, having spent more time out of the office and walking, moving around, than he had in years.

The city was cool; the wind had fingers, and the fingers had nails that scraped. He smelled cooking oil and tortillas and beans, heard the ritualistic lament of *mariachis* practicing the Mexican *rancheras* they already knew, thought about every trivial thing he could get his mind to focus on. He wound up on the far side of the city, as far from home as he could get. In the *confiteria* the woman with the Mayan face was still on duty.

She brought him coffee that he didn't drink. He was, as usual, her only customer, and he watched her return to the radio she had been listening to when he walked in. She glanced at him guessing whether he would be bothered, turned the volume dial deliberately. Angel felt a fatalism that anyone else could have mistaken for wisdom, or insight, or something else that had the outlines of holy inevitability.

The body of Eladio Meza, noted human rights activist, had been found in an arroyo outside the city off the highway going toward the North coast. He had been shot through the head and through the heart. A note had been found in the glove compartment of his car, abandoned near the arroyo. Although they had not yet released the text of the note, police sources told the reporter for Radio Testigo that it appeared to confirm their supposition, which was that Meza had been murdered by a fringe element of the violent left, someone for whom Meza's activism was a form of accommodation. A score had been settled.

Angel listened to the Minister of the Interior and the Commander of the Armed Forces make a joint declaration that this time—this time—the crime would not go unpunished. The investigation would continue until justice was done. Neither man would speculate about other possible motives for the killing. All the rest was testimonials from people who had been too timid to speak in Meza's defense while he was alive.

"He deserved it," Angel railed suddenly at the Mayan woman. She looked at him suspiciously, turned off the radio. To anyone who had no stake in the system Meza was a hero, and now with wings. Angel placed an enormous tip on the table and left the shop. His body wobbled.

He drank but was unable to get drunk. After several hours he did achieve a kind of sober stupor, a condition of enforced passivity that prevented him from violence.

He did not go home. He had the feeling that Pilar would guess his secret and despise him, though that was impossible. He would have to despise himself. He watched the sun come up over the city as if for the last time, walked slowly to work.

He was not surprised when Machicado called in sick. He waited, unable even to pretend to work, until Diaz showed up.

"You've heard, I assume ... " his supervisor said blandly.

Angel tried to read the emotion that flickered across the man's hard, martial face. The antenna ears were motionless; Diaz was professionally calm. It was either quiet triumph or simple watching. He would watch Angel Rojas for as long as it took to assure himself of whatever it was he needed to be sure of.

"That's what the gringos don't realize," Diaz said thoughtfully. "They don't understand how nasty the left is, especially among themselves. They could control the continent if they'd only stop splitting into factions and killing each other. At any rate you can close the file on Eladio Meza, can't you?"

He could. He did.

Before the director of Research left the basement office, he told Angel, "Don't be troubled by what you might think of as wasted effort. You should know that you made an extraordinary contribution with Meza, and it won't go unrewarded. I think I can promise you that, Rojas."

It was not necessary to thank Diaz. Angel watched him go, then turned automatically to the filing cabinet. He opened the drawer, stood rooted with his hand resting on the sheaf of files. There was someone there in the office, behind him.

He thought at first that it was Machicado, showing up late to be the conscience Angel did not require. Then he thought—this was sheer fantasy, the product of his exhaustion—that it was Eladio Meza. Or someone just like him. He could not see him clearly, but he was there.

Angel closed his eyes and was able to detect the man's breathing, steady and slow, regular as a clock. It was not Diaz, or anyone from the Department of Investigations. He had no body, just presence. On an impulse, he walked over to Machicado's desk, took his co-worker's vanity mirror from the top drawer. It had occurred to him for a moment that his nerves might be playing tricks on him, that the presence he felt might be his own. But it wasn't that. When he looked in the mirror he wasn't there.

He placed the mirror carefully face down on top of Machicado's desk. He closed his eyes and held his breath. If he got himself under control, if he reached a point of absolute stillness, he thought, he might be able to catch sight of whoever it was that wasn't there.